THE YEAR OF THE MAFIA

1957. In the upstate town of Apalachin, New York, the leaders of the Mafia gather to carve up the nation. And on a level far below these grandiose godfathers, there's another drama being acted out. Manny Petrone, a mob lieutenant on the way up, is tightening his hold on his territory with all the violent means at his disposal. One of his targets is a stock-car racer and ladies' man named Link, who has been pushed one death too far. In the ferocious fifties, you have to be a little bit crazy to take on the Mafia. Link is. And does . . . in a one-on-one war in which nothing is fair and sex is the deadliest weapon of all. . . .

"JACK KELLY WRITES LIKE A MAN READY FOR A RUMBLE."
—New York Daily News

APALACHIN

JACK KELLY

AN ONYX BOOK

NEW AMERICAN LIBRARY

NAL BOOKS ARE AVAILABLE AT QUANTITY DISCOUNTS WHEN USED TO PROMOTE PRODUCTS OR SERVICES. FOR INFORMATION PLEASE WRITE TO PREMIUM MARKETING DIVISION, NEW AMERICAN LIBRARY, 1633 BROADWAY, NEW YORK, NEW YORK 10019.

This is an authorized reprint of a hardcover edition published by E. P. Dutton, a division of New American Library, and published simultaneously in Canada by Fitzhenry & Whiteside, Ltd., Toronto.

 Onyx is a trademark of New American Library.

SIGNET, SIGNET CLASSIC, MENTOR, ONYX, PLUME, MERIDIAN and NAL BOOKS are published by NAL PENGUIN INC., 1633 Broadway, New York, New York 10019

First Onyx Printing, March, 1988

1 2 3 4 5 6 7 8 9

PRINTED IN THE UNITED STATES OF AMERICA

1957

November 14

Manny's ass ached. They'd been driving since dawn—down the back roads, through the glacier-clawed valleys, past the bottomless Finger Lakes, the hick upstate villages: Canandaigua and Penn Yan, Montour Falls, Cayuta and Catatonk.

A sodden sky hung over the bare husky cornfields. Manny hoped rain wouldn't wash out the barbecue.

"He was the one ordered the kid popped who fingered Willie Sutton," he was telling Leo, his driver. "I ever tell you?"

"No. No, I don't think you did." Leo had listened to Manny tell the story three times before.

"No? This is inside dope. You know Sutton, the bank robber? He'd busted out of a joint in Philly five years earlier. This is 'fifty-two I'm talking about. Willie's living in New York and planning a job, right? Gets on a subway train one day and—I never told you this?—and this Schuster, who's kind of a crime buff, sees him, recognizes who he is, follows him, calls a cop, they collar Sutton. Okay?

"So Schuster's on TV, big hero, interviews, quiz shows. They even give him a watch, a good citizen award. So Anastasia's watching this, right? And old Albert A. says, 'I can't stand squealers.' Course, he

5

has nothing to do with Sutton at all. It's just: 'I can't stand squealers. Hit him. Hit the Jew son of a bitch.' Next thing, Schuster's lying in front of his house in a puddle of brains. Shot him right in the face. Huh? 'Hit him. I can't stand squealers.' Huh? Ha ha.''

Leo laughed. "Crazy fucker. Where'd you hear that?"

"I heard. Really goes to show, don't it? You know, I met him once."

"Anastasia?"

"Yup. I was with Mr. Ruggiero down in New York. Believe me, Albert Anastasia, you wouldn't want to meet a nicer guy. What a joker. But crazy. They called him the Mad Hatter."

"He got his."

"Yeah, they blew him apart in that barber shop there. That was Genovese."

"Did that?"

"Sure. Had it done. That's what this powwow is all about."

Manny was proud. He was proud that Mr. Ruggiero had asked him to attend the parley. He ran a big chunk of Ruggiero's territory along Lake Ontario, but this thing wasn't local. This meeting was bringing in the big guys from New York, from all over the country—California, even. They'd be talking about dividing up Anastasia's thing. They'd be talking about keeping the peace, about creating some order. The whole thing showed how much clout Mr. Ruggiero had. He'd arranged it. They were having it in his territory. He was the peacemaker. Though Manny really knew few of the details, he was proud to be part of it.

Manny smiled to himself. He ran his palm along his hair, slicked back with pomade and still jet black. He was proud of himself: proud of his Roman profile, proud of his tailored suit and imported patent leather shoes. He was even proud of his plump pasta belly. He crossed his short arms over his chest and glanced out at two hunters in red and black plaid probing a hedgerow.

"We almost there?" he said. "My ass is getting sore."

"Another ten, fifteen miles, I think. This thing out in the sticks, or what?"

They'd had to get a map from a gas station to locate the tiny hamlet where the meeting was to be held.

"Yeah. That beer distributor, he's got a house in the woods. It's at his place. Perfect. The weaks down here, they don't know their asses from their Aunt Ednas. Buncha hicks. What could be better?" Manny hated hicks, hated the country. He liked the city—his city. It made him comfortable to see lights at night, to have somewhere to go, things happening. He couldn't stand the gloomy open spaces, the endless darkness of rural nights.

"I hear he's putting on quite a feed," Leo said.

"Open pit. They couldn't get the cuts they wanted around here, so they knew a guy at Armour in Chicago. They're shipping in I don't know how many pounds of their best T-bones and Delmonicos—stuff that usually goes to the swanky restaurants in New York."

"Sounds good."

"Marbled, that's what makes a good steak, when it's marbled just right. Especially for charcoal."

"Makes my mouth water." Leo scratched his iron crew cut. He was a stocky man, dirty around the edges. His nicotine fingers had black nails, his collar and cuffs were dingy, his shoes scuffed, his hairy ears clogged.

Manny slipped a plastic-tipped cigarillo from the pack on the dash and bit at the cellophane. Leo punched the lighter.

"Still busted," Manny said, squirming to take a book of paper matches from his pocket. "I'll have the new car next week. Guy promised."

"Another New Yorker?"

"No, I'm trading up to the Three hundred C, the hardtop. That mother's got a three hundred and seventy-five horse engine. Understand? Three hundred and seventy-five appaloosas under the hood. God, that's power. What I have to have in a car is response. Elegant, okay. But a car's nothing without power."

"Mingya, I can hardly wait."

"Said he had a line on a baby blue one. Tinted."

"Who's that, your cousin?"

"My wife's cousin. Petey Musso. You've met him. Runs a junkyard out in the boondocks. I don't like him, he's a hick. But he's no dope. I put him onto that meat deal I was talking about. Remember?"

"Oh, yeah. That was a great idea, Manny."

"Sure, that meat business. He's already got some hayseeds lined up to supply the product. We just sell it. Could be a big deal. I told Mr. Ruggiero about it. It'll work anywhere. So, in any case, this Musso's picking me up the Chrysler. Tinted, I told him. Gotta be tinted."

"He getting you a good price on it?"

"Yeah." Manny chuckled. "A steal."

They both laughed.

––––––––

Link's '52 Chevy Bel Aire purred through a residential section of the county seat. He cruised easily, his eyes searching for a Chrysler 300C, light blue. He felt a knot of tension near his navel. His left knee vibrated with energy.

Slouched on the passenger side, Ronny asked, "Did you see the car?"

"What car?"

"The death car, man. What a job. I mean, you could sit in the driver's seat and reach over and adjust the idle on the carburetor. I'm not shitting you, that's where the engine ended up. The freaking wheel's bent up like this. The roof—I guess they had to rip it open to get them out."

"I drove past the tree. You could see where he hit the brakes. Went too far into the curve."

"Reeked of beer," Ronny said. "Genny and Topper bottles still on the floor in back. A lot of blood, too. Had to be going—what do you figure?"

"Least seventy when he hit." Link guided the car slowly around a corner. "Should have gone off into the field there, they'd have had a chance. But he locked them up and ate it head on."

"The one girl went through the windshield. They found her about fifty feet beyond the car. I knew her."

"You did?"

"I mean, I knew her around. Just turned eighteen, pretty as hell. My brother's friend dated her a couple of times. He said she had great moves but wouldn't put out for him. I guess she was stuck on that guy, the one who was driving. I saw her down at the Point in a two-piece bathing suit last summer, and I had to go in the water. Real nice. Beautiful legs, with those bulges. She was a redhead—they're always hot. I guess she got messed up bad. Shame, a good-looking girl like that."

"It was quick."

"I'm telling you, just looking at her, I had to go in the water. Those legs."

"Keep your eyes open," Link said. He palmed the wheel and turned the car down an elm-lined street. "Petey claims he spotted it here."

"What is it, that Three hundred?"

"Yeah. Light blue, whitewalls, tinted. Has to be tinted, he says."

"Got the three ninety-two, right?"

"Yup, but it's a monster. That car weighs over forty-three hundred pounds."

"Was it on the street?"

"Maybe up a driveway, I don't know."

They crawled. Debbie Reynolds gushed "Tammy" over the radio. They passed a school bus full of tiny faces.

"Hey, Link, lookit, willya? Look up there."

"See it?"

"No, up there, heading this way. Oh, my God. Slow down, will you? Oh, mama. What a number. And a nurse. She's a nurse. I'm gonna cream my jeans. What a build. And those nurses know how, believe me. Talk about moves. Hey, she's giving us the eye. Nurse, take my temperature. I'm burning."

"Waitress."

"Fuck you, she's a nurse."

"With pompons on her sneakers?"

"So what? Waitress. Look at the way she walks. That is something I'd like to spend eternity with."

"Don't forget the Chrysler."

"My eyeballs are on fire, man."

"She's just a kid with some baby fat."

"I guess a stick of dynamite's just a Zippo lighter with some baby fat. Especially in that white uniform. White and tight. That does it for me. She's a destroyer."

"Just pay attention to business. Petey's antsy to get that car. He's got a customer who doesn't like to wait."

"In Petey's ear, I say. That piece was just my type. What's your type, would you say?"

"No type," Link said. "Wait a minute."

"That it? It's blue. It's tinted."

"That's it. Meet you where we said. If I don't show in half an hour, cruise the main drag a couple of times. I'll flag you down."

"Roger."

Link got out at the corner. Ronny slid behind the wheel and drove off.

Link crossed and began to walk back along the sidewalk. Suddenly the world sprang to life. He felt as if he'd been swimming through mud and now had broken into crystal-clear water. Every sensation took on a resonance of meaning. He felt his weight on the slimy fragrant leaves underfoot. The spit of rain shaken from branches startled him. The motionless curtains in front windows stared at him. The creak of a starling on a wire shot up his nerves. His eyes jumped.

He came even with the Chrysler, glanced at the lock buttons. He moved around the front and stopped by the driver's door. From a tear in the lining of his jacket he extracted a dent-puller. He twisted the threaded end into the key slot and slammed the spool back three times. The lock cylinder came free. He opened the door and got in.

The interior still had a leathery new-car tang. Link worked the dent-puller into the ignition switch. He yanked it out with one stroke, leaving red, black, green, and yellow wires dangling. Sliding the tool under the seat, he took a toggle switch from his pocket. He twisted the bare wire ends onto the terminals. A red light came on below the speedometer.

He felt her coming before he looked up. Motion— every part of her joined in the motion of her walking. Her white skirt stretched and tugged. Her pink jacket, unzipped, flapped open. Her hands fixed a strand of her brown pageboy, pulled at a sleeve, smoothed her collar, hefted the purse that swung from her shoulder. Her mouth beat time on a wad of chewing gum.

Link straightened. He slung his right arm across the top of the seat. He forced a yawn, relaxed his face into a contented smirk. Nice easy car—his car. She noticed him. He let the smirk sag into a leer, looking her up and down. She didn't look away, as he expected, but held on to her gum, eyes grave, watching him. He winked. Get out of here, you little bitch. Her mouth twitched. She hung beside the car, casual, waiting. Link cursed under his breath. He leaned over and rolled down the passenger window.

She brought her face closer, propping her hands on her thighs.

"Whataya know, angel?" Link said.

"You live around here? Where you from?"

"City," he lied.

"New car?"

"Just got it. Want to go for a ride?"

She bounced her shoulder. "Where?"

"Nowhere."

"Okay."

Link unlocked the door. Her smile got in. She smelled of lilac and Juicy Fruit. He surveyed her hard prettiness, her pug nose, lively brown eyes, sharp chin, wide cheekbones. And the mouth. She pushed it out at him. The tumid glossed lips pulsed with her chewing.

He held her eyes with his while he flicked the toggle to turn on the car's starter. Her name was Marsha. She worked at Don & Ella's Route 88 Diner. But she didn't have to be in for an hour—she liked to leave early and walk. Anyway, mornings were Dullsville.

"Good tips?" Link asked, easing the Chrysler onto the street.

"Good and small. And all those truckers with the same old gags and the same old cracks. I tell them I could never love a man with piles and that shuts them up, because they all have them." She giggled.

This was funny, her meeting him, she said, because her horoscope—she was Taurus, the bull—said that she'd be making a new acquaintance and going on a trip. Maybe they should take right off for Howe Caverns or somewhere. Did he believe in that stuff?

"No, I usually lead my own life."

"You're a free spirit. I knew that. Whataya do?"

"Drive stock cars."

"You're kidding."

"Okay."

"No, really, do you? Judas priest, that must be something."

"Yeah, it's something. You know, you've got a nice smile. Reminds me a little of Kim Novak."

She rolled her eyes but couldn't help giving him another flash of wet teeth. He took a pack of cigarettes from his shirt pocket, shook one out, pointed it at her. She reached for it with her lips. He pressed the mother-of-pearl lighter. They both waited for the click. The sweet aroma of tobacco filled the car.

The town quickly gave way to lumpy farmland. Link drove about a mile and pulled into a roadside gravel quarry.

"This guy's a friend of mine," he told her. "I've got to talk to him a second."

Ronny sat in the green Chevy reading *Playboy*. Muffled music drifted from the window. He craned his neck, regarded Link with raised eyebrows.

"You said you weren't feeling well," Link said. "I brought you a nurse." He grinned. Ronny forced a grin. They both nodded their heads at each other, grinning.

"Think this is smart?" Ronny asked.

"She'd love to meet you, buddy."

"Meet me? Link, what is this? You know that broad?"

"She says her name's Marsha. Didn't you say you were aching to?"

"Not if it means spending three years in Auburn."

"Few minutes ago you were talking about eternity."

"Jesus H. Christ. She's seen you. She's gonna get your license number."

"I promised her a ride. I guess I'll have to take her myself."

"Hey, this isn't funny, man. I mean it."

"Well, just act natural, then, or she'll tumble."

"You're crazy, Link. You're a yard and a half over your ass."

"Just trying to have a good time."

Link strolled back to the Chrysler. Ronny hid his face in the magazine.

"What's the matter with him?" Marsha asked.

"Shy around girls. Let's go."

He steered the car onto the pavement and they headed farther into the country. Marsha talked. She liked this kind of weather, fall and all but not too cold. Seemed cozy. The McGuire sisters could really sing, and "Sugartime" was her favorite song ever. Boys her age usually were too shy with a girl, then to cover up they got crude. She preferred a man with a certain amount of maturity. Like Link. How old was he? Twenty-eight? He sure didn't look that old. Maybe because of the way he dressed, or maybe because he made her think of James Dean. James Dean was her favorite movie star ever. When he'd gotten killed in that car crash, she'd cried for a week, and she still would cry if she thought of him for long. She wanted a better job than waiting tables, she said. She could sing. She'd been in glee club in high school. Maybe she could get into a group like the McGuire sisters and have a hit record.

On a straight stretch of road Link punched the gas pedal a couple of times to test the car's acceleration. Its weight strained against the engine for a second, as if a giant rubber band were being stretched. Then the car sprang forward, the momentum providing a breathless surge.

"Hey," Marsha said. "You're a race car driver. How fast can you make it go?"

"Fast enough."

"Let's see."

He eased the car to seventy and held it. It rumbled along easily.

Marsha snapped her gum and smiled. "Do you believe," she asked, "that you can meet somebody you never saw before and know all about them, just like you've been best friends always?"

"Why not?" Link had his head cocked listening to the symphony of efficient sounds coming from the engine.

"And love them? Know you truly love them?"

"Sure. Love's the easy part. It's all the rest of it."

She slid across the seat until her thigh pressed against his. "I know it's going to be that way with us, Link. I know it."

"You do?"

"Mmm-hmm. I know whose car this is, too."

Link fed the engine more gas. The weeds crowding the side of the blacktop became a blur.

"What?"

She stretched a strand of gum to arm's length and gathered it back with her tongue.

"I know whose it is. Old man Messick's. He used to work for the highway department. Now he's retired. Lives a couple of blocks from us. His wife's in the Rosary Altar Society with my mom."

"Isn't that nice."

"He just bought this car. I heard Mrs. Messick telling Mom how she liked the tinted windshield. And Mom said blue was such a sweet color for a car. Robin's egg, she called it."

"Is that what she called it?" Link muscled into a curve. The car drifted into the left lane, gripped the edge of the road. Link had a hot flash but managed to steer the speeding machine back into the straight. He accelerated. The car shuddered for a moment, then smoothed out at a high-pitched whine.

"Boy, is he going to raise a stink," Marsha continued. "He's got friends on the troopers, too. His brand-new car."

Every rise made them weightless. Link drove with both hands lightly gripping the wheel.

"You know," she said, "back when I was thirteen, I and two of my friends, Sandy and Beth, went down to the dolomite quarry. Know where that is? Anyway, the three of us were swimming in our birthday suits— all the kids used to. I guess the highway department had something to do with the quarry, though, because here comes a yellow truck. We don't see him until it's too late: old man Messick. He starts saying, 'You kids know you're not supposed to be in here, I'm going to tell your parents, I'm going to get the cops, this is private property,' and all. I peed, I was so scared."

It didn't seem the car could go any faster, but Link opened up the throttle and it responded.

Marsha chewed more quickly. She never stopped smiling. "Then he sees our clothes. He goes over and picks them up. Says, 'Okay, get out of there.' Course, we're bare naked. 'If you don't,' he says, 'I'm going to take your clothes with me and go call the cops.' So we had to. We climb out of the water. We're trying to cover up. Sandy's crying. And he's standing there saying, 'You girls are old enough to know better,' and how this is a dangerous place and all. And he's looking and looking and looking."

They passed a cherry orchard. The rows of trees whipped by with a machine-gun rhythm. Marsha held her breath for an instant.

She continued, "So he starts saying, like, 'Whose underpants are these?' And he throws them and watches while we put them on. Then he just drives away. We're scared he's gonna tell our folks and we're going to get in trouble. But he never did. Know? He never did."

They were traveling through fluid, hardly touching the tar-patched macadam. Marsha stopped talking. She reached tentatively for the dash.

Link looked at her quickly.

She returned his glance, her eyes peeled, intimate, bursting.

———

Meat. The prehistoric smell of broiling meat wreathed in the stagnant air. It drifted across the lawn and onto the porch of the sprawling house. The men standing in small groups under the bare maples smelled it, the men peering from attic windows smelled it, the two Great Danes chained near the driveway lifted their heads and sniffed the aroma.

Manny stood beside a stone cherub who was urinating into a pool. He was talking to a square-faced man beside him. "So I say, Well, what's the fine? I'll pay it right here. And he says he guesses a buck a mile over the limit. He claims I'm doing fifty-five in a thirty-five, so that's twenty plasters. I give him a Jackson, then slip him an extra five along with it. What's this for? he says. That's to buy your wife a hat to go with her new dress, I tell him. He goes red as a beet. Ha. You know, new dress, twenty-dollar dress. Dumb-ass cop."

"That's good, Manny," the man said. "That's funny. Oh, Jesus, there's Vinnie. I've gotta talk to him. I'll see you around, okay?"

"Sure, sure. Hey, ever come through the city, stop in at the club. Always a good time waiting for you at the Voglia."

"I'll do that."

Manny licked his lips and looked over toward the long barbecue pit that had been constructed of cinder blocks. A chef, complete with white mushroom-shaped hat, was turning the cuts over the coals. Manny was hungry, but he didn't feel like eating. His stomach was griping. He blamed it on the long ride down.

Plus, he had to admit, the fact that Mr. Ruggiero hadn't greeted him when he arrived made him edgy. Hadn't spoken to him, hadn't acknowledged his presence with even a nod. Manny couldn't decide whether it meant anything or not.

Lucky it turned out mild, he thought. A lot of the men milling around the yard wore fashionable silk suits, glen plaids, Broadway sport jackets. They wore suntans that spoke of trips to Havana. They weren't ready for hard weather. If only the rain would hold off—but it had already begun to drizzle.

Manny watched them lining up at the antipasto table in the garage, piling plates with peppers and olives, cheese, prosciutto, and artichoke hearts. He watched them embracing and kissing and jabbering like they were just off the boat. He could speak some halting Italian. But hell, this was America, not Siceelia, not Na-polee.

Nah, he decided, Mr. Ruggiero wasn't mad. Just busy, just occupied with the meeting and all. He decided to walk down to the car to get a new pack of cigarillos. Moving around might help settle his stomach.

Descending the hill, Manny had to smile inwardly at all the Cadillacs. Eleven, twelve, thirteen—like a goddamn funeral. One of the stars in Manny's heaven was his appreciation of the fact that a Cadillac was no class car. A Chrysler New Yorker, or that 300C he was getting, those were class cars, power cars, handling cars, the only type of car you'd catch Manny Petrone riding in. A Cadillac was a nigger car, a big boat. Even these guys, these wise guys, they had some sucker in them. Look at all those Cadillacs.

The cars overflowed the crushed-stone parking lot into a newly mown field. Manny stepped gingerly to avoid soaking his new wingtips in the wet ruts.

"Cops!"

A man was running toward Manny up the private road that led from the highway. He moved haltingly, hampered by his long trench coat.

"Hey, what the hell's happening?" Manny shouted.

"Cops, man!" The other slowed. "The fishmonger who was just here—he went to go and—he run into troopers—they've got the road blocked—right down there!"

"What? Isn't somebody supposed to be watching?"

"I'm watching. And I'm telling. Cops. All over the place. I gotta get up to the house."

Manny followed him along the driveway, not sprinting but walking fast, trotting a few steps, then walking again. The intermittent drops of rain came more steadily.

As he reached the yard, Manny noticed a rifle barrel protruding from one of the upstairs windows. The sight made him feel giddy. Was this happening? Was this really happening? He was already panting from the exertion of mounting the hill.

Now men rushed past him toward the cars. It reminded Manny of after a ball game when everybody scrambled to be the first from the parking lot. They were shouting, barking orders and questions. They kept repeating the word "cops" as if it were a kind of school cheer.

Manny wondered if he'd made a mistake. He should have gotten into his car at the first alarm and driven out. But if the cops—if the road was blocked—if they were down there? He didn't know. He watched a man pull a long-barreled revolver from his jacket and toss it into some high weeds near a replica of the Lourdes grotto.

"Manny, what the hell's going on?" Leo had a napkin draped over his tie, a half-eaten steak sandwich in his fist, and a bulge of partially chewed food in his cheek.

"Where's Mr. Ruggiero?" Manny demanded.

"How should I know?"

"Come on, we have to scram. The cops are all over."

"Where?"

"Everywhere. The road's blocked. Let's go."

"How'll we get through?"

"I don't know. Bust out. Everybody's running."

"Jesus, I thought—"

"Don't. Whatever you do, don't think. I mean it."

They loped a few steps down the driveway. Manny stopped and said, "The iron. Get rid of it."

"What?"

"Chuck it. Now."

"Manny, this is the Colt. This gun cost me."

Manny grabbed him by the collar and started to pull his coat off. Leo twisted out of it, unsnapped the shoulder holster, and catapulted the gun toward the woods.

They reached the car on the run. Leo cranked the engine.

"You're flooding it, goddamn it."

Leo was breathing too hard to answer. He ground the starter again.

A Cadillac came swerving backward up the lane. It

veered into a hedge, cracked down branches, stalled. Six men piled out. They yelled, "No getting through! They're grabbing them!"

Manny felt as if he were sinking in quicksand. He glanced up to the house and saw two men disappear into the forest that surrounded the yard on three sides.

"Come on," he said to Leo. They started up the hill. Manny almost smiled to himself. These guys are supposed to be tough. They run around like chickens with their heads cut off. Use your noodle, you just fade into the woods until the heat's off.

Crossing the yard, Manny put on his camel-hair overcoat. He was glad he'd brought it. Abandoned steaks were still cooking over the coals. Drops of rain sizzled on the hot grate.

The first obstacle was a disintegrating stone wall sprinkled with wet leaves. It was like walking over a pile of greasy bowling balls. Leo almost made it, then tripped on a strand of barbed wire and danced with a shrub. Manny took hold of the wire between thumb and forefinger and stepped gingerly over it. They hurried down a gully, up the other side. They descended a long slope that left them out of sight of the house.

Leo hesitated, gasping for breath.

"Wait up, Manny. I think—" He vomited antipasto and chewed meat.

Feeling queasy, Manny turned away. He was perspiring inside the warm coat.

They moved on. Manny couldn't remember the last time he'd been in a forest. Not since childhood, it seemed. The thick smell of rotting leaves reminded him of the incense they used in church at Easter and at funerals. He stepped into a hole. His shoe filled with cold ink. A thorn snatched at his camel-hair and tore it. Burdocks crowded his pantlegs.

At the top of a short rise they paused.

"We should be almost back to the road," Manny said.

"The road? The road's back that way. You think we're headed for the road?"

"Course. We're making a half circle, like. We came from over there, right?"

"That general direction, yeah."

"From that ridge right there. I remember seeing this tree."

"There's millions of trees," Leo said.

"This one. The road's right down there."

"I thought you said over this way."

"I said we'll veer in that direction."

"Whatever you say, Manny. I'm turned around."

Manny had a sense of direction. In spite of the uniform sky, in spite of the folded landscape that made every direction look the same, Manny could feel the way.

But when the rain began in earnest, a different sensation came over him. Not panic, exactly. An urgency. A desperate need for shelter. He took off his coat and draped it over his head. He didn't run, he strode and skipped. He gave up looking ahead, just watched his footing and took the way of least resistance. Leo struggled to keep up.

At last Manny found a path. Someone had walked here recently. Only a few leaves had fallen over the tracks. Probably led, had to lead right to the road. He followed it for two hundred yards until it disappeared into a tangle of vines and wetland. Manny felt trapped, exposed, forgotten, vulnerable.

A big smile took over his face. Leo, catching up with him, recognized the sign and looked away. Manny smiled and smiled, his eyes brimming over. They stood there for a long time while Manny pulled himself together.

They moved on again, no longer hurrying, offering hunched shoulders to the steady downpour.

By four o'clock the meager light was already draining from the sky.

"Manny, what the hell are we going to do? This is

no joke. We can't go on in the dark. We don't know where the hell we're going. I'm freezing."

"What are we going to do? What are we going to dooo?" Manny mocked. He took out his last cigarillo, unwrapped it, and lit it with the third match he tried. He held it cupped in his hand. He'd been saving it for when they found the road. "How in hell should I know what we're going to do? Huh?"

The rain continued like a stubborn faucet. Manny leaned against a tree. He felt like lying down.

"Wait a minute," Leo said. "I think I heard something. Hear it?"

"No—yes."

"From the house?"

"Crazy? We're five miles from the house by now." Leo flapped his arms and paced.

"No, listen!" Manny whispered. "It's right over there."

"Hey!" Leo shouted. "Hey! Over here."

The sound of breaking twigs moved up the next rise. The two men who crested the hill wore bright orange slickers and the wide-brimmed hats of state troopers. One carried a shotgun, the other a long flashlight. They stopped and looked down on Manny and Leo.

"Ain't you fellas got sense enough," one said, "to come in outa the rain?" They both laughed.

November 18

Petey Musso reached inside his car and tapped the horn to send three ripples of sound across the still air. He was a compact man, with a round face and dark, thinning hair. His eyes moved from the paintless house to the barn, to the splintered corn crib, to the dilapidated shed that had been a milking parlor. No one appeared.

A cat rubbed against his shin. He leaned down to scratch its arched spine. A rooster cracked the silence. Pete liked farms. He breathed the pungent manure, the lush rotting apples and grapes. He could see his breath.

He yawned, pinching his eyebrows together with his fingers. When he looked up again, he was startled to find a man standing close beside him. A boy, really. Pink cheeks. But tall, six two, wearing overalls and rubber boots that looked too big for any feet.

"Uh, Larry, right?" Petey said.

The boy nodded his head once. Straw hair dangled over his forehead. Petey followed him up the slope to the barn.

The inside was like pitch after the white overcast sky. It took Petey a minute to get his bearings. Then the creak of hinges echoed up to the high roof. Another man approached him.

"Good to see you, Petey. Glad you could make it."

"Elton. Cool today."

"Say snow by tonight. Hey, congratulations. Guess I haven't seen you to talk to since."

"Thanks."

"Yeah, old married man. Yessir. Anyway, this is how we're set up here. You see how much room we have. Plus I've got that packing house up the lane that we could fix up if we really go to town."

"You've been at this how long?" Petey asked.

"Six months. They're screaming for it. Supermarkets are screaming for it. Little grocery stores are screaming, they can't compete. Restaurants are screaming. They're all screaming. More the better. But I haven't got the trucks or the connections to expand like that. You can swing it. I'm telling you, you won't be able to sleep at night. They'll be tearing down your door, screaming for this stuff." The lean-faced farmer turned his head and let a tablespoon of tobacco juice plop to the floor.

"How much you moving now?"

"Some. People I know. They like it. No problems. None's come back yet."

"Where?"

"Here and there. I don't want to say exactly, maybe your bride shops one of them."

Larry hawked up a laugh. The older man looked at him without expression.

"But it's edible."

"You wouldn't know it from prime round, Petey. Mostly, it's the way we cut it. Larry studied that in co-op school. He's good and he's fast. You take the best cuts, the rest you grind. Got an electric grinder over there. That goes to the restaurants for burger. Twenty-five-pound packs. They're screaming for good lean burger. That's a moneymaker."

"What about the cost?"

"I'm giving it to you for a flat rate, fifteen cents a pound for everything, and that includes the steaks. You sell it at thirty, forty cents, half a dollar, more. They can't get enough of it. Those guys are always sweating pennies. You're doing them a favor."

"We'll see once we get going. I'm lining up some other suppliers, too. This is your experience, though? Fifty cents?"

"For the best stuff, more. You're still saving them over a regular slaughterhouse."

"Where's the catch?"

"Catch? No catch. What catch?"

"Not exactly legal, is it?"

"No, not strictly. But who's to say? Supermarkets love it. They do have these inspectors—Department of Ag. But they're in business. You sugar their tea, they drink it."

"How do you know?"

"Well, we haven't run into them yet, but that's my understanding. Anyway, with your people, that shouldn't be a problem."

"What's that supposed to mean?"

"This is—Manny Petrone's in this, isn't he?"

Petey crossed his arms and moved his face closer to the other man.

"Hey," Elton protested. "Ain't you some relation to his wife? I practically know Manny myself. Did business with a guy once who was a friend of his. I'm just asking, is all."

"You deal with Petey Musso on this. Period." Petey tapped his own breastbone with a finger.

"Sure, Petey, whatever you say. Your people are your business."

"Keep that in mind."

"I will," he said, splattering more tobacco juice on the floor. "Sure will. Larry."

The boy turned and went though the door where the farmer had entered.

"Don't worry about me, Petey. I know what's what. Larry too. Now, I want to show you how we operate. Come over here."

He led Petey over to a long zinc-topped table. Mallets, saws, chisels, and knives were strewn along the top of it. Half a dozen hooks and a block and tackle hung down from the loft overhead.

"Rigged this up myself," Elton said. "And I'm going to put two more of these setups over there when we get rolling. Here."

Larry slid back a door and entered leading a large, mottled-gray horse. He approached the other two men. The horse's head bobbed each time it stepped gingerly down on its right front hoof.

"Look at this horse," Elton said to Petey. "Ain't he a nice-looking horse? Good-natured. Not a particularly hard-worked horse. That's what you look for. And he's nice and fat from being laid up. Feel him."

Petey liked horses. He put his hand lightly on the taut, electric flesh. The animal turned to look at him with liquid eyes.

"Lot of weight to this horse. Picked him up from a guy down on Miller Road. Hardly cost nothing, 'cause he's lame. Fine horse."

He pulled the block and tackle along its wheeled track until it hung over the horse's spine. Then he slipped two chains under the animal's belly. The horse was used to being harnessed and perked up its ears as if in memory. Elton fastened the chains snugly. The horse stamped its rear hoof.

"Easy," Larry purred. It was the first word the boy'd spoken. He'd put on a rubber apron. He held the horse's head, stroked its muzzle, and cooed and clucked it into tranquillity. Then he slipped off its halter.

"I remember, my old man had a horse very much like this one," Elton said. "We used to hitch him to the sleigh—Jesus, we had a time."

Larry stepped back. One hand brushed the shock of yellow hair away from his eyes. The other took hold of a sledgehammer leaning against the wall. He cupped his left hand and spat into it. He moved directly in front of the horse's face. He brought the hammer to chest level, one hand near its iron head. As he hefted it up, up, he slid both hands to the end of the handle. It hung there for a moment. Tendons corded in his neck.

"Hey!" Petey cried. "What the hell are you doing?"

Petey drove home thinking of Beverly, of her soft Italian eyes and the dimples that flanked her spine. She was no longer pissed. She'd forgiven him that morning. But, damn it, why did she have to wear those scoop-necked sweaters that let everything show when she leaned over? As if her figure didn't come through her clothes to begin with. She liked to flirt. Okay, she had a lively personality. Warm. Great smile. But the guy'd made a crack and she'd laughed. Laughed. That's why he'd had to do it. He hadn't made the welts on purpose. He hadn't used his fists. But he thought what he'd do if he caught her really messing around.

Anyway, she needed it. And that stuff about telling her brother—what a laugh. Frankie Carbo was tough, sure. But he knew you had to keep your woman in line. Plus, Petey and Frankie'd been like that since fifth grade. Besides, Frankie wouldn't be getting out of Elmira for another year and a half. Christ, three years, no beer, no women. But Bev was all right. She wasn't pissed anymore.

He'd first noticed her when she was ten and he was eighteen. Of course, he knew her before that. Frankie's kid sister. Baby of the family. But that summer—he'd been working at the A&P, he remembered—he suddenly noticed her lopsided smile, and those eyes, and the cute suntanned legs. Of course, he didn't dare, then. She was a child. But she sprouted early. Even though she kept her hair tomboy short and acted like a little pest, he watched her. Sometimes, when he hung out at Frankie's, he roughhoused with her. He was surprised by her strength, her bursting energy, the hardness of her flesh. He gradually built a shrine for her in his heart.

He waited. Years of terror and hot, sweating despair. The bleak years of his army hitch. Years when he talked to her for hours on end in his head. When he groomed himself in front of the bathroom mirror for her. When he lay awake nights, tense, thinking of her.

Then their first dates. She was so casual and laughed and jiggled her shoulders at him and said he was getting fat. She fell for Elvis, who Petey thought was a shithead, and she hardly spoke to him for a month. The difference in their ages kept him scrupulous. He'd never urged her to approach his fantasies. And besides, she would have had to tell the priest in confession and she'd have been embarrassed. It hadn't been easy.

Now she was nineteen. They'd been married six weeks. He found out that she knew plenty. But it was just her hot Latin blood, not experience. He made her swear that.

When he arrived home, Petey found a blue Chrysler parked in his driveway. He pulled in beside it and walked around to the back door. Link sat at the kitchen table, his cheek propped on his fist. Beverly was perched on a stool beside the counter.

"Getting a good show?" Petey snapped at Link.

"Oh, for Christ's sake," Beverly said.

"Everybody gets a free show from you, your robe wide open like that? Is that right?"

"Why, you old lady. I swear," she said, pulling her bathrobe over her bare crossed knees. "Naughty, naughty."

"No, I think you're right, Petey," Link said. "Bev's got the stuff. You're lucky you came back when you did. We were just about to head upstairs." He winked at her.

"Hey, think I'm joking? Not in this house, mister. Hear me? Not in this house. I'll take your head off."

Link put down his coffee cup, extended his hand with the fingers spread, and wagged it like a tambourine. "Look, I'm shaking."

"I mean it."

"Come on, tough guy, have a fried cake." Beverly nibbled his ear and wrapped her arms around him from behind. "Coffee?"

Petey consented to be pacified. "Okay, sure."

"What's that on your shirt?" she said. "You just put that one on this morning."

"Blood."

"Blood? Oh, my God. Did you cut yourself? Oh, Petey."

"No, I had to see a guy about that meat business. They were butchering. Ever see that, Link? They use a hammer first, split the skull. Then they hang them up to bleed."

"I used to keep chickens. Them, you'd slice the heads off and they could run around for five minutes, falling down, smashing into things. That was a riot. Only you didn't let them. Bruised the meat."

"How can you talk about it?" Beverly protested. "It's disgusting."

"Disgusting." Petey mimicked her. "Only you should see her put away a rack of ribs."

"But I don't have to think about them suffering."

"They don't suffer," Petey said. "It's quick. Just, seeing it is what I don't like. Messy. The brains, and when they slice the belly."

"Please, Petey."

"And all the insides come spilling out."

"Petey!"

Petey took a bite of doughnut and smiled.

"That the car you want to sell?" he said to Link.

"Beauty, ain't it?"

"Let's have a look." He swallowed some coffee, and the two men went out.

"This dinosaur'll do the ton," Link said. "I tried it."

"Tinted?"

"You said tinted, it's tinted."

"Yeah, looks very good. Let's move it around back." He slid behind the wheel of the Chrysler and drove it through the gate in the board fence that ran behind his house. He jumped out, pushed open the door of a corrugated quonset hut, and backed the car inside.

"Now, is that car good?"

"Petey, come on. Those plates are new. You know how we do the engine numbers. The VIN. It all matches."

They started up the small knoll behind the house. The field was strewn with junked cars lolling in every imaginable posture. Some were stacked in giant Dagwood sandwiches. Others slunk half buried in mud and weeds.

"Just, this one I want to be sure of."

"All the cars I give you are good. Guy gets stopped, messes his pants, goes to confession with the trooper, that's not saying anything about the car, is the car good."

"Hey, that guy was supposed to be all right. Dorf said he was. Turns out to be a jackass."

"You were lucky you had friends on that one." Link pulled up the collar of his corduroy jacket and jammed his hands into the pockets. "Speaking of which, I see your pal in the papers the other day. Hanging out with a bunch of hoods down near Binghamton. They caught him stomping around the woods trying to get away. Where was that, Apalachin?"

"I heard. It was nothing, far as I could see. They weren't doing nothing. Didn't amount to nothing."

"Just like the Elks, right? Little get-together?" Link laughed.

"Free country."

They stood at the top of the puddled lane among the oldest cars, now so eaten and tangled with dry goldenrod and milkweed that they seemed part of the landscape.

"Here's for the car," Petey said, passing Link a wad of bills. "I appreciate you coming through on it. Means something to me."

Link put the money in his pocket without looking at it. "So how's married life been treating you, boy?"

"Making a lazy man of me." He grinned. "It's like my life's finally begun. No more getting ready. This is it. Every day, something special. I get up, it's something special."

"You should take up writing poetry."

"I know, newlyweds and all. But it's more than that."

"Bev's a sweet kid, all right."

"And, you know, I wasn't joking in there, Link. You have a reputation. And I could care less. Except, don't catfoot around my house or I'll kill you."

Link grinned. "First you have to catch me."

Petey nodded solemnly. They started back down the hill.

"So you're getting into the meat business," Link said.

"Just a kind of investment."

"You know how my ma loves short ribs. Maybe you can pick her up something special."

Petey fought off a smile. "Yeah, maybe. You need a lift?"

"Much obliged."

Beverly's brown eyes watched Link through a crack in the curtain as he climbed into Petey's car. From the leaden sky, a single snowflake fell.

December 17

Khrushchev Khrushchev Khrushchev—the man on the clock radio just kept jabbering about Khrushchev. Now a jingle was starting.

"For God's sake." Phyllis groaned. She groped for the knob. "You can trust your car, to the man WHO WEARS—" She turned the volume the wrong way first, then snapped it off.

For God's sake. She cursed Manny for setting the alarm again when he got up. Yeah, she'd told him to, but not today, not when she was feeling like this. He'd done it on purpose. One of his little needles. Ah, the hell with him.

She dislodged the grit from her eyes and scraped her tongue slowly along her upper teeth. Her head was glass crystal. Funny how erotic she always felt when she was hung over. Not anxious for it, just pleasantly prickly. She eased her fingertips over her breasts. They pressed against the silk of the slip she'd fallen asleep in. She gripped her thighs with her palms and tensed first one buttock, then the other. She could still feel the numb warmth of the booze. It churned in her stomach and shot a liquid charge down her.

She wanted to drift back into sleep, but as soon as she closed her eyes a terrible wakefulness came over her. The blankets crushed her. She had to get up.

Her head heaved and her vision fluttered with black spots as she climbed out of bed. She slumped for a moment onto the chair by her vanity, avoiding her image in the big heart-shaped mirror. Her clasped hands sank between her legs and she shivered. She noticed a glass. Watery, but still a trace of amber there, the froth of melted ice cubes. She sipped it. She savored the faint Scotch taste. She poured it into her mouth, gargled, swallowed. And cigarettes, practically a full pack. She lit one, let the smoke out through a yawn. Oh, the day looked promising. Zip-a-dee-doo-dah. Everything going my way.

She took another look at the clock. May would have gotten the kids off to school by now. Manny probably gone downtown. She walked to the window. No, his car still there. Damn. Waiting for her. Another lecture. Gloat. Dig. How you *feel*-ing, Phyllis? Bastard.

Strange car in the driveway, too. Who? Too damn early to have strangers traipsing around the house. Well, hell, she'd show him. Son of a bitch. She'd go down in her slip. Her house. Her damn house as much as his. Walk around any way she damn pleased. He didn't have to do his business here. He could see these people downtown. He couldn't expect her to put on the ritz, ten o'clock in the morning. Let 'em see. He oughta be proud, anyway. Her figure, hell. Any man'd be.

She swaggered as much as she was able without jarring the tender inner surface of her skull. She gripped the side of her narrow waist between thumb and forefinger and wagged her elbow as she descended the stairs.

"Hiya, Phyl."

The voice startled her. She spun around. Petey was sitting in a chair in the corner of the living room. He looked small, looked as if he were making himself small, looked for an instant exactly like the ten-year-old kid she remembered.

"Petey-poo! What a surprise." She put a hand to

her throat and laughed. "What are you doing here? Give us a smacker, huh?"

He rose and shifted his weight from one foot to another as she approached. Kissing him loudly on the cheek, she licked her fingers to wipe the lipstick.

"You caught me in my skivvies," she said. "Don't look too close, you'll see right through."

"I really came to talk to Manny. Something's up. I had to."

"Business, business. What's he—?"

"The maid told me to wait."

"He's probably on the can. Spends half his life there. Hey, how's the bride?"

"Bev's great. She loved Niagara Falls. We went down the Cave of the Winds—you know, where you wear the raincoats? And on the *Maid of the Mist* and all."

"Bet there's something she loves even more. Hanh?"

"Well—"

"Ha ha. Savor the sweet stuff, honey. Believe me, savor it now because it doesn't last. No, I shouldn't say that. Just, it's never as good, never as fresh. You know what I mean."

"We're happy."

"I'll bet. That's a hot little kitten you've got there. But I know you stand up to her, right? Heh heh. Know what they say, a good man is—I mean a hard man is good to find. Ha."

"She's—it's been great, Phyl. I never thought—"

She stood close to him. Her smile dissolved. "Seriously, if you've got it," she almost whispered. "I mean—that flame, when it goes out, you get a special kind of cold. You can't imagine."

Petey nodded.

"Hey, you look kind of tepid. Bev must be wearing you right out. How about a bracer. Join me?"

"I—I still have to see Manny. This business is kind of important."

"One little one? Open your eyes. Pecker you up—I mean perk you up. Ha."

She leaned on the liquor cabinet for a moment. A wave of jitters passed over her, made her grit her teeth. Petey was usually a great kidder. Were his doldrums supposed to mean something? About her? No, usually she saw him when Manny wasn't around. That was it. Manny didn't like him. Petey was all tight-assed because he had to see Manny. Mr. Big.

"You sure?" It came out almost as a shout.

"Well, I really—"

"Hey, don't let me twist your arm. Christ." She splashed Johnnie Walker into her glass and raised it to her mouth.

"Nobody has to twist your arm, do they, Phyllis?" Manny stood in the door of the passageway to the back of the house. He was examining one of his little tipped cigars, holding it at eye level.

"Oh, Mother of Mary. Will you leave me alone?"

"You can count on that. Musso." Manny jerked his head. Before he disappeared he said, "Love your dress, Phyllis."

Petey crossed the room to follow. He hesitated beside Phyllis, jabbed her shoulder lightly with his fist. She smiled wanly. He shrugged, went out.

Manny had covered the knotty pine walls of his office with photos: Manny with his arm around Perry Como the time the singer had played a one-nighter in the city. Manny holding up a three-foot northern pike that somebody else had caught. Manny beside a group of Little Leaguers whose uniforms said Petrone Produce Giants. Phyllis in soft focus wearing a tight evening gown and a Lauren Bacall look. Manny shaking hands with Governor Dewey. Two young boys astride a photographer's ersatz horse. An autographed publicity shot of Dinah Shore blowing a kiss. Manny at the beach in baggy trunks, his arms akimbo. Manny holding a chrome shovel at a ground breaking. They were all framed and arranged in orderly patterns on the walls, broken up by Rotary plaques and Chamber of Commerce scrolls.

Manny settled behind his desk in a chair whose leather back towered two feet over his head. He made his face hard.

"It's about that inspector," Petey began. "You know I told you? Ag inspector?"

"That? I took care of that already. Sent a guy to talk to him. Whataya bothering me about that for, bothering me at home?"

"I know, I know. That's just it. He may die, Manny. Shit. And I've got this farmer on my hands. He's going to point it right to me. The guy dies, how am I going to—? I mean—"

"Wait a minute. What the hell are you talking about?"

"He's going to die, I know it." Petey's voice had a sour twist to it.

"Who?"

"That inspector I told you about. The guy you sent to talk to him? That guy George? He beat the living bejesus out of him. Happened just yesterday. The inspector, they had to take out his spleen. He's got a broken leg. His shoulder's dislocated. All his ribs cracked. Jaw's broken in four places. They think he'll lose an eye. Critical condition."

Manny worked his teeth back and forth on the plastic end of his cigar. "Yesterday?"

"It's in the paper. Big story about it."

"I haven't seen the paper yet." The news took Manny by surprise, and Petey's case of nerves rattled him.

"That inspector gave my man, this hayseed, a summons," Petey said. "Two summonses in the past month. I told you. Plus he kept hanging around the farm. Asked a lot of questions. This guy's a farmer. Dumb ignorant farmer. Any heat, and he'll point it right at me. They're going to put two and two together and say, Hey, he writes a summons, he gets beat to hell. Let's see if there's some connection. And I can see my guy saying, Petey Musso. Petey Musso got me into it. Petey Musso said don't worry. Petey Musso claimed he'd take care of it. All Petey Musso. Talk to Petey Musso. He's the one."

"Calm down. You'll be blubbering in a minute."

"Calm down? What do I do when they come to me? I didn't want that inspector wrecked. I just said, Have somebody talk to him. Have somebody let him know what's what. I didn't think—that wasn't right, was it, Manny? That was a mistake what George Lombardosi did, wasn't it? You said—"

"Don't tell me what I said. Wise up. Anybody asks you, anybody comes to you, you know fuck all. That solves that problem right there, what you're going to say. You know nothing from nothing. Got it?"

"Hey, I'm no canary. I'm just saying, George went around the bend, didn't he?"

"Second, you make the same point to your hick. He starts throwing names, starts shooting his trap, he ends up just like that inspector. See? He opens his mouth, we cut his dork off and shove it in. See? Only first we put it through one of those meat grinders. Get the idea across to him. Even a hick understands if you make it simple."

"Sure I can tell him, but—"

"Don't just tell, show. Show and tell. Lean on him."

"Whataya mean? That's not—I thought this was just a business deal. I thought, you know, inspector showed up we'd give him fifty, a hundred dollars, that's it. Reason with him. I never wanted anything where people were getting stomped on. This was supposed to be business."

"Supposed to be business," Manny sneered. "You're too much, Musso. Know what? What the hell you think business means? Means I screw you before you screw me. People your age didn't get enough taste of the Depression. That inspector needed a lesson. So he was a slow learner. So what?"

"What if he dies?"

"That stuff with the inspector was your fault anyway."

"I said what if he dies? Whataya mean, my fault?"

"He didn't die. Your fault because you let it get out of hand. Let the guy go too far."

"Wait a minute, Manny. We offered him the grease. He didn't buy."

"You didn't let him know the alternative. You weren't direct enough."

"How was I supposed to know? You—I never thought you'd do that, practically kill him. I mean, federal inspector—if he dies they'll have the FBI on it. They'll grab us all. I never wanted people getting hurt."

"They won't grab *us*, my friend."

Petey scratched above his ear. "Ask me," he said, "that Lombardosi's cracked. Way I heard it, he didn't even try to reason with the guy. He just started bashing."

"I didn't ask you. Forget Lombardosi. He's a tool. He's my little finger." He held his pinkie up to illustrate. "Start worrying about Petey Musso."

"The guy's crazy, Manny."

Manny stared silently for a minute. "I thought you were okay."

Petey worked a hangnail loose on his thumb. "I am okay."

"Good. Because what we're talking about here isn't pretend. It isn't something you seen on TV. No movie. No tear-jerker book. This is real." Manny rubbed his palms against each other and smiled. "Do I have to tell you about real? Need a lesson in real? Huh? Like that inspector did?"

"No, I just thought—"

"Hey, that's your big weakness. Leave the mental chinups to somebody who's got the equipment for them. Okay?"

"Yeah. Um, but I think, I mean—I want out. I thought this'd be just a sideline, make some dough off it. I never thought there'd be—that I'd have to—"

"Petey, can I believe my ears? Hmm? You are in on

the ground floor of a very lucrative business. And you want out? Out?"

"I just don't want to."

"Hey, buddy, we have an investment here. What about that? What about the equipment we bought, the band saws and the walk-in coolers and all? What about the trucks? The rest of the people we've got on it? The customers? Listen, all we do is change the business arrangements. Whirlaway Packing goes under. We'll set up another corporation, shift the assets. Lawyers handle all that. We're right back in business in a week or two. I mean, you don't back out of something like this with no reason at all."

"I have a reason. Somebody dies, that's blood on me. The money—"

"So who died?"

"Coulda. And you're telling me, you know, about real and about a lesson and all. Telling me to go lean on a guy. That's not right. Freaking holidays coming up. I'm not gonna."

Manny could feel his body tensing. This was the part he loved.

"You?" he said flatly. "You? You're not gonna? Listen to me, you dumb shit. You know who I am? Hmm? Me? Hmm? Manny Petrone. Manny . . . Petrone." He tapped his chest with two fingers. "You're talking to Manny Petrone. Know who I am? The mover. I make things move. I tell you what to do, you do it, fine. I say jump, you jump, great. But you cross me up, you start telling me, you start trying to tell me what's what, you start thinking you're going to do something other than exactly what I say, you start fucking with me—and I'm going to kill you." He smiled. "Now, I've given you a break because of Phyllis. But you're at the end of your leash right now. And you make me yank, you're going to know it from now to forever, boy. Got it? You're going to be reading about yourself in the paper. Okay? Hear me?"

Petey opened and closed his mouth, nodded.

"And don't worry about your rube friend," Manny continued. "Forget what I said. Don't even talk to him. Don't go near him. I'll take care of it. Don't worry."

"What are you thinking?"

"Hey, I said don't worry. Go back to your junkyard and relax. Have a happy holiday. Know what I mean? Got your Christmas shopping done? Huh? How many days is it now?"

"Manny, listen."

"No. I don't want to listen." He leaned back in his chair and looked away. Petey stood, waited a minute, left the room.

The hard, strong feeling that always bolstered Manny when he set somebody straight faded quickly. His morning coffee, laced with bile, glugged up in the back of his throat.

Lombardosi, that son of a bitch. Manny held a quaking fist over his desk. George Lombardosi. He could practically see the man's face, the little flat bird eyes, the fungus nose, the ax-handle jaw, the skull narrowing up from the ears, the hairline that tangled with his eyebrows when he frowned. He saw it, as always, above him—George stood six inches taller than Manny. He saw it, as always, frozen in that dour, hopeless expression with its hint of moronic anger.

His thoughts slid back to an incident that happened just before the war, an image that always defined George for him. He saw Gladiola Given, a greasy, loud-mouthed woman with a mustache that she actually trimmed and combed. He pictured the three brothels she ran in the city back then, in her after-hours gin mill that stayed open till six in the morning. He remembered her unlimited supply of cumbersome half-witted sons, virtually indistinguishable behind their urban hillbilly faces.

The old bag had agreed with Manny up and down when he'd told her he was consolidating the palm oil and protection in the city. She was with him all the way. For the best, for the best, she kept saying. But one thing and another, between excuses and bald lies and sob stories, she'd never turned him over a penny.

Manny went to see her that night. He took George Lombardosi with him. George already had a reputation from when he'd worked for a guy running Canadian whiskey across the lake during the dry years.

There she sat, the great, gross Gladiola, in her satin and fringe parlor, one of her idiot sons at her feet, a Chinese fan propped against a quart of beer on the tray beside her, a tall Negress, naked except for high heels and a maid's apron, standing behind her kneading her shoulders.

She tried to conciliate him at first. Offered him drinks, his choice of her girls, a taste of her opium pipe. But Manny was insistent. The money. Now. And one of his people inside her speakeasy to keep track of receipts. Plus, as interest, he said, she'd have to give him six girls so that he could start a place of his own in one of the north wards.

The demands irked her. She began to rub her mouth with the back of her wrist. She hated wops, she said. She had specific, insulting things to say about dago women. She commented negatively on Manny's virility. She spat. Her hands became talons. Her nostrils quivered.

She rose. Behind her, the black woman smiled, batted her eyes at Manny. The son got up. A series of grunts erupted from his mouth. Gladiola approached Manny, shaking a forefinger, taking advantage of his hesitation to wind herself into a paroxysm of rage. Manny tried to cover his panic with a grin.

The room pulsed inward. He half turned to George. The big man stepped in front of him. He picked up the blubbering son—no shrimp himself—picked him up at both elbows and slammed him down onto his feet with such force that the kid dropped to the seat of his pants and sat there dazed, his mouth stretching for air.

The old lady turned her wrath on George, her voice

the sound of nails being extracted from hardwood. He looked at her with a look that stopped her in mid-sentence. Without any warning, his fist crashed into her mouth. Before she had time to react, he pulled his arm back six inches and shot it out again, pistonlike, flattening her nose.

Watching her fall, roll, reach for her broken teeth, spurt blood, sob, and cower, Manny knew that a veil had been torn from his eyes. He'd never hit a woman in his life, and he was proud of living up to the cliché or commandment that said you never did. But seeing a man punch a woman with unrestrained force gave him the heady, omnipotent feeling that comes from casting aside long-held principles. Force, he saw, was the core of it all. All of it.

George had been right to hit the woman, but Manny resented him for doing it. George had shown Manny something that Manny knew was valuable, but Manny resented him for giving the lesson. And the resentment was curdled to loathing by the fear that grew from a glimpse of George's cruelty, from the realization that he'd always have to be careful with George.

And now, almost twenty years later, George was screwing up. Despite what he'd told Petey, Manny knew the business with the Agriculture inspector was bad. He wondered if they'd heard about it in the Falls, if Mr. Ruggiero himself would demand an explanation. If it had been the first time, okay. But it wasn't the first time. Manny felt himself being squeezed between two boulders. For a second, he couldn't catch his breath.

"What are these Ag inspectors, anyway?" he asked Leo that evening as Leo drove him home in the new Chrysler. "Federal?"

"What do you mean, like health inspectors? That's state, isn't it?"

"Yeah, maybe. But for meat, I think, they're federal. U.S. grade A, right? That'd be federal. Probably some law—think that'd be FBI?"

"Fucking baloney inspector? Nah."

"I don't know. Shit, they called down from the Falls before lunch, even. I said, Yeah, I heard about it, but everything's okay. Okay how? they said. Okay okay. What was I supposed to tell them? I've been pumping that meat deal to Mr. Ruggiero for two months."

"Too bad you have to take the flack. Fucking George is the one."

"That's it. He's the problem, only he's my problem. Once, I could maybe see. But remember that stuff in Oswego last summer?"

"He said it was a mistake."

"Yeah, accidentally on purpose. Cross the Yalu, you're in fucking China, right? Oswego, where are you? Falcone's. Do you go into a place up there, nice place, and say we'd like to handle your security? Then the owner of the joint has to have a new bridge. Know who paid for it? They say at the Falls, new bridge is no problem for you, is it, Manny? Hundred and thirty bucks to get the guy back his smile. My pocket. George is pushing, y'ask me."

"He was always a bulldozer waiting to go berserk. That's his left bower."

"But I'm saying he's pushing too far. Plus, talk is he's been running his mouth. They love that at the Falls. Oh, boy, do they. What I'm thinking, maybe he has ideas."

"Nah. George? He never had an idea. Just, he's a monster. He's King Kong."

"What about that farmer? You see him this afternoon?"

"Oh, I saw him, me and Gap saw him. We told him how it had to be. He didn't like it at first, then he did like it. We made him like it."

"Good."

"What about George? Should I maybe talk to him a little?"

"No, I think I'll have Carlo talk to him. Carlo understands what's at stake here, and those two are asshole buddies. But I'll tell you something, I'll tell Carlo something, I'm not taking any more crap. I've got enough problems. George wants to spit the bit, he's going to be sorry, I mean it. George, anybody else. Start messing with the mover, start messing with Manny Petrone—"

They pulled into Manny's driveway and stopped.

"What if Carlo sticks up for him?" Leo said.

"Don't what-if me, Leo. This—I can handle this."

"Sure you can."

"Can't I?" The mirthless grin flashed across Manny's face and was gone.

"Sure."

December 22

"Mickey Mouse ears and a gun with a string."

"A gun?" George was sweating.

"I want a gun like Sergeant Preston has, with a string and it shoots caps."

"Oh. Well, well." His beard itched, his back was soaked, and the chubby boy was making his foot go to sleep.

"And some candy."

"Well, there." George wrinkled his nose and twisted it back and forth. He reached up under the whiskers to dig a nail into his jowl.

"Some Sugar Daddies and fireballs and an all-day sucker."

"Ho, yessir!" he boomed at the boy. "You be a good boy and we'll see what old Santa can do! Okay? Huh? You hear me, don't you? Huh?"

The boy nodded his head nervously and arched to the floor. George motioned to a blue-haired woman.

"I think I'll take a break here, Mrs. Doyle. Go out and grab a smoke. It's too hot in this getup."

"But there are only three more, Mr. Lombardosi. And some of the parents are ready to leave." She smiled at him menacingly.

George lifted his hands to heaven but sat back down on the folding metal chair.

"Ho ho, yes. Hello there, little girl. Climb up here on old Santa's knee. Now, what would you like? Hey?"

"A Baby Pee Wee doll," muttered the bright, gangly redhead, squirming to get comfortable.

"A baby peeper doll. Well."

"Pee Wee." She fidgeted some more. "It wets. And a tea set, and a jumper like Nancy's, and bubble bath, and Tinker Toys, and high heels, and—"

"Well, ho ho. Now, that's a pretty big order for old Santa. Have you been a good—"

"And a barrette with sparkles on it."

"—good little girl, hmm? Do your chores, like your mommy tells you?"

"Yes."

"And been good to your brothers and sisters?"

She nodded her head assuredly. She writhed once more to keep from sliding off George's lap.

"Ow!" the girl yelped. She slipped quickly away from him. Her hand went up to her side and she looked at George with desperate eyes. Her lip curled down, pulling her face with it.

"Hey, there. Ho ho. Ho ho ho. What's the matter? Huh? You afraid of old Santy? Are you? Huh?"

His back turned icy. He groped for moisture with his tongue. His hand clawed at the side of his neck beneath the white beard.

The red-haired girl ran away sobbing and pressed her face against her mother's hip.

"Ho ho," George bleated. He barely heard the requests of the last two children. His eyes swept back and forth across the church basement. "Well, ho ho."

George made his way to the lavatory. He hooked the door closed behind him. He ripped off the beard and threw cold water onto his eyes. His fingers wrestled with the buttons of the bulky Santa coat. It fell open, releasing the sour smell of mothballs, perspiration, and mildew.

He eased the large semiautomatic pistol from its holster under his arm. He hefted its weight, flicked the safety off, back on. He raised his eyes to the mirror. He didn't know the face that looked back at him, dripping. It wasn't just the silvery wig and floppy red cap. The face had age written on it in networks of burst capillaries, in purple pouches under the eyes, in lines eroding to wrinkles. It was turning into an old man's face before his eyes. He grimaced. The face grimaced back.

He leaned on the washbasin, forcing air into his lungs. Nothing to be alarmed about. Just the close air. No danger, he told himself. No immediate danger. No need to panic. He finished removing the costume. He replaced the pistol and put on his suit jacket, making sure the buttons were fastened in front. He ran a comb through his hair. He pressed his dentures against his gums. He sighed. Better.

Many of the parishioners had left when he finally emerged from the john. He looked for Bea, spotted her standing close to the door talking to Madeleine. The large room reflected his mood—dismal, stuffy, nearly empty, the tinsel and crepe paper and cardboard angels barely hiding the pipes along the ceiling. He began to cross to his wife.

"George. George, my boy." The man in black called him "boy." "I wanted to thank you. The kids loved it, as usual. Just wonderful. You *are* Santa, you know. Really are. What is this, twenty years almost?"

"Twenty-two. I started when Eugene was three. He'da been twenty-five."

"Amazing. You definitely are Santa. And you don't even need the padding these days, do you?"

"I've gained a few around the middle, okay."

"Been feeling all right?"

"Fine, Father. Kinda close in here. And it's a hectic time of the year for old Santa. Ho ho."

The priest threw back his head in a soundless laugh. "Well, we certainly appreciate it." He interlaced his fingers and kissed them. In a softer voice he said, "We've missed you, George."

"What?"

"At the sacraments. Confession. I have a feeling something's troubling you."

"Well, old Santa. Ho ho. Been busy, Father."

"Yes, but don't you think—"

A twinkly woman tugged at Father DeMarco's sleeve. She had to talk with him about the preparations for midnight mass. A problem had arisen about the manger.

"Have a merry Christmas, Father," George said, moving away. "And a sober new year. Ha ha."

"Carlo's getting the car," Bea told him when he reached her side. "Aren't you feeling well?"

"Why don't they turn the damn heat down in this place? It's hot as hell."

"Oh, Santa, such language." Madeleine laughed. She told people that she looked like Peggy Lee. She had the beauty mark and the blond blond hair, and she wore artificial eyelashes and fire-engine lipstick. Still, the resemblance was slight.

"I was burning up," George mumbled. He helped Bea on with her coat. They moved out the door, Bea waving goodbyes on the way.

The snow that had begun to fall while they were inside brought a sigh from Madeleine. Carlo rolled up in his pride, a long burgundy Imperial. George climbed in beside him. The wives sat in back. They glided along the shiny streets.

"Goddamned Father DeMarco started on me again," George said. "I try to do a good turn playing Santa Claus, and he's gotta start harping, the turd."

"Why, George," Bea clucked. "He's a priest."

"What's his gripe?" Carlo asked.

"Missing mass and all. Same old thing. What's it to him, anyway?"

"Thinking of the dough. Attendance drops off, he don't get as much in the plate."

"No, he knows something."

"Knows something about what?"

"The way he looks at me."

"Georgie," Madeleine said. "I saw you goosing that little Simmons girl. Made her cry."

"Oh, Mad, really," Bea put in.

"You shoulda gotten on line, Mad. Could have sat on old Santa's lap yourself. Nice big candy cane for Christmas."

They laughed. George finished tamping his briar and put a match to it, filling the car with cherry smoke.

"Think I'm kidding?" he said. "I remember when Cindy Colletti was—when she used to climb up on the old knee. Now look. Christ, time is just—I don't know."

"Oh, yeah, I heard," Madeleine said. "It was that Joey Nagle, that basketball player, was what I heard."

"What her old man heard, too. Foul shot. Boy wanted to go to college, too. Ha."

"She seemed like such a nice girl," Bea said. "She used to babysit for Madge Fisher."

"Nice, all right," George said. "Nice knockers."

Carlo suppressed a laugh.

"Hey, back when she was asking me for dollies and tea sets, she was already starting to fill out."

"George, stop."

A few minutes later, the car was parked in George and Bea's driveway. The snow had dusted all the lawns and roofs and shrubs and sidewalks and made the split-level houses seem like echoes, one after another—ghosts fading up the street. The two women went in. George and Carlo stood outside absorbing the quiet.

"Carlo, I have to know. I want you to tell me."

"Tell you what?"

"The talk. What are they saying about me? No, I

know there's talk. I don't feel right about myself. I feel funny. Bad funny. Shaky."

"Just the holidays. They pull everybody down."

"Not the holidays. It's everything. Not one thing has turned out the way I wanted."

"What? You've got the bowling alley. Nice home. You're set."

"No, this isn't the way I wanted it. I can't explain it, but, goddamn it, I'm getting old. Not the way we always used to kid about it. I'm sixty-one and I feel it. And trouble's brewing. Trouble's brewing and I don't think I'm going to be up to it this time."

"You're an ox, George. Listen, that business last week with the meat inspector, that was no good. You know it, I know it. You were supposed to cool the guy out, make him happy. Instead, you treat it like you're back placing pinball machines. But what the hell? He didn't die."

"Lousy punk, mouthing off to me."

"You know Manny. That was his pet idea, that meat operation. I happen to know he got it from a kid name of Musso out there, but he was touting it as his baby. So now he has to eighty-six it, he's pissed. Plus, we're trying to run a business. You have to look at these things: is it good for business or bad for business?"

"Business? Petrone doesn't respect me."

"Sure he does. Everybody respects you, George. They respect you in the Falls."

"I'm telling you, Petrone spits on me. He wanted me to drive one of his meat trucks, give up my territory and deliver meat. George Lombardosi driving a meat wagon? And goddamn horsemeat to boot. Wee-hee-heen!" He whinnied into the night air. Carlo chuckled, frowned.

"Trouble is," Carlo said, "you were on Manny's shit list after that stuff with Falcone's place last summer."

"The hell with Manny. I'm telling him where to get off. I'm finished with that prick."

"You can't be, George. You know that. You can never be finished with Manny."

"I want to know if there's talk. What are they saying? Tell me."

"Well, somebody might say it's time you slowed down, took a vacation. But—"

"Who?"

"I said might."

"DeMarco?"

"What?"

"Father DeMarco?"

"What the hell does he have to do with it?"

"He's in on it. Hates my guts. He's behind it, I'm sure, what's happening to me. Him and his lousy God. Carlo, I told things. In confession, I told things I never should have. Him and his hocus-pocus. See the way he stared at me tonight?"

"Hey, come off it. Don't talk crazy. It's just—"

The look in George's eyes stopped him. All around them the light was seeping up from the white ground and mixing with the darkness above, diluting finally to black. After a long moment, Carlo swatted the big man awkwardly across the shoulders and said, "Let's get some holiday cheer in our stomachs, anyway. That's what we need."

———

"I'm worried, Mad," Bea was saying. "Really worried. I know something's wrong with George, but I just can't put a finger on it. Like, often now I find him sitting up at night. He'll be at the kitchen table at four in the morning. Thinking, he says. I don't like it."

She lit a cigarette. Bea was a slender woman who'd maintained her looks, as well as she could, with a precise and tasteful application of makeup. She favored antique jewelry with heavy, ornate settings.

"You know, I'll bet it's his vitamins," Mad said. "I saw this doctor on Jack Paar the other night and he said most people need more vitamins, but they don't even know it. People with cancer and TB—he'd give them the right vitamins and they were cured. That might be just the thing for George. Really."

"I wish I knew. Sometimes I—oh, here they come."

George and Carlo were taking off their coats in the entryway.

"B.V. and ginger, Mad?" George said. "Bea, sidecar? Cutty for the boys. Okay, Carlo?" He mixed the drinks and passed them around. Before he sat down, he said, "This time of the year, I like to drink one to Eugene. To what he might have been, would have been—to what he was. God bless you, Eugene. We'll never forget you, boy. Never ever."

They all drank. Bea wiped away a tear. Eugene had taken a load of shrapnel when the First Marines were retreating from Chosin Reservoir in Korea. Their other child, Nina, had married a real estate man and moved to California. She invited them out, they invited her back, and the years rolled between them.

"And to our best friends, Carlo and Mad. Merry Christmas."

"To Santa." Madeleine giggled. "And his candy cane."

George got down on his hands and knees and plugged in the tree lights. Then he dropped into his recliner and started his pipe blazing again. Carlo idly examined the Christmas cards that Bea had arranged on an end table. Madeleine and Bea, on the davenport, started talking about Mrs. Colletti and her daughter's short-notice wedding.

Bea felt that only a perfect tree could properly show off her collection of ornaments, some of them a hundred years old. George always tried to find her one. This year he'd chosen a sharp Scotch pine, full and fragrant. George looked over the silver-red balls and intricate tear-shaped ornaments, the glass nightingale perched ready to fly, the tinsel and angel hair. On the top a white bulb blinked inside an elaborate silver and gold star.

Carlo was talking hockey. George listened.

". . . over the blue line. And then Resnick slaps it to Conn, but . . ."

The squat man was dressed impeccably, as always—charcoal double-breasted suit, green silk tie, diamond pin. His wide jaw was beginning to show a shadow.

". . . the goalie was faked on his ass, and they still . . ."

Carlo was ten years younger than George, but they'd been buddies since before the war. Then, Carlo had been smart and gutsy but small-time, a neighborhood hoodlum. George had opened doors for him, put him in touch with the organization. They'd grown as close as bristly men can. And even though Carlo had become Manny's right hand, George still felt protective, especially since Eugene. But an idea was seeping into George's mind. He tried to resist, but slowly it flooded him.

". . . calls a face-off. But, Christ, they line up and . . ."

Thy friend. Lest thy friend. Hadn't Carlo just taken Petrone's side? Hadn't he said "we," him and Petrone? If they wanted to, wouldn't Carlo be the one? The Judas kiss. Carlo, who stood inside his defenses? Carlo, who could tell him, Nothing to worry about? Carlo, who could walk up to him and—and what?

George jerked upright, his face flushed. "It's not you, is it, Carlo?"

The women stopped talking.

"What do you mean?"

"You weren't—that—the deal down there, the—"

"George, relax, will you?" But Carlo's eyes wouldn't leave him alone.

"Now, don't you boys start talking business," Madeleine commanded. "For pity's sake, it's Sunday and three days before Christmas."

She continued her conversation with Bea, something about the big department stores downtown. Her slick red lips opened and closed. George's eyes moved down her neckline. Watched her fingers dance. Took in her meaty calves. Lucky. Carlo was lucky. After Liz had died, he'd gone out and found himself a live wire. Something hot and sassy and new. What if Bea—? He'd do the same. No, he wouldn't. What would he do with warm flesh night after night? Still. Madeleine dangled one of her high-heeled pumps, bouncing it on her toe.

Fine tree. Too many icicles, maybe. They gave it a kind of unnatural glitter. And why did Bea insist on hanging up that limp-bodied Santa with the old face? Must have been stuffed with candy once. But why the haggard look? So foreign. And why that ridiculous crystal flamingo? That wasn't Christmas. That was Florida. While he watched, the tree's branches seemed to grow more gnarled, contorted. The needles reminded him of thorns. The flashing star sent out angry razors of light.

"George?"

"What?"

"I said I talked with Sherry today," Bea repeated. "We have to drop off Diane's present Tuesday. She said about noon. Is that all right?"

"That's your niece?" Madeleine asked.

"Yes, my sister's daughter. And she has the cutest little girl. We're giving her a new bike. Well, George?"

"Guess so. Tell the truth, I forgot all about it."

"Getting old, Georgie," Madeleine said. "Memory's the first to go, legs the last. Still got cute legs? Jack Paar was showing his the other night, I kid you not."

George sucked fiercely at his pipe until he'd created a halo of blue smoke around himself. Carlo made a remark about more drinks. George nodded but didn't move. Carlo took George's glass from his fingers.

The room went dark for a second, but George was the only one who noticed. Bea was smacking her lips the way she did. Her hair'd become gray all of a sudden. He'd noticed it, these last how many years, going gray. But now it was all gray. Even her face, folded in on itself, had turned gray. She used to be beautiful. Innocent as hell. Delicate. Soft brown hair. But she'd become so frail, so dry.

Carlo handed him another Scotch on the rocks. George turned back to the tree. Jesus, didn't the rest of them see it? The tree had become a mass of shrapnel wrapped in barbed wire. Its prickly claws raked the air dangerously. Antlered deer smirked. Noël, the foil letters read. What the hell was Noël?

The juice wavered again, dipped, and came back. The star shot a bullet of light at his eyes. Pulsed. The red bulbs glowed hot. Too hot. The tree writhed, caught fire. Flames crackled up the spiny branches.

"Being awfully quiet, Georgie boy," Madeleine was saying. "Got any new yukkers? Huh? Like that one about the gigolo who drove a hard bargain? Huh?"

"Now, Mad. Is something wrong, George?"

George heard them jabbering about George. Wrong? He turned away from the tree, back. No longer burning. But he could glimpse, just on the edge of his vision, something massive and dangerous. He had to keep alert. Something vague and sad. It threatened to wash over the dikes of his mind, to carry him where he didn't want to go. Not ever.

"No," he said. His voice rose. "No! No! Cock! Piss! God! Fuck! Hell! Damn! Fuck! Shit!" He thudded his fist rhythmically on the arm of his chair. Then he jabbed his pipe back between his teeth.

Madeleine, her eyebrows leaping, looked over at a suddenly restless Carlo. Bea was on her feet, approaching George's chair.

"George? Are you all right?" She dragged the last word into two syllables.

"What the hell do you think?" George rose. He stepped to the front window and pulled the drapes to look at the black sky. Across the street the neighbor's bushes were dotted with blue lights. "You heard what I said."

"No, I didn't understand what you said. I think maybe you'd better lie down."

He turned. "Bea, this is no joke. And don't you give me that look," he added, stabbing his finger at Madeleine.

"Hey, relax, George," Carlo said.

"Don't start getting funny with me, any of you. I know."

"Certainly, George," Bea said. "Just—I think your nerves are on edge." She held her lower lip between her teeth. George hated it when she did that.

"On edge? Ha. Of course I'm on edge. I'm on the edge. I'm talking life and death."

"Now, there's a cheery subject," Madeleine threw in.

George looked at the tree again. The light in the star had gone out. It stood dead on the highest prong, cold, menacing. George stared and stared. Then, suddenly, it burst back into white light, slicing his eyes open.

George's manner changed. It changed the way it had changed so many times, so effectively, in his work. It grew still. Icy.

"You know what I'm talking about," he said flatly to Bea.

"No, dear, I really don't."

"Don't give me that." He took one swift step toward her.

Bea tried to cover up. The tree went. Glass tinkled and broke. The lights blinked twice and died. Madeleine gasped. Bea lay sprawled in the needles.

Carlo froze halfway out of his chair. His eyes followed George's hand inside his coat.

George stood watching him, panting, his forehead beaded, his fist gripping the butt of the pistol.

December 24

"White? I say. White? You're going to get white until you wish you had a little less white. You'll be breaking your back out in the white shoveling the white. So white your car won't start. And the plow comes along and fills in your driveway with white five minutes after you clear the white out of it. You won't be singing white, buddy boy, I say. Still, what the hell, it's Christmas." The fat man picked up another Santa from the plate and bit its head off. "Try one, Link? My mom made them. Molasses."

"No, thanks. I just had lunch."

"They're saying another four to six by tonight. The way it's blowing out there, I pity anybody traveling." He laid a seven of hearts on the eight of clubs.

"Good for business?"

"Sure. Nobody wants to wrestle with this kind of stuff once it's dark. They stop. Me, I put my chains on as soon as it gets over an inch."

"You're smart."

"Go through anything, practically, with chains. Here, let me get your John Henry on the register. You're in six. Turn the heat up all the way and put the fan on. It'll warm right up." He laid the book across his solitaire game. Link signed *Chris Kringle.*

"Here's the key. And Link." Link stopped with his hand on the door. The fat man screwed up one side of his face. "Merry Christmas."

"Same to you."

The afternoon sun hardly made a dent in the dirty cotton sky. Snow swirled nervously, piling in drifts, leaping back into the air.

A clacking whir began when he turned on the heater built into the wall of the motel room. He threw his jacket onto the double bed, pulled the drapes open, and waited.

They were used to these storms that poured across the lake from Canada, whipping a froth of snow. Snow had killed Link's father. Snow and despair over a woman who was not his wife and who was much too young, a woman Link had glimpsed once—black eyes and fever lips bundled in rabbit skin.

He remembered the day, a day much like this one. His father drinking rye until the early darkness, then suddenly rushing out into the squall. His mother's simple "He won't be back." The police there that night, Link fascinated by their cars. The stiff body they carried out of the woods the next afternoon. He just lay down, they said. Lay down and fell asleep. Link's mother had right away opened a beauty parlor in the dining room. The chemicals for the permanents smelled like embalming fluid, but after a while Link couldn't smell them. His mother still did hair.

The heater poured prickly air into the damp room. Colored lights studded the shrubs along the highway. This made how many? Four, five years on Christmas Eve? He smiled. Their own little tradition.

He thought of Sherry, as he often did, when she was a child. He'd known her since she was seven, a golden girl with cobalt eyes and sunshine dimples, sleek arms, and a laugh that was music. All the boys loved her, wanted to tag her in tag and sit by her at lunch and hold her hand on field trips to the zoo. All the girls fought to bask in her glow.

She treated Link as she treated the others then, with playful disdain. But once he asked her for a smooch on a dare. She surprised him with a hard kiss on the mouth and laughed in his face. But he didn't forget, nor did she. Always afterward it was him she privileged by taunting him with her eyes.

In high school her own prettiness turned against her. Her girlfriends' admiration changed to envy. They spit behind her back. Her coyness grew hollow. Boys told lies about her. She turned a hard face to the world. She smoked, wore heavy mascara. Gossip molded her into an arrogant minx.

Her reputation attracted a crowd of swaggering boys who'd fought in the Pacific and knew what was what and drank beer till they fell down. They laughed when a girl said no. Nobody in her class invited her to the Junior Prom. A pristine beauty of sixteen, she found herself being dragged through life without a friend.

Except for Link. He'd always retained his devotion to her, but they hadn't dated because he was a year younger than she. But after he dropped out of school to work in a body shop they gravitated naturally to one another. At first she reveled in his frank infatuation. Later he became her only confidant. On twilight drives in battered, coughing cars they watched the gulls on the lake and she talked. She told him her dreams. She told him what the science teacher tried to get her to do when he kept her after school for a make-up lab. She told him her plans to be in the movies, or a model, or maybe a dancer. She told him about the monster nights when she couldn't sleep and cried till dawn. Unjudging, he handled her with a gentleness she hadn't known before.

Her marriage hadn't ended it. She explained to him why, wept in his arms, left him for good. Suddenly she grew up and closed a door. But even during those years apart, he never doubted. He knew it couldn't be over, not finally. He clipped her newsprint bridal picture for his wallet and waited.

Outside, cars were edging through the blank swirl with their headlights on. Link stood before the warped mirror and ran a comb through his hair, patting the wave with his palm. He returned to the window.

Of course, he'd found substitutes. Girls were his nourishment—hard-sexed dolls and cozy babes with soft thighs, sharp-fingered older women, cheaters, divorcées, and hungry teenagers. Always for a night, for a week, for now. Always casual, for fun, a good time.

When they finally came back together he was stunned by the violence of Sherry's illicit passion. In the hours they stole together she made his nerves light up the way they did when he hooked a car or drove over the limit. Again he became the repository of her tragic secrets. Again they stabbed each other with adolescent fervor.

Now he watched her car roll in, crunch across the

packed snow, park behind the diner. He stepped out into the gasping cold and waved to her. She ran, almost tripped, ran.

"God, I saw a car in the ditch up Damson Road," she said, breathless. "The troopers were there, and a tow truck." She stripped off her scarf, combed her fingers through her hair, shook the dusting of snow from her coat. Her black cowboy shirt was decorated with scroll embroidery and white fringe. "They haven't started sanding yet. Sorry I'm late. Aunt Bea and Uncle George were supposed to be by to drop off Diane's present at noon, and they didn't show up until twelve thirty. I had to give them coffee, chat. They're so nice. Then, this afternoon I have to pick up our turkey at Miller's and do some more grocery shopping—I'm sure it'll be mobbed, and . . ." She realized she was talking too much. "Hell. Merry Christmas, Link."

He smoothed her golden hair back from her temple, grabbed a handful of it, kissed her. With his other hand, he felt the curve of her skirt. She gripped him by his shirt collar. They basked for a moment in each other's eyes.

"What'd they give her?"

"A new bike. They're so thoughtful. Except, Bea told me on the phone that Uncle George has been off lately. Moody. He didn't say two words while they were there. Usually, he's all ho ho around Christmas."

"Going through the change."

"Maybe. Bea had a big black and blue mark down the side of her face. She said she got it falling on the ice. I wonder."

She sighed. She wrapped her arms around his neck and laid her head flat on his chest.

"Missed you, angel," he said.

"Oh, Link, thank God. I've been cold for weeks."

"How about a drink?"

"Sure."

He took a pint of apricot brandy from a paper bag.

She found two plastic glasses in the bathroom. He unwrapped the cellophane and poured each half full.

"To us," he said.

"Another year. I love you."

They drank. Sherry felt restless. She kept walking to the window to check the snow. She talked and talked. Asked about his mother. Told about Diane's teacher at school. About the tree they'd bought at one of those cut-your-own places. About how quiet Dave became around the holidays—worse than usual. About what she planned for dinner the next day when Dave's parents came. About her sister, who was expecting her first. Her fingers kept twisting her wedding band.

"I got a little something for you," she said.

"Sherry, I told you."

"No, really, it's nothing. Here."

He untied the ribbon, tore the paper from the flat box. He took out the black leather gloves and put one on. The other dangled at his wrist. He waved to her. "Thanks, I needed them, too."

"Sure you did. They fit?" She loved his hands—big hands, bony and muscular, always dotted with scars and scabs and cuts, but with sensitive fingers and fine nails—intelligent, knowing hands.

"Sure. Here's something for Diane." He handed her a slender unwrapped box.

"Link. Oh, Link, this is gorgeous." She cradled the silver and turquoise cross, examined the slim silver chain. "This is too much. Really. She'll . . . how can I . . . ?"

"Tell Dave? You saved it out of your grocery money."

"You shouldn't have. She's going to absolutely love it. You know how she adores turquoise."

He swallowed the rest of his brandy and began to untuck her shirt. "I have a present for you, too."

She let her head drop back, ran her nails down his scalp, and laughed.

"Let me get ready," she said.

She went into the bathroom and closed the door. She never liked to be undressed by someone else, even him. Not that she was shy—it was just a habit. She preferred to prepare alone.

Watching herself in the cracked mirror over the sink, she brushed her hair. Her present. He knew. Just what I wanted. Needed. And deserved, goddamn it.

Twelve Christmases this would be with Dave. She'd married him for Diane's sake. Married him because her life had slipped and slipped to the point where she didn't know for sure the father of the child inside her. Married him for herself, too. For someone to hold onto. She'd stayed with him for Diane's sake. For someone to go out and get the tree. For someone to buy the presents, pay the bills, be there.

She began to unbutton her blouse.

Married him because back then Link was a cocky young hell-raiser without a future. Dave Ryan was a man, a working man, a serious man, a respectable man, a solid man. And Dave was a man who worshiped her beauty as something sacred. Their marriage had been preordained. He'd rescued her, carried her bodily into adulthood. Link had offered only wildness and passion, fast cars and giddy times.

She folded the blouse and laid it across the edge of the tub.

Diane was an exact replica of Sherry as a child—the lemon silk of her hair, the eyes, the cocked brow, the smile, the streak of stubbornness. For five years Sherry had never thought of spending Christmas Eves in the bathrooms of steamy motels.

But one autumn, when Diane was just starting kindergarten, Dave asked her to have the oil changed; he was a stickler for manufacturers' recommendations. Her heart fluttered when she saw Link at the Cities Service station. They were polite, tense. Casually, he asked her to go for a drive with him while she waited. She couldn't stop herself from saying yes, from practically shouting yes. Then it was natural, automatic. He drove her back a long dirt road. The sun was shining. They talked the way they'd always talked. She poured out her frustration and longing. He said all the right things. She could still remember the musty smell of the back seat.

She slid her skirt down. She stepped out of her half-slip.

After that, Link became the focus of her life. She planned their furtive meetings weeks in advance. Anticipated. Couldn't eat the day before. Visions of Link screamed in her head during the quiet times.

Their rendezvous were adventures. When his mother was away, Sherry would drive to a shopping center in another town and leave her car. He'd pick her up and take her home. They'd bounce on the squeaking brass bed that had been his parents', that his mother kept in the room she'd abandoned after his father's death.

She sat on the toilet cover, unsnapped her stockings from her garter belt, rolled them down.

Link was an enigma, a tender and knowing man as a boy but, as a man, forever a boy. Careless, sometimes cold, yet always unwavering in his devotion to her. He was a ladies' man, but he said he had never loved anyone but her and she knew he meant it. Quiet, a poet when only she could hear. She felt that their souls had mingled, but when she looked into his cool gray eyes, she looked into unknown depths.

She arched to unfasten her bra.

He knew how to talk to her. He knew the exact words that would twist her thinking away from the dangerous paths. He flattered her mercilessly. With a look and a word, he could make lightning shoot low in her belly. His talk reassured her, gave her hope, set her to panting. And most of all, he knew how to lie to her. He was a thief and he knew how to lie.

She hooked her thumbs under the elastic of her panties.

And he had hard, muscled arms. Lean, relentless

hips. Powerful shoulders. A tattoo on his bicep—a red rose with a blue stem and thorns that were too long. And those lovely sweet hands.

She touched her mouth with lipstick, smoothed her lips together, smiled at herself. Turning, she examined the ghostly shadow of her bathing suit against last summer's tan. She slipped her ring off, left it on top of the toilet cistern, and opened the bathroom door.

December 25

Manny hunkered on all fours behind an overstuffed chair. He wore a white shirt, loosely knotted tie, and a headband sporting a single feather. In his hand he clutched a small bow and an arrow with a suction-cup tip. He peered slowly around the corner of the chair.

"Pow! Pow! Pow!" a voice shrieked behind him. "I got you. You're dead."

"I'm going to get you."

"You can't. You're dead," the boy insisted. He grabbed Manny's tie. "I'm taking you to the hoosegow. You dumb Injun."

Manny crawled along behind the pajamaed youngster. The boy made him climb between the television set and the couch.

"Squaw," Manny said. "Oh, squaw. Help your brave escape. Pass me that knife there. The rubber knife, right over there. Hurry."

"I'm no squaw," Phyllis said. "I'm the saloon keeper."

"You're Miss Kitty, Mom," the boy told her.

"Right." She took another swallow of her highball.

"Stevie, want to see snot under my microscope?" his older brother called from the dining room.

"Yeah."

Manny climbed off the floor and dropped his weight into a chair. "You're in a good mood today," he said.

"I have a headache."

"That your cure?"

Phyllis smiled coldly.

"Just don't get out of control, okay?"

"It's Christmas, goddamn it. Supposed to stay sober on Christmas?" She drained her glass. Chimes sounded. "Who's that?"

Manny rose and started toward the door. "Probably Sam. I'm riding down to the club with him."

"What?" she said in a stage whisper. "You're going to your whorehouse and leaving me with these?" She jerked her head toward the next room. "On Christmas?"

"Watch your mouth. It's a social club. There'll be some guys there I want to see."

"Whorehouse."

Before Manny opened the door, Phyllis was on her way to the powder room off the kitchen.

"Mom? Can we go out? I want to try out my coaster."

"No. I mean, yes. Make sure Stevie wears his snowsuit. And buckle your boots. All the way."

Returning with newly rouged lips, Phyllis stopped to pour herself a fresh drink. She heard a man's voice saying, ". . . the one who suffers. Because people see him walking around and they start to think."

"Shargoff?" Manny said.

"Yeah. Damn Jew. Has that place on Norton Boulevard. Part of Lombardosi's. But George—what's with him?"

"I know what you mean."

"Something's gotta give, Manny. Shargoff'll spoil the barrel, I'm telling you. Lombardosi'd better—why, hello, Phyllis."

"Good to see you, Sam."

"Merry Christmas." He stood. Offering her cheek, she pressed against him. "You're looking ravishing as usual," he said. "I was afraid Chief Hubba Hubba here had maybe scalped you."

"I forgot I had my headdress on." Manny chuckled.

Phyllis slid her arm around Sam's waist. "He's quite a buck, all right. A real Comanche."

"Phyllis is the saloon girl. Right up her alley, I'd say. Aren't you going to offer our guest some firewater, Miss Kitty?"

"No, really, Manny," Sam said. "A little early for me. Thanks anyway."

"For most of us."

"But not for me, is that it?" Phyllis said.

"No, not for you."

"I'm a lush, is that what you're trying to say, redskin?"

"Phyllis, come on."

"Am I a lush, Sam?" She rubbed her hip against his.

"Why, no, no *sir*, you're a sport, is all."

"A sport. Hear that, Manny? Have I got a great figure, Sam? Melt-'em-down eyes? Perfect teeth? Dynamite legs? Hanh? And cheekbones? Hanh?"

"Sure you do."

"Flatterer." She moved away from him, taking a big swallow of her drink.

A second later, she stood in the middle of the room alone. Mutilated wrapping paper still littered the floor.

She fled into the kitchen. She made herself another drink, pouring the rye by fingers, to hell with the shot glass. Plenty of ice—she loved to suck on ice. The bright snow hurt her eyes when she looked out. The refrigerator stopped running. An avalanche of silence fell on her. Fingers tickled the back of her neck.

She dreaded having to see the decorations again, the poinsettia, the wreath, the ribbons, the lime-green nightgown Manny'd given her, the donkeys, the sheep, the angels, the plaster Jesus sprawling in the hay. She sat at the kitchen table.

Sam. How she loved to seduce him in front of Manny. So innocent. Peck on the cheek. She'd felt him tense when she touched him. Whole different story when he had her alone. Whole different ball game. She chuckled. He couldn't lay off her then. He was putty in her hands. Well, not putty exactly. She laughed to herself again. Yes, putty. Ha. She was in good form. Too bad nobody to share it with, to laugh with. A man with a good laugh was what she needed. A real laugh. Sam was nothing but a punk. Manny looked sideways at him, he wet himself.

All punks. All wanted a taste of the forbidden fruit. Petrone's wife. All cringed if Manny so much as sneezed. She didn't need them. She didn't. Did not. No.

Well, what if she did? Healthy. Anybody'd tell you it was healthy. Doctor, even. Handsome doctor. He'd say, young woman, older husband, boring husband who didn't know the word fun. Natural and healthy. Best.

She didn't consider herself a mother. Hated those two brats. No, not hate. Just, she was too vibrant. She'd read the word in a beauty magazine. Vibrant. And young. And with a figure probably no other mother of two had in the world, a figure that every woman, sixteen to sixty, dreamed of having. A blessing. Her figure was a blessing. It was.

Yes, and she needed to grab. Life, you had to grab. Want fun, you grab it. Nothing wrong with grabbing. She'd been grabbed enough—ha ha—she was going to grab back. Grab. Life in a nutshell. Grab. Grab, grab, grab.

The enormity of this alcoholic truth dawned on her, sank in, and vanished. Grab. She tipped her head back and drained her glass. Some of the drink dribbled from her chin, dripped onto her neck, traced a line down her chest.

She looked. Her pride and joy. Pride on the left, joy on the right. How many times had she used that line? Tweedledum and Tweedledee. Amos and Andy. Smith and Wesson, somebody said. Concealed weapons. Pair of queens, ace in the hole. Oh, ho. They'd paid their way.

Not that she didn't sympathize with the girls who wrote Ann Landers and said that flat-chested girls ought to realize that their full-bosomed sisters had problems too, what with cracks and wolf whistles and all. But she'd always liked it when men looked, and they'd been looking for a long time. Still looked. Plenty. Especially since she wasn't one of those amazons, but actually had slender hips and looked terrific in a bathing suit. Even Manny had gone wild over them, at first.

At first. But after she'd had Stevie, he'd forgotten about fun. He seemed to think of her only as another possession, like his car, or his diamond watch, or his silver-plated putter. Something-I-got-you-can't-have. Lookee, no touchee. Damn fink.

She hated him. Hated husband, hated kids. Nice thought for Christmas morning. And slobbering drunk. Well, the hell with them. The hell with the men she made look like children, too. Made crawl. Made beg for mercy. Didn't need them.

Christmas. It had been Christmas when her own father had given her the doll house. He'd made it with his own hands. Spent hours on it, he must have. With the teeny-tiny furniture and the teeny-tiny curtains, the little windows, rugs, dishes. Made it with his own hands. Gave it to her to help her dream, his little girl, his little Phyl.

His own hands. His own hands. She loved the way those words drew up a tide in her. She loved to stir her soul, to feel the sadness creep up her, set her afire, rise into her throat, flood her mouth, lap brimming at her eyes. She could conjure it by calling on memories: the doll house—his own hands—the time her father'd taken her out when she was thirteen and had let her wear high heels and taste a cocktail, just the two of them—the time she'd found him weeping behind the garage. She would let it gather and build, then release it all at once. It would gush from her in pounding, burning spasms and leave her spent and blissful.

Not that Phyllis was maudlin. She'd rarely gone to

see the old man in the nursing home during his sick years. And though she'd cried for show at his funeral, she'd been relieved to be rid of him. She never visited his grave.

She spit the ice cube back into her glass. She went upstairs, grimacing as she passed the tree. She teetered opening the bureau drawer. She reached among her lingerie and from the cup of one of her bras drew out a brown glass bottle. She held it up to the light. She went to the bed and pulled back the covers and poured the yellow capsules onto the sheet. She spent half an hour counting the pills, lining them up like soldiers, playing with a dose of barbiturate that she was sure could kill a horse. Then she put them back.

1958

"I'm trying to get her for the club," Manny said. "Wait'll you see her act. Knots, man. You won't believe your eyes. Knots."

"She can dance?" Carlo asked. He sipped his Cutty. His hand adjusted his onyx cuff link. They were seated at a table in a low-ceilinged tavern. The amber candles on the tables and blue bulbs under the bar bottles provided the only light.

"Dance? Dance? My God. She's something I've never seen before, and that's saying something. I'm going to get her for the club, I swear it. I'll introduce you to her."

Carlo smoothed a cuticle with his thumbnail and watched Manny light a small cigar.

"But what I was saying," Manny said. "I was in the service, the reserves, until they found out about my heart murmur. One of the things they teach you, the battle's not won on the battlefield. No, the battle's won in the minds of the enemy. Let's say there's a million Russians over the next hill. Okay? Just you and a couple of your buddies on this side with BB guns. But you line up your shot—*bam!*—hit the general in the pecker. He panics, thinks he's outnumbered, calls a retreat. See what I mean? You win even though, push came to shove, the odds are all against you. Psychology wins, not brute strength. Get my point?"

"Pretty basic stuff."

"Sure it's basic. Strike hard, strike quick, strike where it hurts. Make an example. Teach these weaks how to think. That's what's important. Not a hundred bucks or five hundred bucks. They start thinking wrong, we've got a mess on our hands. Of course it's basic. It's fundamental."

"So what's the point?"

"Point is, George doesn't seem to be getting the message. He hasn't got things straight in his head."

"Come on, Manny. He's been at it for years."

"Then why's he letting this go? Since Thanksgiving this has been dragging. What the hell would you think, you're one of the guys who does pay his dues? Think you're a total sucker. Think maybe nothing'll happen to you if you stop paying. You can't let them start thinking that. You have to make an example. You warn them, then you make an example. Clear the air. Lombardosi's gotta make an example of this Shargoff."

"He knows that."

"Knows it, why doesn't he do it?"

"He's being cautious. Shargoff's no big deal. After that meat inspector, maybe he feels he lost his head a little."

"My ass. Hiya, Billy." Manny waved to a man sitting down two tables over. "My ass. Know what I think? George has ideas about his own thing."

"No, he wouldn't—"

"Listen, that deal with the meat was going to be a feather in my cap. But I had to shut the whole thing down. Took on extra trucks, people, I had to shut it down cold. Had to eat crow in the Falls. Thing with Falcone. I'm wondering if George isn't talking to this Shargoff, you know, on the side."

"Not George."

"Then why is he giving these guys ideas? They all

start to get ideas, where are we? Lombardosi can't handle, to hell with him."

"To hell with him?"

"If he can't do his job."

"Don't say to hell with him, Manny. George? He goes back. He didn't crawl out from under a rock last week. He was around before you pulled the city together. When things were iffy, he gave you this." He patted his right bicep.

"Sure he did. I know. He's a gorilla. I appreciate sometimes you want a gorilla. But that's just it. He's got the brains of an ape. You need more ammunition than that, especially when you're handling a Jew."

"He's no stupe."

"Tell me about it."

"He's not."

"Carlo, you and I are businessmen. Aren't we? Isn't that our future? George is stuck in the past. Maybe he's still useful, but I'm thinking he needs a keeper."

"He won't go work for somebody else. Not now."

"For you he would. You could pass him jobs, things you're sure he can handle."

"Manny, the man has pride."

"I'm trying to do him a favor, let him stay at all. Maybe he's getting senile. What is he, anyway?"

"Around sixty."

"Looks older. Maybe he oughta go down to Florida, retire."

"He hates the heat."

"Tell me about the heat. I'm the one with the heat. You hear? Remember that business last fall? Apalachin? Well, they've got this commission down in Albany. I'm subpoenaed for next month. My lawyer says it could be dangerous. It's not a court. They can do anything. Make up the rules as they go along. Like at those Kefauver hearings. They can make you look bad, smear you. You can't have any dirt under your nails. Understand? Talk to George. He'll listen to you."

"I talk to him."

"Make sure he gets it, I mean. I don't want to come close to him before I'm finished in Albany. Tell him to cut the crap. Give Shargoff one last chance. Then—after Albany—fix him. Fix him. I know Jews and I'll tell you something. Hey, there she is. There's Donna. See her?"

"That kid?"

"Can you believe it? Her. She'll be on in a minute. Oh, she'll kill you."

The girl's Prince Valiant haircut, bulky sweater, and knee socks made her look like a babysitter. She crossed in front of the bar without looking around and passed through a door beside the jukebox.

"Oh, yeah," Manny said, stubbing out the remains of his cigarillo. "Jews, they're too smart for their own good. Don't want to go along. They're all that way, wisenheimers. Know more than you do, they think. I mean, I can see this Shargoff saying, 'What'll they do for a couple hundred a week? They won't bother. I'll pocket the difference.' See? That's all they think about, money. And he's right, if Lombardosi thinks the same way. What's he, run skin flicks?"

"Yeah. Moves a little dope on the side."

"Whatever. He's making his and, being a Jew, he wants to keep it. Says, I'll hold off and see what happens. Misses a month, Lombardosi's not on his ass. Next thing, he figures he won't pay, period. Ain't long, he's saying to his pals, 'Look at me. I told them dagos where to get off.' See? That's just what he's doing. I know. I hear."

"All George has to do is spit, the guy's back in line."

"Why doesn't he, then? Why didn't he yesterday? Why do I have to push? Why can't he take care of his own?"

"Maybe you're worrying up something that's no big deal."

Manny put his elbows on the table and leaned partway over. "I say it's a big deal."

"Okay, I'll talk to him."

"I know you will. You're can-do, Carlo. I appreciate. I appreciate what you've done in the markets, too. What you've shown. Not just me, but they appreciate it in the Falls, too, the produce situation. You don't go wild, just get things done. That's what we're looking for, a business attitude."

Carlo nodded.

"Hey, here she comes. Drink up, we'll get another round. Nance?" Manny pointed at the waitress and made a circle over the table with his finger.

The dancer tottered on stiletto heels toward a small platform in the corner of the room. She wore a sequined toga and a spiked crown. She carried a police flashlight. Violet lips and large brown eyes dominated her delicate face. Scattered applause greeted her. She didn't look around.

"She's patriotic, see?" Manny said. "Statue of Liberty. This'll knock you out. Thanks, babe." He handed the waitress a dollar tip.

The girl climbed onto the platform and positioned herself, her right hand holding high the glowing red flashlight, her left clutching at the opening of her toga, her face tilted innocently upward. The jukebox died and a recording of "God Bless America" began to play over the loudspeakers. A yellow spotlight illuminated her.

She began to turn slowly around, taking tiny steps that made her seem to glide. She could have been in a school play.

"Stand beside her," Manny hummed, "and guide her."

Talk to George, Carlo thought. Funny idea. He remembered George first taking him to meet Manny twenty years ago. What an occasion, actually shaking hands with the Man, with the Mover—the "Crowned Prince," George called him.

And Manny called George Mr. Lombardosi back then, treated him with deference. George was already known from Buffalo to Boston for his brawn. He'd crushed a man's face with his hand, they said. He'd killed a guy with a heart punch. His fist had splintered an oak door. He was Manny Petrone's personal strong-arm. Now Manny was saying to hell with George and was sending Carlo to talk to him.

The first anthem reached its climax and faded into a version of "The Battle Hymn of the Republic" with a bump-and-grind beat. Donna dropped her Miss Liberty pose and slithered out of her toga. She faced the audience defiantly in red-and-white-striped underwear and navy blue stockings sparkling with rhinestones. Somebody in back hooted.

Carlo thought of George's look, of the way he had of making his eyes go dead. You knew instantly that he was capable of anything. That look, his bulk, and his reputation meant that George could stare down anybody on earth. Carlo had earned his bones, all right. He'd done his share of the heavy work. But he couldn't quiet his imagination the way George could. Couldn't summon the abandon that terrified.

Carlo edged forward. The girl rolled her stockings down to her knees, stretched a leg backward, pulled the ankle up to her shoulder, and slipped the blue nylon off, placing the scanty shoe back on her bare foot. She played with her G-string, stretching it to the snapping point with enormous gestures.

Carlo was used to strippers who flaunted rippling flesh. This girl's breasts were compact, the rouged nipples buttons. But she had a way of moving her lithe, startlingly flexible body that made him keep shifting in his chair. She played a counterpoint to the sluggish rhythm of the music with the knobs of her shoulders. She grew blatant, using the beam of the flashlight to caress herself.

George had muscle, but muscle was a tool, a com-

modity. Manny knew it, so did Carlo. Brains fetched
the premium price. Brains and connections. Politics.

Carlo had the brains to see the potential in the
produce market. He hadn't spoiled it with a heavy
hand. He'd brought the buyers, the distributors, the
suppliers into line step by step. Quiet and steady. No
brawls, almost none. Just daily pressure.

Now the market was his. He ran Manny's wholesale
operation. What he said went. People asked his per-
mission. From long habit, he'd even grown to like the
cold mornings, the predawn chill when the broccoli
and onions, the potatoes and lettuce and peppers arrived. He had his base. He was making his connections. Not hurrying, just becoming known, bending an
ear, helping the right people, building up credit in the
bank of favors.

Donna arched her back, her raised arms swimming,
swimming. She put her hands on the floor behind her
and swayed. She lifted a leg and pointed it at the
ceiling. She kept stretching it. Her other leg rose. She
hovered in a handstand. Then she brought the first leg
all the way over and slid it between her hands, bouncing into a full split. Someone screamed.

Carlo looked at Manny. Manny's face was an eager
puppy's, engrossed in the tease. He'd used George,
but he would never understand him. Manny didn't
know, really, enough about hurting people, about real
pain. He'd gone too far on bluff and threat. He'd let
others carry his baggage.

She was repeating the move. Tendons stood out in
her thighs. But instead of putting her hands down, she
kept swimming. Men were rising in their seats. She
kept swimming. She bent farther, farther, until she
was only half a woman—taut legs and straining pelvis.
Then she arched her neck and her head came up past
her calves. She completed an impossible circle. She
grabbed her ankles. She eased up farther. Her face
stared from between her knees. A mocking, leering

smile spread across her mouth. Her glassy eyes reflected the light. She winked.

Carlo didn't like the situation Manny was pushing him into. He knew there was more to it than just some hearing in Albany. Manny was afraid of George, and with reason. And something was bothering George, too, deep down. Carlo didn't want to be the middle man. He liked George and owed him, but he answered to Manny. And he knew, in the end, that Manny was right. George had to fall into line.

The girl straightened. The music pounded to a crescendo. She turned, bent forward, and shivered her naked buttocks. Men were pounding tables. She whipped up applause with thrusts of her hips. Turning again, she reached out to them. But as her arms stretched forward, her shoulders began to arch backward one more time. Her fingers beckoned, her head and torso dropped away. The light shone for a second on her isolated legs, then blinked out.

She hopped quickly down and gathered her robe. Clapping and whistling and groaning followed her back to her dressing room.

"What an act," Manny said, laughing and wiping a tear from his eye. "Did I tell you? Can she tie herself in knots? I'm going to get her. I really am."

February 27

Testimony of Manfred R. Petrone before the Select Subcommittee on Labor Racketeering of the Senate of the State of New York.

Subcommittee chairman, Senator Lawton S. Van Dyne.

Chief counsel to the subcommittee, Mr. Donald P. Racine.

Attorney to Mr. Petrone, Mr. Winslow H. Jacobs.

RACINE: Have you ever gone by any other name, Mr. Petrone?

PETRONE: What do you mean?

RACINE: Ever used an alias?

PETRONE: No, never.

RACINE: Pagliaro? Never called yourself Michael Pagliaro?

PETRONE: Well, I can't recall.

RACINE: Weren't you arrested under that name? Convicted of armed robbery?

PETRONE: Oh, when I was a kid, you mean. I thought you were talking about as an adult.

RACINE: Did you use that name, Pagliaro, or didn't you?

PETRONE: Maybe I did, it was a long time ago.

RACINE: Do I have to bring in the police records, Mr. Petrone?

PETRONE: I might have given that name. That was my mother's, my grandmother's maiden name, Pagliara.

RACINE: What business are you in, Mr. Petrone?

PETRONE: Distribution. Produce, mainly. I do some general-purpose trucking. And I have some real estate that I take care of myself. Plus a kiddie park, a small one.

RACINE: An amusement park?

PETRONE: A kiddie park. Rides, spook house, arcade.

RACINE: Aren't you also involved in a laundry, a linen supply type of . . .

PETRONE: (inaudible)

RACINE: Please speak up.

PETRONE: A business associate of mine, I said. He runs that. I'm not—I just have some money in it. He asked me, I gave him some money. Plus, I lease him trucks.

RACINE: It's an investment?

PETRONE: You could call it that.

RACINE: Don't you also have an investment in a firm known as Whirlaway Packing Company, Incorporated?

PETRONE: Not anymore, counselor. That operation is defunct. Kaput.

RACINE: But you did have, did you not? You were the principal behind the company, weren't you?

PETRONE: It was a corporation. I was part owner.

RACINE: Majority owner.

PETRONE: Have it your way.

RACINE: During December of last year, wasn't Whirlaway Packing twice cited by the Department of Agriculture for selling adulterated product? And wasn't the inspector who wrote those citations threatened? Wasn't he told to, quote, lay off of Whirlaway, unquote? Wasn't he afterward brutally beaten? Wasn't he required by the severity of his injuries to remain in the hospital for a period of more than five weeks?

PETRONE: I wouldn't know, counselor.

RACINE: You know nothing about this inspector or the crime perpetrated against him?

PETRONE: I don't . . . just a minute, please. (pause) I don't choose to answer that question, respectfully, counselor, by my rights under the fifth amendment to the constitution.

RACINE: Do—

PETRONE: The U.S. constitution.

RACINE: Do you deny that Whirlaway Packing received the citations?

PETRONE: I heard something about that, yes.

RACINE: What were they for?

PETRONE: Like you say, for adultery. (laughter)

RACINE: For selling horse meat for human consumption, correct?

JACOBS: My client—if I may say a word here—my client has already given his reason for not wishing to pursue this line of questioning, counselor. Mr. Petrone was not directly involved in the operation of the company you refer to. And due to certain upcoming litigation, I don't feel that he can be impelled to offer testimony on the subject at this time.

RACINE: Horse meat, Mr. Petrone?

PETRONE: Must have been a mistake made, is all I can say.

RACINE: A horse mistaken for a steer?

PETRONE: I'm afraid I'm a city boy, counselor. I wouldn't know about those things.

RACINE: Are you involved with the rackets, Mr. Petrone?

JACOBS: Now, just a minute—

SENATOR VAN DYNE: Let the witness answer the question.

PETRONE: No, I'm not in any rackets.

RACINE: You swear to that?

PETRONE: Well, what do you call a racket? Everybody's got a racket. You make money on a deal, immediately it becomes a racket. The stockmarket, that's a racket. (laughter)

RACINE: Let's look into your background for a moment, Mr. Petrone. On July 17, 1948, Superior Court, State of New York, you were indicted for conspiracy to murder one Anthony Stromoni, correct?

PETRONE: And acquitted.

RACINE: Not acquitted, sir. The charges were dropped after a key witness changed his story. On January 5, 1951, you were arrested for statutory rape and second-degree assault. You eventually pleaded to lewd behavior and were fined one hundred dollars.

PETRONE: Woman problems.

RACINE: October 11, 1954, drunk and disorderly, assaulting a police officer, resisting arrest. Reduced to disorderly conduct, two hundred dollars' fine.

PETRONE: That was my birthday.

RACINE: April 22, 1955, Manfred R. Petrone charged with unlawful imprisonment of one Salvador Noto. Mr. Noto was killed in an automobile accident two days before the trial was to have begun. Charges dismissed.

PETRONE: God rest his soul.

RACINE: November 3, 1956, in Federal Court you were indicted for seven violations of the Mann Act. At the same time, in New York Supreme Court, for operating a house of prostitution. Case on continuance.

PETRONE: I should . . . (inaudible)

RACINE: What was that?

PETRONE: I should have you as my lawyer, Mr. Racine. You've got these things down pat. (laughter)

RACINE: You don't dispute the fact that these charges have been brought against you?

PETRONE: I've never been . . . I refuse to answer on the grounds of the fifth amendment.

RACINE: Now, Mr. Petrone, the subcommittee would like to find out about the events of last November 14. At approximately four thirty P.M. of that day, you were apprehended, along with an associate of yours, wandering through the forest in the rain about two miles from the home of one Joseph Barbara in the town of Apalachin in Tioga County.

PETRONE: Are you asking or telling?

RACINE: Do you deny the fact?

PETRONE: Why should I?

RACINE: When the officers asked you to give an explanation of your presence, you indicated that you had been visiting Mr. Barbara, had decided to take a stroll in the woods, and had become lost.

PETRONE: One tree looks like another to me.

RACINE: You frequently take walks through the forest during a downpour?

PETRONE: That's right. I guess I'm kind of a romantic. (laughter)

RACINE: Why did you choose that particular day to visit Mr. Barbara?

PETRONE: Well, you see, Joe'd been having problems with his ticker. Had a heart attack. So my friend and I decided to drop by and cheer him up.

RACINE: When you arrived at Mr. Barbara's home, did you find anyone else there?

PETRONE: Well, his son, Joe, Junior, I think he was there.

RACINE: Anyone else?

PETRONE: A few guys, I don't know.

RACINE: Does the name Vito Genovese, known as Don Vitone, mean anything to you?

PETRONE: No, nothing, except—

RACINE: Except what?

PETRONE: I think I read about him in the papers once.

RACINE: How about Joseph Profaci?

PETRONE: I draw a blank.

RACINE: Weren't Mr. Profaci and Mr. Genovese also visiting Mr. Barbara that day? Aren't those two gentlemen notorious as leaders of the New York City underworld?

PETRONE: I wouldn't know, counselor. If you say they are, I'll believe you.

RACINE: Are you familiar with a man named Lewis Santos, of Havana, Cuba? Wasn't he there that day?

PETRONE: I wouldn't know.

RACINE: State police records say he was. Would you happen to know if Mr. Frank DeSimone of Downey, California, dropped by to wish Mr. Barbara well that same day?

PETRONE: I wouldn't question your information.

RACINE: Didn't you recognize any of them? Didn't you eat a steak sandwich with any of them?

PETRONE: Not to my knowledge. I didn't have time to eat.

RACINE: Before the police blocked the access road to Mr. Barbara's property and you fled in panic?

PETRONE: Before I went for a walk.

RACINE: But all of these men were gathered there that day and you didn't run into any of them?

PETRONE: I might have without knowing it.

RACINE: Fifty-eight men, you must have seen some of them.

PETRONE: I saw a few guys around, I told you. I don't know everybody.

RACINE: Any idea why these men were there?

PETRONE: Joe has plenty of friends.

RACINE: Friends from New Jersey, Pennsylvania,

Ohio, Missouri, Florida, from as far away as California? And they all congregate at his home on the same day?

PETRONE: Just a coincidence, I guess.

RACINE: Just a coincidence? Are you asking the subcommittee to believe that?

PETRONE: I'm not asking the subcommittee to believe anything.

RACINE: Isn't it true—

PETRONE: Just a minute. Just hold on, counselor. Senator Van Dyne, let me remind you of something. I'm a citizen of this state. I pay taxes. I have a family. You asked me to come down here, answer questions. I came. You asked me to cooperate. I'm cooperating. But I demand the respect due any other citizen, any other taxpayer. I'm not going to sit here and swallow a bunch of phony insinuations. Now, if we can—

RACINE: Mr. Petrone, I'd remind you—

PETRONE: I'm not going to be a patsy. I'm a businessman, get it?

SENATOR VAN DYNE: Mr. Petrone, the subcommittee appreciates your cooperation. Counselor will confine himself to questions of fact.

RACINE: Are you familiar with Mr. Barbara's occupation?

PETRONE: Joe? I think he has some beer accounts and works for Canada Dry or something.

RACINE: Are you aware that he has been arrested three times for homicide?

PETRONE: Is that my business? I'm not my brother's keeper. And he ain't my brother.

RACINE: Stefano Ruggiero, known as the Niagara Powerhouse: do you know him?

PETRONE: The name doesn't ring a bell.

RACINE: Was he in attendance at Mr. Barbara's house that day?

PETRONE: I just said, I don't know the man.

RACINE: I would advise you to weigh your answer more carefully, Mr. Petrone. Certain members of the

Niagara County Sheriff's Department are prepared to testify that you were observed visiting the Ruggiero Funeral Chapel on Porter Road in Niagara Falls on July twenty-eighth of last year. At that time, no corpses were laid out at the chapel. Could you explain that visit? Or do you deny it took place?

PETRONE: That's . . . just a minute, counselor. (pause)

JACOBS: My client respectfully declines to answer that question on the grounds of his constitutional rights under the fifth amendment.

RACINE: Have you been assigned a territory, Mr. Petrone?

PETRONE: I don't know what you mean by that. What territory?

RACINE: Has anyone told you that you can act as the boss of a certain part of this state? Has anyone given you the right to operate illicit businesses in that area—gambling, prostitution, narcotics? Has anyone authorized you to collect tribute from other businesses, both legal and illegal, in this area we're talking about, by means of extortion and strong-arm tactics? Are you, in your turn, required to pass on some of your revenues to another party as a fee for that person's support and material aid?

PETRONE: This is ridiculous.

RACINE: Aren't you part of a conspiracy against the laws of this state, Mr. Petrone?

PETRONE: No, I'm . . . I refuse to answer that. You're trying to hook me.

RACINE: Isn't it true, Mr. Petrone, that the meeting of more than fifty men from all over North America last November was far from being the coincidence that you allege? Didn't those men, and you with them, gather in order to promote a vast conspiracy?

PETRONE: I refuse to answer that under the grounds of the fifth amendment.

RACINE: Didn't those men, and you with them, come together in order to coordinate and organize their crimes?

PETRONE: Refuse under the grounds of the fifth.

RACINE: Don't those crimes include theft, bribery, prostitution, intimidation, and murder?

PETRONE: Come on, the fifth.

RACINE: Isn't this nation being afflicted by the cancer of an enormous and insidious criminal conspiracy, Mr. Petrone?

PETRONE: No answer, same grounds.

RACINE: Doesn't this one conspiracy go by many different names?

PETRONE: The fifth amendment.

RACINE: Isn't it called the Office or the Syndicate?

PETRONE: The fifth.

RACINE: Isn't it also known as the Outfit? The Arm?

PETRONE: Fifth.

RACINE: The Mafia?

PETRONE: Counselor, I respectfully plead the fifth amendment.

April 23

"Goddamn, Link, we're a couple of acrobats." Sherry felt with her hands along the dashboard of the dark car.

"We've had enough practice."

"Grab my cigarettes, will you? They must be in back."

"Where?"

"In my jacket. Give me that, too. I feel chilled."

"Want me to close the window?"

"No, I like the peepers. Makes me think of spring."

"Mating season."

A flame illuminated her face, then Link's. "He's already got the hole dug," she said.

"Hole? What hole?"

"I told you. The fallout shelter. Dave sent off for the plans from Civil Defense. We're gonna have the first

bomb shelter on the block—and a beauty, too. Chemi-
cal toilet. Canned food—he's getting his own canning
equipment. Drums of drinking water. Geiger counter."

"You'll be living in style if the bomb goes off."

"Oh, it's going to go off. He's got Diane waking up
with nightmares. Every time the fire siren sounds, she
thinks it's the end of the world. War's just a matter of
time, Dave insists."

"What isn't?"

"I guess they saw a movie on it at work. You know
what it's going to cost, this shelter? Hundreds and
hundreds of dollars. We were supposed to be going to
the Thousand Islands this summer. Now that's out. The
money's going into concrete. And he spends all his time
either out digging or making plans, what he'll do."

"He's at work tonight?"

"Four to twelve."

"How's he take that swing shift, anyway? Days,
nights."

"I guess he's used to it, they've had him on it so
long."

"That'd make you want to hide in a hole. Me, I'd tell
them where to stick it."

"You? When was the last time you worked any kind
of a shift?"

"Oh, let's see."

"You're terrible. I was counting on that vacation.
Diane will throw a royal pout. She gets ants in her
pants sitting around the house in the summer."

"She's growing up."

"Can you believe she started pestering me for a bra?
What do you need with a bra? I said. Well, she has to
have one. Susan Miller has had one for three months.
And Miss Eaton, the gym teacher, says that if girls
don't wear bras, their boobies sag. Well, first you have
to have something to sag, Miss Lollapalooza, I said."

"You had them at that age."

"Twelve? I did not."

"What about that tangerine-colored sweater you used to wear in seventh grade?"

"Oh, you remember that?"

"Used to lie awake nights, thinking about it."

"I hate to imagine some little snot-nosed kid getting hotted up over Diane. But I guess sooner or later it happens."

"She has your looks."

"More than that. Sometimes I see that gimme gleam in her eye and I know it all too well. Or I notice her admiring herself in the mirror, or walking, or talking to one of her friends—it's me all over again. I see it, but I can't—I don't know how to steer her away from it. She has the makings of a hellcat, Link. It scares me."

"She'll get through. You did."

"But she's not going to end up the way I did."

"Things so bad?"

"Yes, they're bad. Sometimes I think you have the mind of a child, Link. I look around, it makes me want to cry. My marriage has added up to a big zero. And I tried. I had Dave's parents over for dinner every Sunday. I washed and darned and cooked and cleaned. Shit, I look at these women, with their supermarkets, and their televisions, and their housework, and their gossip, and their clothes, and their recipes, and their husbands, and their families. And I just cannot fit in. I can't. I don't have a hope in the world. Except Diane. And I know she's already slipping away. It happens. I know."

"I'm right here with you, angel."

"Are you? Oh, Christ, I love you, Link. But are you? Other men's cars, other men's women. That's you. I know I'm not the only one."

"The only one I ever loved. Only broad who's ever done it to me. Any others, well. . . . And the cars, that just gives me a thrill. I just feel more alive when I'm stealing."

A low cloud splattered the car with rain for a few

seconds, then moved on. The peepers took a deep breath, began anew.

"I've been thinking about us lately, Link. Thinking and thinking. I wanted to tell you."

"Tell me what?"

"I've decided. We'll have to—this will have to be the last. I cannot continue, not the way things are."

"Worried about Dave?"

"I care about Dave. In spite of all the distance between us, I care. If he ever knew, he'd be hurt."

"He knows."

"Does not. But the thing is, Dave hurts anyway. He was born hurting. I don't want to make it worse, but that hasn't stopped me."

"What's stopping you?"

"Diane. She's barely five years younger than I was when I had her, for Christ's sake. She's going to start figuring why Mommy goes out so often when Daddy's at work. She's going to know."

"You don't want her to know?"

"Only a man would ask that. How could I control her? It would pull the rug out from under her if she found out now. I want to see her fall in love, really in love, and walk down the aisle in a big church wedding and make it. I don't want to give her the idea that marriage is a sell, that you can cheat your way out. I don't want her to think her old lady's a tramp. I don't want her to feel what I feel sometimes, that emptiness. I want her to fit. And that isn't all. It's you, too."

"Me?"

"Diane loves you. Didn't you know? She tells her girlfriends 'I've got a guy.' She has your name written all over the inside of her school binder. That time she got to ride in your car at the races, I thought I'd never hear the end of it. Link this and Link that. I know it's a childish thing, but it's good for her to have a crush. Dave tries, but he's never been able to get close to her. He's too cold. You give her somebody to look up to.

And if she ever found out about us, she'd hate my guts. She comes first, Link."

"So we drop it? Just: been good to know you?"

"I have to do it that way, baby. We can't be just friends."

"This was the farewell performance?"

"I didn't mean to, even tonight. I wanted to talk to you."

"I forced you?"

"Something forced me."

"Haven't we been careful? Haven't we gone out of our way?"

"It's not a question of being careful. She'll know. We can't hide it."

He clasped his hands behind his neck and rolled his head back.

"My feelings won't change, Link."

"It's easy for you to say now. Your legs haven't even cooled off. Going to teach Dave some new tricks?"

"Don't, Link."

"Okay. I see your point. You're right. You're dead right."

"I want you to understand."

"I understand."

"Tell me."

"What?"

"That you've always loved me, even when we were kids."

Her eyes glistened in the dark. Link turned over the ignition, made a three-point turn on the dirt road, and took her home.

June 7

Petey kicked his mud-clotted boots against the back steps. Stamping inside, he pried them off. He shook the rain from his greasy jacket and hung it up. The kitchen was overflowing with the aroma of baking. He padded across the linoleum, opened the refrigerator, picked up a hacked ham bone, and grabbed a bottle of Coke. He continued into the small living room. After playing with the rabbit ears for five minutes, he managed to stabilize a fuzzy picture on the television screen. He settled into his chair opposite the set, licked the fat from his fingers, and swallowed some pop.

Beverly's arms were wrapped around a bundle of laundry as she came downstairs. She brushed against one of the antenna prongs. The picture tangled.

"Hey, watch it, willya? Look what you did. Took me an hour to get that picture."

"Stuff yourself. Why don't you get an aerial? Want reception, you need an aerial. Everybody knows that."

"I'm getting an aerial. Think I'm going to climb up on the roof, put up a freaking aerial in the rain? Fix it."

"I've got a cake in the oven. You said you wanted chocolate cake. I'm trying to make you one."

"I'll put cake in your oven. Fix it."

Still holding the laundry, she grabbed the tip of the rabbit ear and moved it. The picture danced and flickered. She batted at the wire again. The antenna fell to the floor. The image began to do somersaults.

"Oh, for the love of Mary and Joseph. You stupid cow!"

"Bonehead! How'd you think I'd like it if my girlfriends found out my husband sat around all day watching soap operas? Huh? How would that look? Kinda funny, y'ask me."

"Who asked you? Just fix the goddamn picture. And hurry up, I'm missing it."

She dropped the laundry and picked up the rabbit ears. She twisted them twice without resolving the picture. Then she ripped the wires loose and hurled the contraption across the room.

"Here, genius, fix it yourself."

"Why you scum! You dirty little bitch." He jabbed his middle finger in the air and slapped his bicep.

"What's that, your age or your I.Q.?" she screamed. "Or number of white parents?" The gap in her terrycloth robe revealed a buff-colored slip.

"I don't have to take this crap. Not from a whore like you." Dropping the ham, Petey climbed out of his chair and bounded across the room. Beverly didn't raise her hand quickly enough. She took the slap squarely on her cheek. His knuckles immediately snapped her head back the other way. He kept his hand raised and lifted his chin at her. She spat.

"You pig!" Petey yelled.

He tried to pin her arms. Beverly took sacramental Knox gelatine and sharpened her nails daily with emery boards. Her right hand sliced the side of his neck. He wrestled her, spun, flung her into an end table. She toppled a lamp as she fell. He rushed at her. She aimed a bare heel at his groin. He sidestepped.

"Your mother should have had an abortion!" he shouted.

"Yours did. You!"

"Fat ass!"

"Skinny dick!"

"You—" He managed to grab hold of her ankle. He dragged her around the room. She kicked wildly. He heaved. She rolled into the corner of the couch. Panting, he swabbed his neck with his palm. His eyes rounded at the handful of blood.

"Look at this. Look. You did this. You."

She got to her knees, watching him. "You guinea bastard!"

Petey wiped blood onto his hand twice more, looking at it each time. "I'm going to kill you. You bitch! You damn bitch!"

"No!"

He moved quickly, catching her by the hair and twisting her head back. She gasped.

"Look at this." He rubbed the blood onto her face. "Look what you did."

Beverly tried to loosen his hand, but he twisted harder, pulling her onto her back. He sat on her, pressed her arms to the carpet with his knees. He slapped her cheeks, softly at first, then harder and harder. Her neck writhed.

"Say uncle. Say uncle!" he said.

She bared her teeth, hissed.

"Mess up my program, you're going to say uncle." His arm moved back and forth rhythmically, gaining momentum.

"Mother!" she screamed. "You goddamn motherfucker!"

Petey stopped slapping. He reached back, grasped the hem of her slip, yanked. It tore. "Goddamn you to hell, Bev! I mean it."

"Petey!"

He released her arms. "I mean it."

"Petey!"

Twenty mintues later the sharp odor of burning cake and the insistent buzz of the doorbell aroused them both from their stupor. Petey swore. He stood up, zipping his fly. Beverly rushed for the kitchen.

They rarely used the front door. All their friends came around to the back or looked for Petey in the yard. On his way, he straightened the table and replaced the lamp. Its shade still hung askew.

"George," Petey said on opening the door. "Good to see you. Yeah, come on in." He shook hands with the hulking man and stepped back.

"You were expecting me, weren't you?"

"Sure I was. Didn't know exactly when, is all."

"I told you, two."

"Is it that late already? I guess it is. So, what's new, George, boy? How you keeping?"

"Not too bad. Yourself?"

"No complaints. You've never seen the place before,

have you? Things are—well, Bev was just cleaning.
Bev, you decent?"

"I'm upstairs, hon," her voice said.

"Come on, George. Don't mind this disaster area."

Beneath his raincoat, George wore a pin-striped suit
and bow tie. He didn't remove his hat. He stepped over
the laundry and followed Petey into the kitchen.

"Bev was baking and I guess it turned out a tragedy.
You know how brides are." He laughed.

"You're happy, married?"

"Oh, sure," Petey said, rubbing the clotted blood
from his neck with a dishrag. "Have you met Bev?
She's upstairs. I can—"

"I'd just as soon get our business taken care of."

"Oh, sure. That's fine."

Petey slipped his boots and jacket back on and led
the way outside. George paid no attention to the mud
that smeared his spit-polished Florsheims.

Inside the quonset hut, they squeezed around two
cars and past the assorted grilles, bumpers, fenders, fan
belts, tires, hubcaps, and steering wheels that dangled
from the walls and ceiling. They crossed the grease-
packed floor to a workbench that ran most of the length
of one side. A dissected engine sprawled amid its in-
nards on top. Petey reached underneath and pulled out
half an oil drum. He pushed away the paper and soiled
rags and lifted a burlap sack onto the bench. His hand
yanked the chain that hung from an incandescent bulb.

"Ever use one of these before?"

"In a car once, yeah."

"Did it work? Ha, stupid question. Think—that's the
main thing. Think before you act. Think before you
make any move."

"I don't think?"

"Sure you do."

"So stop mouthing off."

"Relax." Petey withdrew a plywood box from the
bag. "It's all in here. Battery, clock, cap, eight sticks.
Just what you wanted. The lid slides like this. Neat?"

George, his face frozen in a frown, looked down at the cluster of red cylinders, the one-handed clock.

"This, the beauty of this device is its simplicity. I designed it myself. I handled this stuff in the service. Corps of Engineers."

"My boy was in the service."

"I knew him."

"Eugene? You knew Eugene?"

"Not personally, but—he played basketball, didn't he?"

"Guard. They won the county."

"I was a couple of years ahead of him in school. Shame."

George stared at him.

"It fires at six. You want ten minutes, you set it at four. Half an hour, at twelve. Here." He wound the clock twice, held it to his ear, then twisted a knob on the back. A loud click sounded. George threw his hands to his face.

"Relax, I know what I'm doing. You put the red wire here, the green one there. See? Last of all, just before you close it, you push this switch up. See, this little one here. Up. Then it's ready. Simple?"

George's jaw muscles were working, but he said nothing.

"If you can, wedge it somewhere. Crevice, doorway, anywhere. That focuses the force."

"How big?"

"Bang? Take the front of a house off. With luck, maybe the back too. Lot of force there, way you wanted it. My advice is, sit with it before and go over it at least three times, what you're going to do. Rehearse. Make sure. Then, when you place it, walk, don't run."

"I don't run."

"No. Now, I suggest you use this. Just an old feed bag. It'll look like trash. Pack some rags around it, newspapers. That'll keep it dry and cut the sound of the clock. Nobody'll notice. Okay?"

George watched him repack the box and place it into the sack.

"Hundred dollars." Petey took the money the other man counted into his hand. "Great. Say, this your own thing, or for the boss?"

"What do you mean?"

"Manny in this?"

"Yeah, no, why?"

"I don't mind a word. I do good work, I like credit."

"I thought he was your cousin."

"His wife, she is. Manny, I think, is a little pissed off after that meat deal last winter."

"What about it?"

"Don't get me wrong. I'm on your side. I think the jerk needed to be tenderized. Just—"

"Just what?"

"Didn't go down, that's all."

George narrowed his eyes and rolled his upper lip back. "Don't stink. Crap. Fuck," he said, tearing each word from his throat. "Fucking shit bastard. Cock. Damn. Eat. God."

Petey wrinkled his nose and lifted his brows. He noticed a line of saliva rolling down George's chin. He nodded.

"Yeah, okay. And I'll have the car for you Monday night. Don't worry."

As George went out, he clunked the sack against the doorway. Petey winced.

June 9

"Splish splash, I was takin' a bath," Ronny sang. "Heard that? Bobby Darin. Bobby, baby. Yeah, it was a Saturday—"

"I wish we'd found something before school let out."

Link was driving. The yellow bus ahead blinked stupidly as it disgorged children.

"Oh, I was takin' a bath. . . . Hey, lookit that little number. No straight lines, huh? Ooo, how do they walk in those skirts? Tight dresses and lipstick—dah dah dah, dah-dah. I wish I was back in school. Man, oh man, do I wish."

"You hated school."

"Hated it then. Dig that blonde, Link. With the saddle shoes. Cool, man. I'll carry your books, honey. I'll carry you." They started moving again. "Hated it then, but they didn't have this talent back then. These chickies are hot. Slow down. Lookit her walk. Those legs. Does she or doesn't she? Hey, babe."

"What makes you think you'd score any easier than you did the first time around?"

"Knowing what I know now, I'm talking about. Put me back in school knowing what I know now. I'd be a wolf. I'd have them for breakfast."

"You would?"

"Sure. When I was in school, be honest with you, I didn't know the direction to first base. Just stood there with the bat in my hands. Went down looking. Knowing what I know now, I'd be driving in runs right and left. And believe me, these young babes are worth the price of emission. Ha ha ha."

"So why are you always striking out, DiMaggio?"

"I said, if I was back in school. If. Way it is, broads my age are all married. Or else they're dogs. Or, I think some of them do it with their girlfriends."

"So be a cherry picker."

"Uh-uh. I like to look, but I'm not ending up in the slammer for statutory. No, sir."

"Know what your problem is, Ronny?"

"Maybe I'm oversexed."

"No, you're really just a mother-grabber at heart."

"So you're a dipshit. So what?"

"No, I mean it. To you, all females are your mother. From a distance, you go gaga. But up close, it's yes, ma'am—no, ma'am—sorry, ma'am. I've seen you. You please and thank-you them until they puke."

"Bull."

"No bull. Every one you meet, you're struck dumb. Like you've just been born. You want to tear them apart, but as soon as you come within touching distance, you're in church. You're afraid they'll spank you. That's why you have such trouble getting laid."

"Come off it. What are you, Dr. Joyce Brothers?"

"I'm just telling you. They want a daddy, not a little boy. How old are you, twenty-four? And always short of tail."

"Five. Listen, I've got standards, Link. I'm particular. They have to be top shelf or I don't mess with them. If I was seventeen again, I'd have the pick of the litter."

"Knowing what you know now."

"Right."

Sunlight broke from between clouds. Link steered into the parking lot of a small supermarket.

"This looks okay. See, the entrance is around the corner there. We'll wait a minute, then check keys."

" 'You can trust your car to—' Going to paint this?"

"No. Change the plates and unload it tonight. It's a job car."

"For who?"

Link shrugged. A woman rounded the corner of the store, a bulging bag of groceries in one arm, a bouncing child attached to her hand. She got into a station wagon and drove out. A gray Buick looped in and parked at the end of a row. The woman who emerged wore high heels and pink toreador pants. She patted her hair as she walked toward the store.

Ronny looked at Link.

Link nodded. "Eye it, try it, buy it," he said.

Ronny climbed out, made his way through two rows of cars, circled back. He walked directly to the Buick, opened the door, slid behind the wheel. Link started the engine of his car. Ronny began to back slowly out of the space.

The woman in the pink pants appeared around the corner of the store. She walked with an impatient wiggle. Suddenly, she stopped and gazed, mystified, as she watched her car roll down the aisle toward the exit. She began to run, taking fragile steps on her precarious heels.

Intent on maneuvering the unfamiliar car, Ronny failed to notice the woman approach. Link sounded three short bursts on his horn. Three more. Oblivious, Ronny sat waiting to merge into traffic.

Before he got a chance, the woman was on him. Link heard her say, "Hey, you!" He watched her lips snarl. She flung her left arm into the car. He saw Ronny's hands go up. The car jerked forward, lurched to a stop, barely avoiding a collision. The woman approached the window again. She tried to reach inside. Ronny was rolling up the glass. She battered it. The traffic cleared.The car surged ahead with a loud squeal and disppeared up the road. The woman tottered after it for a few steps. She looked frantically around. Then she turned and headed back toward the store.

Link cruised out of the lot and drove away at a moderate pace. A quarter hour later, he arrived at the spot they'd decided on, a dirt patch beside a back road. Fishermen parked there when they were trying for bullheads in the meandering stream below. The gray Buick sat innocently in the sunlight, empty.

Link parked beside it. He sat for a minute, drumming his fingers on the roof of his car. He got out, opened his trunk, removed a pair of license plates. He bent down behind the other car and began to unscrew the plate holder.

Ronny's face was still ashen when he emerged from the willow saplings and high grass that sheltered the turnoff.

"Shit a brick, man," he said. "Whyn't you warn me?"

"I gave you the three toots. Twice. You didn't even look around."

"Goddamn. She saw me. Looked right at me. That ain't cool. Probably talking to the cops this minute. What the hell could I do? Was I supposed to say, 'Oh, is this yours? Why, I have one just like it. So sorry. My mistake.'"

"You're getting a shiner. She connect?"

"Yeah, she connected. Caught me right here. I could hardly see to drive."

Link laughed.

"Hey, this is serious. Damn bitch. What am I going to do?"

"What's to do?"

"Know what she was after? This." He held up a white leather purse.

"Any dough?"

"Twenty-eight bucks."

"Yours, champ. Buy a steak for that eye."

"Oh, fun-ny. I've been sweating barbed wire all the way over here. Kept waiting for a gumball machine to show in the mirror."

"Dame's got a left. You have to give her credit."

"I'm telling you, she looked me square in the face."

"Forget it. Stop whining. I won't tell anybody you got beat up by a skirt. Put a couple of stones in that and toss it in the creek."

Ronny picked up a fist-sized rock and jammed it into the handbag. He swung it by its strap, let go, listened for the splash.

"Want to hear something really funny?" he said. "She had a rubber in there. No kidding. Tucked in her billfold. Goddamn Trojan. I thought only guys carried them. She must be hot for it. And, you know, she wasn't half bad, either. Did you get a look at her? Decent bod. Very decent. A real live wire. I should have said, 'Hey, babe. Get in here. I don't want your car, I want you. My ICBM's ready to blast off. Let's make whoopee.' Maybe she would have said, 'All right, do it to me, cool daddy. I'm yours.' Oh, yeah."

He grinned. His eye was swollen nearly closed.

———

"I keep thinking back, Carlo," George said. "Keep going over every damn woman I ever had. Every whore, every B-girl, every tramp. Which one? Which one gave it to me?"

"The doc's sure? Syph?" They sat at a table beside the rail that separated the small bar from ten bowling lanes. George wore a cardigan and a flannel shirt, Carlo a tie.

"Some kind of syph. Parcheesi or something. Twenty—thirty years, it takes. Gets into your blood, then it hides. Waits. Eats from the inside, like the Reds in this country. Sooner or later, it hits your brain. Begins to rot you, inside out."

"Give you anything for it?"

"He gave me some shots. I'm supposed to go have some more. But at this stage it's too late. When you first get it okay. But nothing can put back the rotted part, or stop it spreading."

"I'm sorry, George."

"My old man dropped dead at a lathe when he was fifty-two. I can't complain. Thing is, it's not like a bum heart, where you can take it easy, pamper it. It's there, inside, waiting. And it can screw up everything, make you go off your head. Sometimes, I feel it. I look in the mirror and it's not me looking back."

One of the bowlers hopped backward on one leg, waving his arms, trying to change the course of the ball he'd just rolled.

"And Bea. Other night, she was washing dishes and I started in on something, talking trash the way I do. It made sense to me at the time, but—anyway, I look over to see if she's getting it, and she's cringing. As if I was pointing a gun at her. I wanted to laugh. Looked like a cartoon character. Then I realized. She's afraid of you, I said. Afraid. Bea's afraid of you. That's a damn lonely feeling, Carlo."

"It's the sickness, though. It's not you."

"The sickness is me now."

"What's the doc say to do?"

"Nothing I can do. It's going to get worse."

"Shame. Real shame."

"I've been feeling it coming on ever since Eugene was killed. When that happened, I knew things were going to turn sour."

Carlo clicked his tongue and looked down at his empty beer glass.

"Patsy," George said to the bartender, "couple more. Funny thing, though, what you remember. Like this one broad before the war. Ugly? Face all pimples, peroxide blonde with an inch of black roots, marshmallow ass. I must have been wall-eyed when I picked her up. Don't even remember doing it, just the next morning. Hotel had dirty sheets. I opened my eyes and she's standing there in the raw, looking through a rip in the shade. I think it was raining. She comes over to the bed, stands there scratching her bush. She says, 'George, you'da made a hell of a priest.' And she wasn't joking. She wasn't making fun of me. She says, 'Father Lombardosi, it's got a nice ring to it.' Says I'd look good in black, that I had a way with people, be good in confession. And, you know, I'd once thought, when I was little, of being a priest in order to make it up to my ma. Whether I told this bag about that or what, I don't know. But it comes back to me, her saying that. Funny. Hell of a priest. Wonder if it was her?"

The bartender brought two more beers to the table.

"I know how those things stick in your mind," Carlo said.

"But what difference does it make where I caught it or who I caught it from? What am I going to do, look up some hooker from thirty years ago and beat her face in? Some grandma? Ever think of that? Women you had in your salad days are grandmas?"

"No, I never thought of that."

"Maybe not you. For some reason, I think if I knew, it would at least make some sense out of the whole thing, tie it together. Say, if it was the most beautiful dame you ever had. Except, none of them were all that beautiful up close. Not the ones I had. Not even the flashy ones. It's stupid. I just have to swallow it. I've swallowed everything else, haven't I? What's been put on my plate, I've swallowed it." George lit his pipe, making wet sounds.

Carlo watched the ball of one of the bowlers plow straight through the head pin and leave the seven-ten split. He looked back at George's sagging face. Syphilis. Syphilis was what got Capone, they said. Tough for George. Tough for Carlo, too. He'd have to make some hard choices. He asked, "So what are you going to do?"

"Now? Fight. I'm a fighter, I can fight this. It doesn't hurt or anything, thank God. I have to learn to control myself."

"Maybe you should think about slowing down, letting someone else take the knocks."

"And watch Petrone grab my business and turn it over to some young jackass? What would I live on, this? Taxes and all, I'm lucky if I break even on this place."

"I'm sure we could come up with some arrangement."

"Carlo, don't kid a kidder. You know and I know, if it's not in your fist, you haven't got it. I can still handle fine, thanks. I don't need help from Petrone or from you or from anybody. I'm not ready to roll over and play dead. I might just end up kicking Petrone's precious ass."

"Don't talk that way, George. Don't ever talk that way to me." But he knew George was right. You don't put yourself at someone's mercy, not in their world. Mercy was for weaks.

When George didn't respond, Carlo asked, "You've taken care of that thing with Shargoff, haven't you?"

"Stinky Shargoff? What about him?"

"I told you a long time ago. Manny's been grousing about the bad example, the way you're letting him go."

"Petrone's a goddamn old woman. Can I run my business or not? He wanted an example, he's going to get an example. It's all set. It's all set for tomorrow morning."

"What is?"

"*Kaboom!* Know that place Shargoff operates on Norton? I'm going to blow the fucker up."

"What are you talking about?"

"Eight sticks. I'm going to make the big *kaboom*. Shargoff will come around, all right. But I'm thinking of Manny too. Lombardosi's no punk. This'll teach him. Lombardosi makes heap big noise in this town yet. You fuck with Lombardosi—*kaboom*."

"I don't know, George. Dynamite? Somebody gets hurt, heat'll be on all over town."

"Nobody's there during the day. I checked. The action's all after dark. See, what I'm after is the *kaboom*. I could go twist Shargoff's arm off, he'd come around. But Manny, seems he doesn't go for that anymore. That silly-assed baloney inspector last year who I called a bad name, Petrone was all over me."

"You put the man in the hospital."

"I kicked his ass, sure. But with Shargoff, it'll be different. *Kaboom*. Teach him and teach anybody, you mess with George Lombardosi, you're screwed, baby. *Kaboom*. Screwed, blewed, and tattooed. Ha ha. *Kaboomsie*."

Carlo felt as if he were holding a conversation with a ventriloquist. "I think you'd better let me check with Manny first," he said. "We'll see if—"

"*We'll* see? You keep talking about *we*, Carlo. I thought you and I was *we*."

"That's what I mean. Maybe we can go over and talk to Shargoff together."

George squinted. "Hold my hand or something? Come on. Anyway, like I said, it's set for tomorrow morning. You'll hear it, the big noise. They'll hear it all over the city. People will be going, What was that? Petrone, he'll hear it."

"George, I'm telling you, you're overdoing it. You're using a howitzer on a mosquito. How much does Shargoff owe?"

"Not the point. Didn't you tell me how Manny said to make an example? Didn't you? Not the money, an example. Teach them how to think? I've been making examples all my life, and he's telling me. I'll show him an example. Him and that damn priest of his."

"Priest?"

"DeMarco. Manny knows Father DeMarco. Did you realize that? Manny's not in our parish, but he knows our priest. The two of them, they're plotting something."

"Like what? A rake-off on communion wafers?"

"Ever notice the way DeMarco stares at you? I caught him peeking out of the sacristy before mass last Sunday."

"You're going to church now?"

"Huh? Oh, yeah, lately I have been. Yeah. Tell the truth, I want to keep a watch on that guy."

"Who?"

"Who? DeMarco, I just said. Giving me the old fish eye from the sacristy. And I think that he, that he was the one who gave me this parcheesi, this syph. Remember how they used to always say, go with a woman not your wife, you'll catch it? Well, I think they make sure you do. Wear those black suits. Give you the curse. Infect you. Eat you alive with their diseases. Expect you to come crawling, asking them to forgive and forget. They never forget. They make you so you can't trust yourself. That eye. Smiling at me. Plotting.

Him and Petrone. Getting inside me. Can't trust myself anymore. Not anymore. Not anymore."

"Slow down, George. Relax."

"Relax?"

"You're getting upset. Take it slow, will you?"

"I'm right, aren't I?"

"How do you figure? DeMarco wasn't around thirty years ago. You caught it off some broad."

George massaged his eyes with his fingertips. Carlo watched the last two bowlers pack their balls and shoes. A heavy silence took the place of the rumble of pins.

George sighed. "Summer comes," he said, "nobody bowls. Know what I'm going to do? Cover the lanes with plywood and throw sock hops."

"What?"

"Sock hops. For kids. No booze or nothing. Just have records, maybe bring in a combo, and let them dance, have a good time."

"You serious?"

"Sure. I don't make nothing running the lanes in summer. But you get two—three hundred kids in here, buck a head, you're doing okay. Clear. And sell lots of pop. Besides, I like kids. Always liked kids."

June 10

The old street. His street. Home. George listened to the ticking from the bag beside him on the seat of the gray Buick. He'd wound the clock and made the connections and set the switch before he left. He'd given himself forty-five minutes. He felt it was better like that. If something happened on the way, it happened because God wanted it to happen. Plus, he wouldn't have to mess with it later.

Hulking black clouds were pacing overhead. The

kind of day he'd hoped for. He felt that he was on a mission, that his stolen car was a sacred vehicle. The sense of calling burst in his chest. The whispered ticking crashed in his ears.

His street. The place where his family's house had stood was a vacuum of urban renewal. But they hadn't yet gotten around to building one of the drab brick cubicles that lined the rest of the block. The cement stairs that had led to his front porch now stood amid the rubble like a tombstone. All the faces now were black.

Not all. There was Eddie Bagioni. Rudy's Pal. George rolled down the window. Little Eddie Bagioni.

Hey, Lombardosi!

Hiya, Eddie.

Whataya doing?

Collecting pop bottles. Look. Penny each. I found six in a trash can on Stegner Street.

Those are all covered with dog piss. I wouldn't touch those if you paid me a million dollars. Hey, Rudy, look who's here. Fatty Lombardosi. He's trying to make some money.

Fuck a duck, Fatty. Whataya wasting your time for? Ask your old friend Rudy. He'll help you out. Won't I, guys? I help out my pals. Here. Here's fifty cents. Forget the bottles, Fatty. Nice fifty-cent piece.

I've already got these, so—

I said forget them.

The sound of shattering glass tore the air.

Don't you say thanks, Fatty? Eddie whined. Rudy give you four bits, you didn't say thanks. Did he, guys?

What's it for?

For being a nice guy, jerko, Rudy said. We're friends, ain't we? Siamo amici.

I guess, yeah. Thanks.

Listen, friend. How about doing your friend Rudy a friendly little favor?

What?

Well, you know Wheezer's brother Norman, don't you? The idiot? The retard? Huh? Norman don't get on with girls much, you know. Does he, Wheeze? Maybe it's the way he smells, I don't know. Anyway, he's always running his flag up the pole, but he never gets any fun. And we was thinking. Be nice to give him some fun for a change. Sort of a birthday present. Not that it's his birthday, but he don't know the diff. So I said, I bet Fatty Lombardosi would do that. He might even like it.

Do what?

You'll see. No, now don't try to get away. What you think I give you the fifty cents for? Nothing? You've gotta. Bring him along, guys. Wheezer, go get Norman. You've gotta, Fatty.

Come on, Fatty. You'll love it. Hold him. I'll break your arm. No, you don't. Lookit him. Yeah, Fatty. Fatty, Fatty, two-by-four, couldn't get through the bathroom door, so he did it on the floor. Fatty, Fatty, two-by-four. Fatty. Fatty.

George licked his lips. A Negro boy rode past on his tricycle. The sky was dropping. He started the engine and drove on.

All the familiar streets, changed now. Only the trees remained as always, bursting with the sticky golden green of early summer. Trees and memories. Memories of memories. Incidents lost like the darkening images in reflections of parallel mirrors, yet now bursting into false clarity.

Bless me, Father, for I have sinned. It has been five weeks since my last confession. Five weeks.

Yes, my son. What is it, my son?

Father, they made me.

Yes, my son. What is it, my son?

They made me, Father.

No one can make you sin, my son. If you deny guilt, God denies absolution. You are unclean. You are foul

*and unclean and unnatural. You have done what is foul
and unclean and unnatural. Unnatural.*

But I didn't want to.

*Vile. Impure. Do not blame others for your sin.
Your sin. Your sin.*

O my God, I am heartily sorry . . .

Unclean. Unnatural.

. . . for having offended thee.

He parked under a maple tree. He wanted to slide
back the wooden cover and look at the clock, but he
wouldn't let himself. The mounting tension exploded
time. Minutes became interminable. Seconds lingered.
The air clogged with the smell of sap and rain.

Rudy was the first.

The sky turned suddenly black. Black, but with a
line of morning brightness at the horizon. Thunder
heaved in the distance.

The first one. The first one where you couldn't go
back.

*Georgie. How they hanging, buddy? Still throwing
them dumbbells around? Heard you hooked up with
Petrone. Couldn't believe it. I thought you were neighborhood. Couldn't believe you'd tie in with that punk.
Listen, you and me go way back. This Petrone's squeezing some guys we both've known for a long time. I
mean squeezing. That ain't right. There's room. You
agree with me, plenty of room for everybody, right?*

Just so much room, Rudy.

*I'm talking practically family here. I mean, don't get
me wrong, I'm willing to reason. Sure, Manny wants to
reason, I'll be the first to sit down with him. Wants a
cut, I'll think about it. I want to see what's in it for me,
natch. Maybe it's good business, I don't know. We can
talk. Just, I don't like the elbows. I don't like pressure.
I don't like my friends getting kneed in the kidneys. I
don't like threats. You know me, you know that. I
don't knuckle under to threats.*

I know you, Rudy.

Don't look at me that way. I'm warning you. Hey, we'll talk. We'll straighten this out. Live and let live. Petrone understands. He's got brains. Now what the hell is that for? Come on. Don't clown around. Think flashing a gun will get you respect? Huh? I knew you when you were nothing. Remember? Guns don't scare me. I've got friends here. Maybe Petrone's not so all-powerful. Fucking punk. Better think twice about waving a gun in my face, Lombardosi. I see through you. No, wait. It's all money, right? Manny just wants the cash, doesn't he? Didn't he mention a deal? We'll talk about it. Just money. We don't need this, do we? Did he tell you to? Did he? Listen. Listen to me. I'm willing to make a deal. There's no point. You can't—George, please. I didn't. I'm sorry. So help me God, I'm sorry. Just don't. George. Please. Don't. Oh, God, don't.

No going back. Lost acts. The first drops fell warm on George's neck as he crossed the street. He clutched the precious burlap sack under his arm. He trotted up the steps, a man seeking shelter from the imminent downpour.

He placed the package in the corner of the alcove—gently, as if depositing an infant on the doorstep of a stranger. He felt so calm he couldn't understand the trembling of his hands. He was startled by the *dit-dah* of his heart, which took up the ticking from inside the box and amplified it, accelerated it. The splatter from the sky was growing violent.

Descending the steps he forced himself not to look around. He watched someone's hand, his own, rise and slur a sign of the cross in the air. The dampness soaked through. His shoulders turned cold.

He returned to the cocoon of the car. He clenched his teeth against the chill. Rain battered the roof with a white roar. Sheets ran down the windshield. The glass began to fog. He lowered the window an inch. Cold sprayed his face. He breathed wet wool.

The cloudburst drew a breath, hesitated, then lashed

out with sharp gusts. George removed his pipe from his pocket and clamped it unlit between his teeth. A twig and a few young leaves fell onto the drenched pavement. An umbrella appeared on the opposite side of the street. It moved slowly, tilted against the wind. A squat woman in black was making a vain, waddling attempt to escape the deluge.

George pressed his palms against the wheel. The inevitability of it made him smile. He bared his teeth.

She stopped in the alcove. She searched in her bag. Finally, she drew something out—a black mantilla. She put her hands up to pin it to her hair.

George's smile wouldn't stop. It opened up his face, consumed his cheeks, his eyes, his forehead, peeled back along his skull, letting the storm pour into his head.

Then the first crack of lightning. The naked roar of thunder. The bulb of flame. The roiling black smoke. The thudding wave that rocked the car. The lost act.

A moment later, the click, the sprinkle of stained glass pebbles.

June 20

"Manny!" Phyllis traced the curves of her mouth with red. "Man-ny!"

"What?" he shouted from the bathroom.

"I want a new TV, one of those portable ones. We can keep it in here and get some rest. Watch the news in bed. Not have to sit up." She eased the lipstick again across her full lower lip. "Did you hear me?"

"You want a portable television."

"The Hendersons have one, and Lois says they get a lot of use out of it." She put her fingers at the corners of her eyes and slanted them upward to see how she'd look as an oriental. Exotic. "Hear me, Manny?"

"She got, I want. Just like a kid." He came into the bedroom wiping dabs of lather from his face. "Where's my tie?

"What tie?"

"The striped one. The one I had out. Oh, there it is."

"Where you left it."

"Hey, Phyllis, don't. Just don t, okay? I've got a lot on my mind."

"Oh, yeah. Widdle boy gonna get his gweat big gold star. Such a good widdle boy."

"Laugh your head off. After that crap in Albany, half the City Club wouldn't speak to me. This, they're admitting they were wrong."

"You twisted their goddamn arms."

"So? It's all politics."

"Bunch of fat farts with hairy noses. And the wives. Holy hell. 'Phyllis, dear, wouldn't you like to work on a committee to put mums around all the public johns?'"

"Stokely Simpson, he's a real fat fart."

"You're jealous because Stokely knows how to dance."

"I can dance."

"At the podiatrists' ball." She finished powdering her nose and moved the puff down her throat and into the cleft of her underwired bra.

"Just keep yourself under control tonight, hear me?"

"Why, whatever do you mean?" She smoothed her slip and went to the closet.

"I mean don't juice yourself into a scene."

"Screw you."

"Come on. We're supposed to be pillars. You can't be an upstanding member of the community if you can't stand up."

"You kill me, Manny."

"I'm not joking."

"No, jokes are fun. You don't know what fun is."

She draped four different dresses over her, meditating on each one, before she decided. She said, "Did you talk to Rick, the way I asked you to?"

"What?"

"I told you, I heard him upchucking in the bathroom last week at three in the morning. I know they're drinking beer, him and that Logan boy."

"Few beers going to kill him?"

"Manny, he's eleven years old."

"I drank hard liquor with my old man at that age. And it wasn't even legal. Maybe you oughta worry about the kind of example you're setting him. Ever think of that?"

"Talk to him. You're his father."

"When I have time, I will." Manny held his breath and buttoned his shirt over his belly. Chimes sounded from the living room.

"That'll be Leo."

"I don't understand this, Manny. Why can't I go with you?"

"I told you, I have to straighten out a problem with one of the shop stewards beforehand. He's picking me up. Then he'll drop me at the hall."

"Why not come back? We can go from here."

"I haven't got time. I want to get there early, mix with the Joes before the feed."

"But I don't like being in the same car with that swine Leo. He's filthy. You can smell him. Doesn't he ever take a bath?"

"That's enough. I told you, I have things on my mind."

"I'm sick of you, Manny."

"I'm double sick of you. And I'm sick of your crap. I'm not putting up with it tonight, believe me."

A voice at the door said, "Leo's here."

"Have him wait in the den, May. Give him a drink. I'll be right there." He slipped his vest on and balanced the tie around his neck. "Hear me, Phyllis? You're going to be nice tonight. Hear me?"

Manny went out. Phyllis pulled her stockings on. She admired her slender ankles, the curve of her calves. Watching in the mirror, she tugged the neckline of her dress down. She smoothed her eyebrows, adjusted the wave of her dark auburn hair, smiled. She placed her palms on the backs of her hips, turned slowly from side to side, smiled again.

"Hey, Manny," Leo was saying. "Got any ice?"

"May! Bring some ice in here for Leo, will you?"

The dough-faced woman appeared with an aluminum tray and poured cubes into a bucket on the sideboard. She went out. Leo dropped three cubes into his glass.

"Well?" Manny said.

"I checked with Chi Chi. He's ready."

"Everything? Loaded?"

"I double-checked—the gloves, everything."

"This guy you got the dope from, he's all right?"

"Been drinking there for years. Gary knows him. Says they're putting on dances for kids on weekends, no bowling. Our man always gets there a little after eight. And no matter which way he takes, he's gotta cross the Wellington Street Bridge, go up along the park there. Perfect. No houses or nothing."

"Chi Chi knows?"

"I did a dry run with him the other night. He's a good kid."

"Okay. We'll meet in the parking lot at the hall. He's clear what to do after?"

"I went over it about a hundred times. I'm telling you, he's a good kid."

Manny rubbed his mouth with the back of his hand.

"You sure you don't want me along, Manny?"

"No. No, my show. This baby's my show all the way."

"If you say so. Remember, though, he always has that cannon on him. You can't give him time."

"Don't worry. He won't have any time."

———

George smiled at the blond head beside him in the car. He said, "How's school? How's school? Did you get a good report card?"

"Today was our last day," Diane answered. "Boy, am I glad. I hate school."

"You shouldn't ever hate."

"Why? School stinks. Know what happened, Uncle George? Mrs. Crowley—who I have for reading lit? —she got into a fight."

"A teacher? Woman teacher?"

"Yep. This big girl, Lesley—I think she's a sophomore—was putting on lipstick at her locker and Mrs. Crowley was hall monitor and she slapped Lesley's hand and her compact fell on the floor and broke. So Lesley hit Mrs. Crowley right in the face and they started fighting. They fell down and were screaming and all."

"That's not nice."

"I hate Mrs. Crowley. All the kids there were watching and cheering. Until these men teachers came and picked up Lesley. Then Mrs. Crowley slapped her in the face real hard. And Lesley got expelled. I wouldn't care if I got expelled. I think it's cool."

"Oh, no. You have to behave yourself. You're always a little lady, aren't you? Aren't you? A good girl?"

"Yes, Uncle George."

A little angel, he thought. A little angel in her starched white blouse, her bobby socks, her blue satin bow. So eager and delicate. He loved children.

"Uncle George, how come the moon follows you when you're in a car? How come it goes along with you?"

"It likes you, I guess. Yeah, the moon likes you."

The heavy cream-colored moon raced along the horizon. It hurdled barns and sliced through forests to keep up with them, always staring.

For an instant, George felt himself loosen. He was coming apart. Night was rushing into his head. He groaned. He clenched his jaw and frowned at the road ahead.

"Will there be city kids at this dance? My friend Pam says city kids are cool."

"Lots of kids, there'll be lots of kids there."

"I wish I had more kids to play with."

"You like boys? Do you? You starting to like boys now?"

"Sandy says boys have cooties."

Her laugh reminded George of her mother's laugh. It was lower pitched than you'd expect, with an edge to it. It gave him a funny feeling.

"Cooties?"

"They do have cooties, boys in my grade. I hate them. I like my swimming teacher, though. I'm going to start lessons again week after next. I'm in intermediates this year. Those guys who teach swimming lessons are cool. But I really and truly want to marry a race car driver."

They were following a road that paralleled the shore of the lake. Occasionally they veered close to the water. George glanced out at the calm surface. Like an endless sheet of glass, it reflected the sheen of the fading twilight.

"Race?"

'You know, like at the speedway? Mom took me once. It was so loud you couldn't even hear. And they had crackups and all. And then between races once they let the kids go out onto the track so you could ride in a race car, whichever one you wanted. Did you ever ride in a race car, Uncle George?"

"Clap erasers?"

"*Race* car. I got to go in this one, the Fugitive. That's my favorite. You know, they didn't go real fast or anything. Just, the kids got to sit in them and go around. Did you know they only have one seat inside? They have these bars and all, but only one person can sit. I didn't know that. I thought they were like a regular car."

George gave another low moan. His fingers were claws. The bottom was dropping out. He couldn't help it. It dropped and dropped. His arms, legs, the organs in his belly weren't him any longer. Another car sped past, glared at him with its lights.

He switched his own lights on.

Diane was watching out her window. She was hugging her knee. Her little patent leather shoe gleamed. Then she made a quick arc with her head, throwing her bangs out of her eyes. It was a woman's gesture. Like her laugh, it made George shiver.

"Do you ride your bike? Huh? Do you? Do you?" He hadn't meant to shout.

She squinted at him, her mouth moving hesitantly.

"That bike old Santa gave you for Christmas? Huh? That two-wheeler? Ho ho. Shiny two-wheeler under the tree? Huh? Been a good girl? Huh?"

One of her eyebrows rose. Sherry used the same expression. George forced himself to chuckle.

"I sent you a thank-you note," Diane said. "Didn't you get it?"

"Sure. Old Santa will see what he can do. I mean, have you been riding it? It's fun, isn't it?"

"I can ride it. But Dad won't let me ride in the road, and our sidewalk's too short and the driveway's all stones. I want to ride it to Pam's house, but Dad says I can't because I might get hit by a car."

They were moving out of the farmland, past suburban homes.

"You mind your dad."

"Uncle George, how come the Russians hate us? Dad says they want to drop bombs on us. Then they'll come over here and we won't have any more summer vacation from school. Christmas vacation, either."

"The Russians? It's because they're Reds. They're all Reds. They're dirty, fucking Reds. They're goddamn, fucking— No. No, I mean—"

She'd pushed to the far edge of the seat and was looking at him out of the corner of her eye.

"That's not nice," he said. "Never use those words. You see, Diane, you get old, see? And you don't know what you're thinking in your own mind. You—somebody—you hear things. Like people talking inside your head. You don't know what they're saying. It's just, you have to try not to listen. Maybe say a prayer. It's when you get old."

She wasn't paying attention. She bent her fingers around the vent window to feel the wind. She said, "Dad works nights a lot, so you have to be real quiet when he's sleeping during the day."

They both fell silent. They had reached the city now. At a traffic light, George lit his pipe and puffed it to a red glow. Diane liked to lean her head on the back of the seat and watch out the window at the trees and the yellow streetlights going by overhead.

"Is Mom pretty?" she asked.

George grunted, sucking on his pipe.

"I think she is," Diane went on. "Pam's mother, and Susan's mother, and a lot of kids' mothers are old. They look old. I think Mom's the prettiest."

They were turning onto the wide bridge that crossed the river. Old-fashioned lampposts paraded by on its edge. The milky sky opened above them.

"There's the—! Oh, no. Shooey, I saw the evening star, but then I saw another one. When you see two, you can't say it. Uncle George, do you believe in 'Star light, star bright, first star I see tonight'? Then you cross your fingers and make a wish? And it comes true?"

"Look at the stars. See 'em? See the stars?" George wasn't answering her. He sighed.

"Only it has to be just one, the first one. If you see two at the same time, it's too late."

"Too late. Yes, that's right, it's too late."

Diane slouched again and looked up. They turned down a street lined with trees. Under the leafy canopy it was already night. George drove slowly, leaning forward.

"We almost there?"

"Almost."

They were following the gorge of the river. Diane

watched some kids playing in the park along its edge on their right. She thought of the boys who'd be at the dance. Her friend Pam would be there. Pam's mother was going shopping and would take them home later.

Diane wanted to kiss a boy to see what it was like. Not on the cheek. Not play. For real.

They stopped at a traffic light. She wished they'd get there.

A loud crack made her hunch her shoulders. A firecracker. Or like a man she'd seen crack a bullwhip in an assembly at school. It made her eyes water, she was so startled.

The car jerked forward. Diane slid half onto the floor. Her knee gashed against the heater. It stung. It was bleeding.

"Uncle George!"

They were going very fast. The car swerved. She banged hard against the door. The handle for the window dug into her shoulder.

They kept going faster. They bounced. She clutched the dashboard. She pulled herself up. A jolt slammed her mouth into the glove compartment. She raised her chin and could see out the front.

They weren't on the road. Big bushes were rushing toward them. Her mouth opened, but she couldn't breathe or make a sound. I wish I may, she thought.

The bushes tore their fingernails along the car and disappeared. Ahead it was black. They were flying. All black. Breathless and smooth, they were flying. Flying.

I wish I might.

———

Link gripped the wheel as if it were a live snake. He angled the Fugitive onto the banked dirt track. He played with the clutch the way a jockey plays with the reins of a skittish Thoroughbred. The car surged, eased forward, halted, lurched, pranced, pawed, shivered.

He took his place in the pack. The racers were

lining up behind the shiny pace car like convicts forming a procession behind a prison chaplain. They were a mean lot, their doors welded shut, fenders hammered and patched, fat black tires bulging out in back. They were blank-eyed, cauliflower-eared, thick-tongued, loud and merciless.

"Coming onto the track now," a voice shouted over the public address system, "for our seventy-five-lap late-model feature. That's Cal Vanderstyne in Howie's Collision number Twenty-seven. Next, in the white Buick . . ." Static, hacking engines, and a cheering crowd washed away the announcements. But those who filled the bleachers knew the racers by heart. They knew the drivers: Sparky and Lloyd and Bucky and Link and Moose and Junior and Butch. They knew the cars: number 17, the yellow Devastator; number 99, Hell on Wheels, a grape-colored DeSoto; the green-and-black Fugitive, lucky 7; Spitfire, a Ford painted the metallic gold of a radiator; number 1188, the blood-red Dead Man's Hand.

The cars were now marching around the quarter-mile clay oval. Floodlights squinted at them through clouds of moths and june bugs. The slow parade lurched forward, the cars lagged and spurted, nudged each other with steel elbows, kicked up dust, blasted flames out their exhaust pipes, and made faces with their toothless grilles.

After two laps, the pace car accelerated and eased off the back straight.

The racers, suddenly finding the bits loose on their palates, began to pick up speed. Eyes turned to the figure in white coveralls who waited on a platform halfway down the front stretch. As the cars wound into the last turn, he held up his left hand like a man cautioning a tidal wave. Then his right arm whipped out a green flag and cracked it.

Noisy and rambunctious up to now, the cars suddenly exploded into deafening insanity. The starter's flag excited all the vehicles to frenzy. They surged down the short straightaway at breakneck speed. Just as they seemed certain to blast off the track, they cut hard to the left and slid sideways around the banked dirt. Tires wavered and clawed in the soft clay, then grabbed and sent the cars hurtling down the back-stretch. In the dim far corner, the fenders of two cars came together. Metal tore. A Buick careened wildly, found its footing, leaped back into the herd. The stampede continued.

Link flew into the turn. Blood pulsed in the steering wheel. He jerked it to the left. He fishtailed. He yanked the wheel to the right. He fluttered it back and forth. Braked with his heel as he throttled with his toe. Punched in the clutch. Shifted. Felt the pressure of his seat as the car tore forward. Listened to the howl of his engine among the furious screams of the other cars. Glanced at the tach. At the car beside him. Wrestled into the next turn.

Inside the dust, inside the mist of oil, the smell of gasoline and burning rubber, inside the fumes, the clods of clay, the riot of detonating engines, inside the heat, inside the rabid shrieks of the metallic beasts, inside, at the center, Link began to dance. The world beyond the oval track no longer existed. The dirt hollow consumed him. It was a savage dance, a centrifugal, wrenching, barbaric dance. But with its own rhythm, its own wild grace. Dancing, he guided the hurtling car through the chaos before him. He fought for position. He crowded opponents to the rail. He banged quarter panels. He shot through openings. He held off challenges. He maneuvered. He dove low under a car ahead.

Lap followed lap. The leaders became nearly indistinguishable from the stragglers as the faster cars lapped the slower ones.

Link moved into third place. In first was Walt Forman's Flame Thrower, an orange Lincoln, number 13. Moose Nemo held second in his lavender Ford.

Without warning, a tan Chevy broke into a spin on

the curve. Another galloping racer clipped its fender. The Chevy skidded sideways onto the infield. It raised an explosion of dust. The second car, Tiny Phillips's black Plymouth, ran up the curve and clobbered the guard rail. A third car piled into it. They both waltzed in a long arc as the others dodged and swerved to avoid the pileup. The entire incident took only two seconds. The crowd jumped up as one, craned to see.

The yellow flag went out. A yellow light flashed on the backstretch. After a brief scramble for position, the remaining cars slowed to a crawl. Their engines panted in the relative hush that descended on the track. Link pulled his goggles up and wiped sweat from his eyes.

Waving arms heralded the survival of the drivers caught in the spasm. Two wreckers swooped out to tend to the maimed and crippled. The Chevy limped to the pits under its own power. The others were dragged back, consoled by applause and the announcer's cheery "They'll be back!"

The reunited pack crawled nervously down the back straight of the cleared track. The green light blinked on. Engines roared. The cars accelerated in a mass. They surged around the fourth turn. The starter again whipped out the green banner. The uproar continued.

Above, a pregnant moon lookd down on the broiling jewel of action among the sleeping orchards. Across the countryside, the sound of the engines carried clearly for ten miles before it became indistinguishable from the drone of insects.

Link made an outside run at Moose Nemo before every turn. The Fugitive's engine gave him a yard lead at the end of the straight, but Moose had the groove and would ride Link up the bank of the curve, hold the better traction, and rush down onto the next straight ahead. Link asked the car for more power, but he couldn't get position on the turn. Then the Ford appeared to have beat him off. He was a half car length behind on the stretch, and Nemo was pulling away.

Just before the two cars slid into the turn, Link hit his brakes. Nemo, anticipating another challenge on his right, had begun to drift up the bank. Link stomped on the accelerator and careened to the inside. Moose tried to correct his mistake. His car threatened rebellion as he urged it downward.

Link felt his own car begin to float. He kept applying the whip as he skidded, nearly weightless. By the end of the straight, Nemo was breathing his exhaust.

The Flame Thrower held a quarter-lap lead. Link concentrated on driving the groove during the next few circuits. Patches of rubber and sprayed oil and loose dirt created slippery spots on the turns. He looked for the firm track, set his car up, took the turn, piled down the straight. He began to close on the orange car ahead, but time was running out.

The crowd divided into two factions. Link was the fair-haired boy. Ladies' favorite. Cool, wry, slick. Walt Forman was a bull-necked, dirty-mouthed, hard-drinking old-timer. He'd pumped gas at Knapp's Gulf for as long as anybody could remember, and he'd always driven the Knapp's Gulf Flame Thrower. Farmhands, truck drivers, and volunteer firemen loved him.

Link was now following within inches of Forman's bumper. Before each turn, he'd bang the Lincoln from behind, just hard enough. But number 13 held off the challenge, and Link could do nothing but wait. He went low and nudged the other car's fender as they negotiated the corner. He skidded onto the sloppy part of the track and lost time regaining his balance on the stretch.

The two cars rushed bumper to bumper off the front turn. The starter snapped out the white flag—last lap. The spectators screamed and stomped. Link surged to the outside, and they barreled into the turn with Link's headlights at Forman's passenger door. The Flame Thrower's skidding rear end slammed into Link's door, jolting his elbow. Link tried to hold on as they slid around the turn, but he felt the big orange car ease ahead. The two cars howled down the back straight almost touching.

On the last turn, Link let the Fugitive ride up to give him a clear track to the finish. He saw the orange fender shimmying an arm's reach away. Still pumping the brakes, he fed the engine more gas, more. He let the steering wheel spin back through his hands as he hit the final stretch. His car leaped forward. It pounced to within inches of Forman's leading bumper. But the Lincoln had just as much power and a better angle. Forman opened up his throttle. He streaked across the line. The starter waved the checkered flag.

"She's here," Ronny said to Link as soon as he turned off the engine. "I saw her when I went to get a brew. She wants to talk to you."

"What about Marsha?" Link unstrapped himself and climbed through the window.

"She was with me. She saw her."

"You take care of her tonight, understand?"

"Marsha? Link, I can't do that. I mean—"

"She likes you." He took a sponge and squeezed water over his head.

"Sure, as a friend, maybe. But, to actually—you know."

"What are you going to do, marry her and have ten kids and worry about all the grandchildren visiting on Thanksgiving? Just take her home." He dried his face with a paper towel and pointed to the car. "I'm hearing a tapping noise. I think we should lift the head and go over the valves again. Moved good, though. You've got that chassis set up nice."

"I thought you were going to take him coming off of it."

"The guy was ticking, that's all."

Ronny stayed back to load the car onto its trailer.

Marsha waited just outside the pits, her mouth tensed

between a smile and a pout. "Judas priest, Link, I wanted you to win so bad I could taste it."

"Yeah, well, I gave it my best. He had the car—tonight, anyway. . . . Listen, angel, I've got some business to take care of. I don't think I'll be able to take you out."

"Sherry?"

"That's it."

"She's just stringing you, Link. She don't care a damn."

"Sure she does. She loves me."

"She said she didn't want to see you no more." Marsha chomped furiously on her gum. "You told me."

"Her life made her say that, her situation. What we have goes farther than situations. Didn't I tell you two people have a chance—maybe?"

She was holding onto his finger, squeezing it. "But she's married. She's a married woman."

"Married doesn't mean anything. I'm talking about people, about me and her."

"But Link."

"It's love, angel. You have to give it every chance you can, because the rest is a load of crap."

"But you told me you liked me. You wanted me."

"I told you the truth all along. I never promised you anything but a fast ride. You don't get that, start complaining. Okay?"

"Yeah, but shoot."

He slipped an arm around her shag sweater and pressed his mouth onto her lips.

"Hey, Romeo!"

Link winked at Marsha and turned.

"How'd you fuckin' like eating my farts, lover boy?" Walt Forman said. His sausage fingers were wrapped around the neck of a bottle of Four Roses. Two grinning pals stood beside him.

"You were really getting on the throttle tonight, Walt," Link said.

"Damn right. And listen to me—you fuckin' bang my car again, I'll use your fuckin' head for a fuckin' football."

"That right, Walt?"

"Fuckin' A, it's right. Any shit-eater that bends my metal gets his fuckin' ass handed to him."

"I'll keep that in mind."

Coming out of the gate, Ronny stepped in front of the hard-bellied driver. "Your crank is what's bent, Forman. You're asleep out there half the time. We should be talking to your insurance company."

"Why you fuckin' little douche bag—"

"Shove it up your ass, man—if you can find it."

Forman knocked Ronny backward with the heel of his hand. "I'm gonna fuck you up, you fuckin' little prick."

Forman's friends grinned some more and muttered encouragement. Others gathered to watch.

Ronny beckoned with cupped fingers. "Come on, you dipshit. I'll make you eat bicycle seats."

"Hold it, Ronny." Link stepped between them. "Walt, you're a sore winner, you know that?"

"Who the fuck you think you're—"

"Wait a minute. You drove a real nice race. I'm a student of the art. I appreciate. Nobody handles a car like you do, except maybe Lee Petty. And nobody's got a car that can match the Flame Thrower. Not around here. Congratulations." He held out his hand.

Forman frowned. "Link, are you fuckin' me?"

"No, Walt, I'm definitely not fucking you. Maybe I'll neck with you, but that's as far as I'll go." He smiled.

Everyone laughed. Forman frowned more deeply, then broke into a raspy guffaw.

"Oh, shit," he said. "But I'm serious about that banging. You gotta fuckin' give me room to race. I'm not kidding."

"You never kid, Walt." Link smiled again as the big man and his friends moved away. He used his fist to stroke Marsha's cheek. He glanced at Ronny, nodded, and walked toward the bleachers.

He picked his way up through the crowd toward the blond hair, lifting his chin to those who yelled out greetings and consolation.

"Here's trouble." The hefty woman in the gray sweatshirt nudged Sherry in the ribs. Then she stood and threw an arm around Link's neck and massaged him with her softness. "Now why in hell couldn't you beat that nasty old Walt Forman, huh? We're screaming our heads off for you up here. This one's gripping my arm so hard I've got black and blue marks."

"Next time, Frieda."

"Next time, next time. Link, you're breaking our hearts. You really are. We come out to see you win. You're our boy. You lose, we all lose. We want to see at least somebody make good. Somebody from our gang. At least one. Right, Sherry?"

She met his eyes.

"That's not the only reason, is it, Frieda?" Link asked.

"Why, Link."

"How much?"

"Five bucks. But so did Sherry. We don't back you just with our mouths, baby. We . . ."

Her words were obliterated by a pair of modifieds that came wailing onto the track for the next race.

". . . hard feelings," Frieda was saying. "Buy you a beer at Andy's. You've got time, haven't you, Sherry?"

She shook her head. "I really have to get back. Diane'll be home at eleven thirty and Dave's on the graveyard."

"Just one, that's all. Don't we owe it to our boy here? He's such a devil, such a sweetheart."

With magnified snarls, the new gang of cars began to line up. Frieda pecked Link's cheek and beamed. She pulled him down beside her.

The race cars strutted past on their pace lap and

prepared to mix it up. Sherry leaned across her friend and said, "Link, I want you to understand that . . ."

But now the race began. All conversation was shattered by the explosion of sound from the track. Link held Sherry's eyes and jerked his head toward the exit. He got up, squeezed Frieda's shoulder, and made his way down the bleachers without looking back. When he reached the bottom, Sherry stood and followed him.

In Link's car, heading north along a back road, she said, "I'm leaving Dave."

"For good?"

"He's not there anymore. He's just visiting. Just sizing things up—me, Diane."

"Isn't that the way he always was?"

"He was always quiet. He was always distant. But these past few months—I've noticed it since you and I've been apart—he's hardened. At dinner, he might ask Diane about school or about her baton twirling. But then it's silence. Not just silence, pain hanging in the air. He stares at his plate, eats. Christ."

"You fight?"

"I wish we did. If he'd hit me, even, anything to clear the air. But you have to have something in common. We don't. We're polite, the way you are with somebody you don t know."

"He's saving it for another lifetime."

"And that damn bomb shelter. I told you about that. He's obsessed with it. Our backyard's a mess. He spends all his time out there, down in the ground. He's pouring concrete now. But if I say anything about it, about how much it costs and all, he feeds me a line about radiation and fallout and half-lives. That's what I'm living, a half-life."

"What'll you do?"

Sherry looked out the window at the ghosts of apple trees parading in the fields.

"I don't want to hurt him. He's been good to me. He's been there when I needed him. And he's always loved Diane. But I just can't take it anymore. My nerves can't take it. The loneliness, the strangeness, the cold. I need someone, Link. Someone who's warm and alive and human. Someone I can get drunk with and laugh with and argue with and make love with. For real, not just going through the motions.

Link turned onto a dirt lane. They crossed the inky spikes laid down in the moonlight by a row of poplars. They passed a vineyard, stopped on a low bluff overlooking the lake. Sherry ran her nail around the latch of the glove compartment.

"I know how this sounds, Link. I'm not really trying to make you say yes or no. It's just, I have nobody. Nobody I can open up with the way I can with you."

"I know."

"I mean, maybe I am asking. I'm a mother. I have to make a home for Diane. I have to think of her first."

"Sure you do. This definite?"

"I'm decided. How, when—I'm not sure yet."

"I'll be waiting."

"Will you?"

"Whatever happens, you know I'll always be here. I'll always be here for you, Sherry."

"God, I hope so, Link. It's been hell not seeing you. I can't tell you."

"So here I am."

She touched his mouth with her fingers.

"Let's take a dip," he said.

They scrambled down the clay onto the beach. The lazy swells were waving streamers of moonlight, lapping the shore with tiny hisses. The small stones crunched under their feet. They crouched at the edge.

"Not bad," Link said.

"It's freezing."

"Be warm once you get in."

"I'll watch."

He pried his shoes off, pulled his tee shirt over his head, unzipped his pants. She watched as he waded.

She admired his muscular back, the line of tan at his waist. He dove. The black glass rippled and fell still. She waited. Moments passed. Just as a spark of panic flickered in her throat, he broke the surface. His wet shout echoed from the bluffs and took off across the lake toward Canada.

"Come on in. Have some fun."

She hesitated. Link rolled onto his back and spurted water from his mouth.

She smiled, unbuttoned her blouse.

Her blond hair and blond skin glowed in the pale light. The cold black water touched her ankles, her knees. A choppy wave splashed her thighs. She hugged herself. She took another step. She couldn't keep from giggling.

Link moved toward her, only his eyes above the water.

"Link."

He came on, froglike.

"I mean it, Link."

He bubbled nearer.

"Link, don't you splash!"

He splashed.

———

"It's easy, says the rabbi, you've just gotta remember where the stones are."

The crowd whooped as one. The speaker puffed out his cheeks and rolled his eyes toward the ceiling of the hall.

"But, seriously, folks, seriously. Our honored guest tonight knows there's no walking on water. When it comes to beautifying our parks, when it comes to supporting our Little League programs, when it comes to raising a voice that our state legislators really listen to, when it comes to sponsoring tours to show important businessmen that our city is a great place to set up shop, when it comes to lending a hand when a hand is needed, our recipient has been there, and he's been there with his sleeves rolled up and a smile on his face. You all know him. He's a great, great guy. And I'm honored to introduce to you the City Club's Citizen of Achievement, ladies and gentlemen, Mr. Manny Petrone." Applause washed the room.

"Thanks, Ed. Thank you. That was nice. Well, Ed's introduction made me out to be such a swell guy, I wasn't sure whether I was supposed to be ten feet tall or ten feet under. Ha. But in all sincerity, folks, I want to thank the members of the City Club for this very special honor. I'm sure there are many more deserving than I am, but all the same I'm glad that a few of the little things I've done are having some effect on making this city a better place to live and work in. Thanks. Thank you. I won't stand up here jabbering because I'm no big public speaker. Besides, I want to finish before the highballs wear off. Ha ha.

"But Ed did mention our distinguished representatives down in the state capital there. And, as most of you know, I haven't always seen eye to eye with them. They're not all bad, by a long shot. I see Joe Eggleston sitting out there, and you all know what he's done over the years for the city and county. That's right, take a bow, Joe. But as for the majority of them, I think I have to agree with the remark I heard where somebody said, 'Of course we're having a lot of ups and downs in this state. We've got a bunch of yo-yos in office.' Ha ha.

"But truly and seriously, what they're afraid of in Albany is us. All of us. Every citizen who won't put up with a bunch of grifters snooping into his private life. Every citizen who has enough brains to know that we're the bosses and not them. We pay their damn salaries. We send them down there. And we can call them back, come November. Right? That's right.

"Now, I don't want to get too political, but I had to get that in. And once again, I want to thank you all for coming out, thank our City Club, especially my friends on the award committee who stuffed the ballot box on my behalf. Ha." He waved both hands at someone down front.

"And while I'm up here," he continued, "I have a little surprise I'd like to announce. Would Father DeMarco step over here, please? Father. Most of you know Father Anthony DeMarco, pastor of St. Anselm's in the seventh ward, longtime booster of the City Club, and a hell of a nice guy to boot. Father's going to give the benediction here. But first, I'm sure you've all heard of the terrible tragedy that occurred at St. Anselm's a week or so ago, a terrible act of criminal vandalism that took the life of one of Father's parishioners and did serious damage to his church. I know you were all as pissed off about that as I was and hope, as I do, that those responsible will be brought to justice. But in the meantime, a few of us—Jackie Molloy, Charlie Endino, and some others—we've gotten together a fund to raise some money to show that our community cares. We've all chipped in some dough and hope to be raising more. So I want to take this opportunity to present Father DeMarco with this check for eight hundred dollars toward the repair of St. Anselm's. There you go, Father."

"Thank you, Mr. Petrone. I really am surprised, and I'm deeply touched by your generosity. I can assure you that this money will go a long way toward raising both the new facade of our church and the spirits of our parishioners. Thank you very much. Thank you all. Now, if you will join me in giving thanks to Him who is all-generous."

They sighed Amen in relief after the long prayer. A clamor of clinking glasses, forks, and plates joined the rising swell of renewed conversation. A four-piece combo began playing "Stardust" beside the bar in back. Men loosened their ties, stretched, and lit long cigars. Women trekked to the ladies' room in small groups.

"I'm really overwhelmed, Manny," the priest said,

leaning over Manny's shoulder. "This is certainly a fine gesture on your part."

"Least I could do, Father. Hear anything more about—you know, what was behind that business?"

"I'm sorry to say it remains a complete mystery. I mean, bombing a church?"

"Ask me, I'd say it's niggers. You know, I have some real estate in your ward. And we've been getting niggers coming around, wanting to buy into a white block. Just move right in. Some of them get real sore. That, ask me, is your problem. They figure they'll wreck the place one way or another."

"Yes, well, we most certainly do appreciate your efforts."

"Nothing, Father."

The priest returned to his place near the end of the table.

"Let me be the first to kiss the Citizen of Achievement," Phyllis said. "What a thrill." She pulled him into her perfume and smeared red across his cheek.

"Knock it off. What the hell are you drinking?"

"What the hell are you drinking? I'm drinking Manhattans. So? Something wrong with me kissing my husband?"

"You're getting to be a real lush, you know it? And it isn't funny anymore, Phyllis. It really isn't."

"The way you charm a girl, Manny. What the hell are we here for anyway? I thought we'd have some fun."

"I told you, I have to talk to people. Now, you better sober up or I'm calling a cab and sending you home."

"Like hell."

"Phyllis, listen to me. This is for real. Sticks and stones. Savvy? Another night, we'll go out somewhere private, have a ball. Tonight, it's public. I'm drinking ginger ale, for Christ's sake. I have to stay on top of things. Don't screw it up. Okay, baby?"

She turned away with a look of sour resignation. A

rotund man moved across the rostrum and flashed brown teeth at Manny.

"Judge Walker. Good to see you." Manny held out his hand without standing up.

"Bill, Manny. Congratulations."

"Thanks. Pull up a chair, Bill. My wife, Phyllis."

"Hello, Mrs. Petrone. Delighted. You know, they put on a good spread here. The roast beef was not bad at all. Better than I get at home lots of times. Ha ha."

"Yeah, they do a good job. How's everything up your way, Bill? Running uncontested this year?"

"Don't I wish. How I hate having to squeeze meat. Only thing worse is answering a lot of ridiculous questions from ignorant reporters. And those television boys, they're always trying to trip you up."

"Anything we can do, Bill, we won't forgive you if you don't give a yell."

"That's white of you, Manny. I'll see how things shape up. Oh, and I wanted to tell you, your name came up the other day."

"Oh, yeah?"

"Assistant D.A. name of Sanderson. They had some kind of disturbance down at the farmers' market. I don't know, just some hooliganism, far as I could see. Somebody's stand was damaged. One fellow landed in the hospital. Okay? But Sanderson's yapping about there's something behind it, some conspiracy. He's saying Manny Petrone's this and Manny Petrone's that, and there's a plot to shake down the stands, and why don't they look into it, and this one's afraid to talk, and so on. Anyway, I said, Why don't you boys concentrate on bringing in indictments on the real criminals instead of harassing businessmen?"

"You know why it is, though, don't you, Bill?"

"Well I—"

"Name. They all want to make a name. Purely political."

"Don't I know it, Manny."

"Course, I appreciate your telling me. Think anything'll come out of it?"

"Very doubtful. This guy has no say. He's just jabbering. But I figured you'd be interested, just to know."

"You're right there. I hate misunderstandings."

"I know what you mean. Look, take care of yourself, Manny. And, you know, you deserve it." He pointed to the plaque beside Manny's dessert plate.

"Thanks, Bill. And tell the missus I was asking."

"Will do. Mrs. Petrone, nice seeing you."

Phyllis pushed her lower lip at him as he walked away. "If this is better than he gets at home, his wife must be serving him baked condoms."

"Say, Phyllis, do me a favor, will you? Take a trip to the powder room. This guy's been waiting to see me, and it's, you know, private, like."

"I need a drink anyway."

She stepped down and made her way past the long tables. Groups of people sat talking over coffee and cocktails. She reached the bar and ordered a Manhattan. A haze of smoke hung in the stale air. The band was plodding through "Lady of Spain." She moved to the edge of the dance floor and leaned against a pillar, sucking her maraschino cherry.

Up front, she saw Manny and a tall dog-faced man talking. Manny held his hands out, his fingers tightly curled. The other man couldn't stop nodding.

"Hello, Phyllis. Enjoying the party?" Stokely Simpson had absorbed a lifetime of Ivy League before flunking out of Princeton his sophomore year. The blond-haired lawyer still had fuzzy baby cheeks at thirty-five.

"Sure, Stokely. I love to mix it up with a bunch of deadheads. Lots of laughs."

"I guess a crew of horny tomcats wasn't available, so they had to settle for this band."

"Aren't you going to offer to buy me a drink?"

"I thought you already had one."

She tipped her head back and drained the cocktail. "I just finished it."

Stokely went to the bar and ordered two drinks.

"Manny must have been pretty surprised to be named the Citizen of Achievement," he said.

"He was just overwhelmed, Stokely."

"Not too many gangsters are so honored."

"Well, he had to beat out all the crooked lawyers."

"It was no lawyer who blasted St. Anselm's, my dear. But word's going around that it was one of your husband's thugs."

"That's crazy."

"Sure it is."

"What do you know?"

"Only heresay, love. Decidedly inadmissible. Care to dance?"

The small dance floor was crowded with shuffling couples. The band moved into a jerky bossa nova. Booze washed through Phyllis's brain. Stokely rubbed against her. She didn't try to stop him. His palms were moist. The tune ended. A few dancers applauded listlessly.

"How can anyone dance to this noise?" Phyllis complained too loudly. Stokely held her elbow. They maneuvered over to the end of the bar where they'd left their drinks. "That's too jittery for me. I like a nice fox trot."

"Fox trot's old-fashioned now, Phyllis."

"I'm an old-fashioned girl."

"Sure. Know why? Know why you're an old-fashioned girl? Because you're full of bitters. Ha ha ha."

Her eyelids drooped for a second. She looked at him. "Stokely, how come nothing's fun anymore? I'm too young to be running downhill."

"You're just in a bad mood."

"No, it's me and Manny. It's war now. He doesn't love me. I can't remember that he ever loved me. Does he? Would you say that man loves me?"

"I wouldn't want to venture a guess. What's he say?"

"He says I'm a lush. He never wants to have any fun. It's all so dry and predictable. There's no spark, no life. Is that a marriage?"

"I dare say that describes a pretty good portion of all marriages, yes."

"Oh, you're cute."

"Ready for another?"

"I shouldn't. Sure."

Stokely turned to the bartender. Phyllis glanced around. The fog of smoke and breath and used air was growing thicker. The band was oozing a ballad that blended with the hiss of conversation. Someone laughed. She felt warm, pins-and-needles warm.

"I'm starting to feel better," she said, sipping her new drink. "Hell with Manny Petrone. I feel damn good. 'Don't drink, Phyllis. You're a lush, Phyllis.' What the hell is this, church?"

"That's the spirit."

"That's the spirits, you mean." They clicked glasses. She laughed. A drop of amber liquor wet her chin. She noticed Stokely looking down her. She smiled. She felt his hand low on her hip.

"If only it wasn't for the kids," she said.

"Then what?"

"I'd leave that bastard in a minute. I'd really have some fun."

"No, you wouldn't."

"I would. I would too. Don't tell me."

A fat man with a boil on his neck glided by, dancing, Phyllis thought, with his daughter.

"Don't hang that line on your old pal, Phyllis. You love being Mrs. Petrone. It lends you that crucial component of true feminine charm—danger. You're forbidden fruit and you play it for all it's worth. Your husband is a cobra and you've got the flute. The performance fascinates some men, and I mean yours truly. But without him you're just another pretty face playing off-key."

"That's a load of crap, Stokely, and you know it. I don't need Manny to make men sit up and roll over and play dead and fetch and beg. Except for the kids, I'd be gone."

"That's a good story to put yourself to sleep with as you get old."

"Old? Hell with you. I just turned thirty-one. Is that old? I had Rick when I was twenty. I just turned thirty-one and I hate my husband's guts. Understand?"

"You're not alone. They all hate him. All the smiling, cringing dupes that kneel and kiss his feet. They hate him because he pulls the strings, because he's what they'd like to be. But hate is one of the strongest attractions in the world. Don't you agree?"

"You're talking trash."

"Am I? You sleep with men right and left, Phyllis. No, I know you do. You told me, remember? You let them diddle you, then you hate them for not telling your husband where to get off. And you hate Manny because you can't do without him, and because he gets his at a whorehouse, and because he treats you like a display hankie."

"Where do you figure you have the right to talk to me that way?"

"I figure I have it coming to me, sweetie, because of the risk I run being with you. You know, all Manny has to do is suspect that I've had my hand on your ass and I've got a couple of broken legs or worse. I know it. I love it."

Phyllis laughed. "You're right, too. Could go to Manny and say you tried to rape me. And then? Hanh?"

"Why 'tried'?"

She grinned and bit her lower lip and took another swallow of liquor.

"I feel warm, Stokely. Let's get some air. You have a car, don't you?"

"Cool off, darling. We're not alone."

"Got a leak in your inner tube?"

"You're incredible, Phyllis. Always in heat."

"Killjoy. Buy me a drink."

He ordered her another Manhattan. The band started to play again. Stokely talked close to her ear. Some of what he said was dirty. Some of it she didn't catch. He laughed. Other men, a few with their women, came up to them and talked. They all laughed. They laughed a lot. Phyllis laughed. She didn't know what they were laughing at, but she joined in the contagion.

The air suddenly clogged. Phyllis became aware of herself breathing. The whole room was breathing with her. She looked for a place to sit down. Without excusing herself, she wandered toward the door.

Outside she dropped her head back and tried to focus on the queasy moon. She sat on the concrete steps between two pillars. She swallowed acid. The wave of nausea passed. She closed her eyes and felt herself rising. She savored the sensation, wished she could keep rising, float to heaven. Purgatory, float at least to purgatory. A thin squeak of a laugh escaped from her throat.

Opening her eyes, she was surprised to find a drink still in her hand. She promptly poured it into her mouth. Immediately, remorse swept over her. Her brain heaved. She didn't vomit, she never did. But her skin turned clammy and she trembled. She threw the glass onto the sidewalk. The shatter pleased her. The hell with them.

She rose unsteadily and made her way back inside. As she entered, her spirits collapsed. From the trickle of music that had reached her on the steps, she'd constructed an image of a lusty nightclub, with men in tuxedos doing the quickstep and leggy girls selling cigarettes from trays. Instead, the drab hall, the rows of long tables covered with white paper, the humorless women in Sunday dresses, the stink of cigars and perfume, all the lusterless reality made her want a drink. Bad.

When she had one safely in hand, she moved into a corner. The lights at the rear of the hall had dimmed, but the speakers' table was still bright. Manny continued to shake hands, talk, and laugh.

Watching him from that distance, she realized how little he was. Really quite a small man. Funny to see his strutting manner. His paunch. His slick black hair. The jerky way he moved his hands. Such a small man. Teeny tiny.

And they all thought he was so tough. So smart. But he didn't even know that his wife—his own wife—was the most attractive, the most exquisite, the most refined, the most passionate, the most unhappy woman in the world. Didn't know about the men who'd— She chuckled to herself. Manny Petrone's private property. His display hankie. Even a twit like Stokely Simpson could blow his nose on it.

On the dais, Manny threw his head back and opened his mouth. A city councilman with a face like a raw pork chop removed his glasses to wipe tears of laughter from his eyes. She saw Leo motioning to Manny. Filthy Leo. He looked sick.

Manny broke away from the group behind the podium and went to confer with Leo. Probably Leo wanted to go home because he was sick. But he had to ask Manny. Please, boss. Good. At least they wouldn't have him in the car on the way home.

Manny didn't like it. Leo was making him upset. She could tell from his face, the way he moved. Very upset. She'd known those danger signals since the first days of their marriage.

The hell with him, that little man. Little Mr. Big. Mr. Stick-in-the-Mud. Mr. No-Fun. She downed the dregs of her drink and looked around. A man in a smoke-gray suit caught her eye, a friend of Stokely's. They'd been introduced, but Phyllis couldn't remember his name. She smiled. He smiled. He walked over and asked her to dance. He called her Phyllis. They danced. He looked at her from beneath heavy eyelids. She felt warm again.

The band began to weep "Love Me Tender." They spun lazily around the floor. The room, the other dancers blurred. She closed her eyes. Applause. The music faded but the room continued to spin. She clutched his arm. The band struck up a chord. They were jostled. Suddenly, he wasn't there anymore. Manny stood in his place, face grim. Her feet were numb.

"Phyllis, we're going."

"Oh, hiya, Manny. Wanna dance?"

"I said we're going. Now."

"Going? Going where? I'm having fun. Fun. Ever hear of it?"

"You're drunk. Come on."

"No. Who're you? Hanh?" She waved him away and started to turn. She ran into a wall. Leo. She felt pressure on her wrist. She looked down at Leo's dirty fingernails. Manny took her other arm. She was flying.

The booze lit her up with a rush. She reeled. Leo held her up while Manny retrieved their coats.

They were outside. Milk washed the sky. She sucked the tepid, fragrant air. Manny opened the car door and threw something into the back seat. Phyllis felt her brain loosen and tumble. It felt good.

Manny was talking to her. She made an effort to focus on his face. Suddenly, his hand came out of nowhere and jolted her cheek. Again. She couldn't feel the sting, but she knew her eyes were wet. They guided her into the car. She fell across the back seat. Manny sat in front with Leo.

Phyllis gripped her mouth with her hand and wheezed. She felt something poking her hip. Rolling over, she pulled it out from under her. A plaque: Citizen of Achievement.

———

"Cold?"

"Kind of." She was leaning back, letting her hair

stream out the open window. Link was smoking a cigarette, driving quickly. "I hope Diane isn't home yet."

"She have a date?"

"Come on. She's meeting her girlfriend at a sock hop. My uncle has a bowling alley in the city. He put in a dance floor, plays records for the kids. He loves kids. Came all the way out here to pick Diane up. Her friend's mother is bringing them home."

"Remember that dance at school, the time we got caught making out in the girls' locker room?"

"I remember."

"Seems like yesterday."

"Yesterday a million years ago."

"You had the moves."

"The moves. I was pretty smart back then. I was so smart I thought you had to put that kid stuff behind you. I thought you couldn't stake your life on those feelings that shook you up and poured you out. Oh, I was smart."

"But we still have the whole works, don't we? Didn't we just find that out?"

"I only hope it's not too late. All these years I've thought you couldn't live in never-never land, that you had to balance your books, count your change, pay your taxes. Dave offered me that—so I thought. God help me, I just wanted what would be right for Diane."

"I know."

"I was wrong. That's the playacting, all that responsibility and security and holding back. That's pretend. What's real is—us. I want Diane to know that now. I want her to know that love—real, hot, bloody, man-and-woman love—is the only thing. I want her to know that all the cardboard marriages and connect-the-dots people shaking their fingers are what's phony. That you don't need a bomb shelter, or a regular job, or a lot of new clothes—if you can only get lucky."

He stroked her knee. "Another thing she oughta know—her mom's one swell babe."

She paused. "Link, I have a secret to tell you. A big secret."

"What?"

"Not now, but soon."

"The mystery woman."

She laughed, ran her fingers through her hair. "Oh, Christ, I'm happy for a change."

They sped on.

"Car there," he said.

She lived in the last of three small ranch houses on a country road. The clay soil held water and made the lawns coarse and patchy.

"Dave's?"

"Nope, it's a police car. State trooper."

"Oh, Link, they couldn't be looking for you, could they?"

"I don't see how."

"Let me off at the driveway and go on."

"What's the point? I run, it looks bad."

"What are those other cars? That one's from Channel Eight."

Link pulled into the driveway and parked behind the black-and-white police cruiser. Standing on the lawn with the trooper, a man was holding a bulky movie camera across his shoulders. Another hefted a large photographic light and battery pack. Two men in suits were talking to a woman wearing a bathrobe.

They all moved toward the car. Link shut off the engine. Sherry slammed her door. Crickets were pulsing in the marshy fields.

"Marge, what's going on?"

The woman, who lived next door, had been crying. She started to say something, then bit her fist and just looked.

Link knew the trooper. "What's the matter, Lonnie?"

"Bad business." He turned to Sherry. "You're Mrs. Ryan?"

"Yes." Sherry was shaking. "Is it Dave? Has something happened to Dave?"

"I'm afraid I have very bad news for you, Mrs. Ryan. It's your daughter."

"Diane?"

"There's been an accident. A shooting, actually."

"Oh, God."

"She did go out tonight?"

"She was supposed to be getting home right now. Pam's mother, Pam Foster, her mother was bringing them. What's happened? Tell me!"

"Your daughter was riding in a car with George Lombardosi, who I understand was your uncle."

"Yes, he is. Uncle George."

"Someone opened fire on him. He was shot. The car ran off the road, down a ravine."

"Oh, my God. Oh, Diane. Is she all right? I mean, is she in the hospital? Is she hurt? Oh, God."

"She was rushed to St. Mary's emergency room. They tried. There was nothing they could do."

"When can I see her? Jesus Christ. Diane."

"She passed away on the operating table, Mrs. Ryan."

"Oh, God. Link, we've got to get to the hospital right away. Before it's too late. Which hospital did you say? Oh, we have to hurry. God, I cannot believe this is happening. Diane!"

"Sherry." Link gripped her arm. She was rigid.

"It's Diane, Link. Diane's been hurt. I have to go see her. She's hurt. She's hurt bad. Oh, God. They're operating on her."

"Sherry."

"I'm very sorry, Mrs. Ryan. It's one of those things. It's tragic."

"Oh, Sherry," the bathrobed woman wailed, trying to choke off her sobs. "Trust in God, honey. He's taken her to Him."

"Liar!" Sherry screamed. Link held her as she lurched forward. The woman shrank into her tears. "Oh, Jesus, Diane."

"Mrs. Ryan, how do you feel about this tragedy? Do you have any idea what might be behind it?" The reporter had quietly directed the camera. Now the light burst into a phosphorous glare and the whir began. Sherry, her face twisted, stared into the brightness. The other reporters crowded around.

"Was Diane your only child, Mrs. Ryan?"

"Do you know of any connections your uncle might have had with criminal elements in the city?"

"Do you think the police will—"

Link held up a hand to shade his eyes. "Lonnie, can't you stop this?"

"Are you the girl's father?" the reporter asked, turning the microphone toward Link. "Or are you—"

Link lunged forward. The reporter went down hard. The cameraman stepped back, still filming. The man with the light stumbled, sending the beam of white careening around the yard.

Two other reporters tried to grab Link and hold onto their note pads at the same time. He landed a straight right on one man's eye socket.

"Get the mother!" the cameraman shouted. "The mother!" The light beam swung back into Sherry's face. She watched the struggle impassively. Link managed to deliver an uppercut that brought the other reporter to his knees before the trooper wrapped him in a bear hug.

"Shut off that goddamn light!" the trooper shouted.

"We need tears."

"I said shut it off!"

The light died. Link stopped struggling.

"I'm pressing charges, officer. I want this man placed under arrest." The reporter's eye was puffed and bleeding.

"Can it."

"Al," the cameraman barked to his assistant, "here comes a car. Maybe that's the father."

The men heaved their equipment up the driveway and began to film. In the bleached light, Dave Ryan's face was ghostlike. A tall, angular man, he wore his black hair in a long crew cut. He was dressed in a green work shirt and baggy pants.

"Mr. Ryan? Did you talk with your daughter before she died?"

"Do you know of any reason?"

"What are your feelings?"

Dave saw no one, spoke to no one. He passed the reporters without haste. He walked up the driveway. He stopped beside Sherry and put his hand on the back of her neck.

"Dave? It's not true, is it? It's not true."

"I went to the hospital as soon as I heard. Diane's gone, Sherry."

Her face crumpled. She pressed it against Dave's shoulder and wrapped her arms around him. He enfolded her and led her into the house.

The reporters trudged to their cars. The neighbor woman, still sobbing, crossed the lawn toward her own home. Link stood alone with the trooper.

"Know what happened, Lonnie?"

"I understand the guy ran with a mob in the city. Somebody wanted him dead. Car went down a steep drop after they shot him."

"He died?"

He nodded. "Took it right in the face."

"Doesn't seem right. Doesn't seem possible, even. Little kid like that. You know?"

"It's not right. It's just the way things go. You a friend of the family?"

"Yeah."

"I hate these calls. Just like an auto fatality. What can you say? No reason behind it. Just, out of the blue. Just, a shame."

"Think they'll get whoever did it?"

"I hope to God they do. But—"

"What?"

"These gangs, you can never get anybody to talk. You could know who did it—can't build a case."

"He deserves the chair."

"Sure. Sure he does."

Link walked back to his car. Carefully, he backed across the lawn, around Dave's car, and onto the road. He drove about half a mile before he pulled off and stopped. He hid his eyes with his hand, though there was no one to see.

When his chest loosened, he opened the windows on both sides of the car and lit a cigarette. He punched the accelerator. His tires screeched three times. He hurtled through the dark along the deserted country road. The moon was setting when he finally arrived home.

June 23

"Just dry a young girl's tears, Manny. That's all I'm asking." Althea was a large, shapeless woman adrift in the middle years. She had a habit of continually reaching inside her dress to adjust the straps that suspended her big bosom. Her narrow eyes watched Manny closely.

They sat together on a chintz-covered sofa in the library of the Voglia Social Club. The club, which Manny owned, occupied a spacious Victorian house in a section of the city now going to seed. Manny used it as a place to meet and entertain friends and business associates. It also brought in a respectable income as a brothel for "well-recommended" customers. Manny called the small back parlor the library, even though its only reading material consisted of stacks of worn *National Geographics* and *Reader's Digests*.

He flicked an ash from his little plastic-tipped cigar.

"What? What's supposed to be the big deal?"

"You know. The big deal is her heart is broken. She was expecting you last week. She prepared, she waited, and you ignored her. You went with that party girl."

She spoke in her habitually conspiratorial tone even though they had the room to themselves.

"So? So what? Earl brought those girls over. They were a lot of fun. That Debbie, she was fun. Hear that joke she told, the one about the sausage? We had a good time. So what?"

"A good time? Manny, you don't understand Donna. She's a sensitive girl. She's new, she's not sure of herself. You ignore her. You go with a tramp. She feels cheap. Lonely. All you have to do—something a little special. Say you're sorry. Give her some token."

He sipped his Bristol Cream. Thoughts that had played tennis in his mind for the past three days arose, volleyed their worn ball back and forth, and subsided. Nothing helped his sour stomach.

"Come on, will you, Althea?"

"Believe me, I'm giving you the best advice. She loves you. You're practically a god to her. Did you know that?"

"Look, I come down here, you know what for? To get away from problems like this. To find some—I don't know—some simplicity. My wife is really turning the screws these days. She won't let up on me. Some kid, twenty-two years old, I'm supposed to say I'm sorry? I'm supposed to buy her a diamond tiara? She's a businesswoman, is my opinion. I'm not saying we don't get along. I'm not saying I don't like what she does. But the idea I should be faithful to her, that's a laugh. That's non compos mentis."

"No, no, no. I know you, Manny. I know exactly what you're thinking. You think she's a whore. You think, treat her as such and let her keep her mouth shut. Fine. But I'm trying to give you wisdom. A woman isn't a whore just because she takes things from men. She becomes a whore when the man treats her that way and she goes along. A man of intelligence, a man of dignity—a man like you—knows how much better it is when he can treat her like a lady. Because then he receives the affection, the services of a lady.

Think how tender she is, her golden-brown eyes, her little hips, the way she whispers to you, breathes your name. For some men, all that is nothing. They're happy with a cow, a dirty sheep. For you, tenderness is worth preserving, something human. A little care, a little gentleness, a small gift. Such an insignificant price to pay. The rewards will be great, believe you me Bob."

Thinking of Donna, Manny had to agree.

"Bullshit," he said. "The kid needs to be spanked."

"Spanked, Manny? Manny, Manny, you're upset. I've seen it these past few days. You're not yourself. Look at you, you're biting your nails. Is it something you'd like to talk about? Tell Althea."

"No. I mean, maybe I am a little edgy. Working too hard. I need to unwind." He forced a laugh.

"Excellent. Go to her tonight. She's waiting for you. Apologize. It won't hurt. You can make her a very happy girl. And she'll help you unwind, you know she will."

"I can't. I'm meeting Leo here. We have business to discuss."

"After."

"I can't stay that late. I told you, Phyllis is on the warpath."

"Then let me be your messenger, your messenger of love. Let me tell her that you long to be with her but are tied up with urgent business. Give me some pledge to take to her. Something that says, I care for you, you're mine, always. Believe me, Manny, I'm steering you in the right direction, for your sake."

"Cash?"

"To buy some love token."

"Forget it, Althea. Think I'm made of money?"

When Leo appeared ten minutes later, Manny was just replacing his wallet. "Tomorrow for sure, tell her," he said.

Leo asked Althea to make a bourbon on the rocks. She brought it to him. He stirred it with his finger. He and Manny crossed to a small office near the kitchen. Manny turned the bolt and sat on the cracked leather couch. Leo straddled a chair, facing him.

"There's practically nobody here," Manny said.

"Monday night's always dead."

"Don't give me that. Guys are staying away."

"This George thing has them all looking over their shoulders. They know he was your people."

"What about Chi Chi?"

Leo shook his head. "Like I said, over the weekend I couldn't find him. Lying low, not answering his phone, not around. But today I caught up with him at his place. He's having kittens, Manny. I had to slap him around a little to get his attention."

"What the hell's his problem?"

"The kid. The job, fine, he got a kick out of it. But Saturday he saw in the papers about the kid. He went wacko."

"Why?"

Leo looked at Manny's averted eyes, hesitated. "Because of the kid. You killed a kid."

"What? What kid? I didn't kill any kid. Don't say that. George is the one. Lombardosi. Driving around with a kid in his car? That's crazy. That's wrong. That's sick. He's the one responsible. George, not me. The kid's blood is on his hands, not mine. He drove down that ditch, not me. Him."

"Except, George ain't here anymore. He don't have to worry."

"I do?"

"Nah, it'll blow over. Just, about Chi Chi, I mean."

"Leo, I'm going out of my skin over this. They already called me from the Falls. I have to go up there the end of the week."

"How bad?" Leo asked.

"Five different places we're supposed to be taking care of got hit Saturday night. No license, after hours, gambling, petty crap like that. That's no coincidence.

The papers have nothing else in them—front page day after day. It's on TV every night."

"Things will cool off."

"But I have to answer to the Falls for it. For all of it. They want to know what happened, why. What the goddamn hell am I going to tell them?"

"Tell them it wasn't your fault."

"You're fucking right it wasn't my fault. George new—he knew he was in for it. So he drives around with a damn kid in his car. Idiot. Sick fucking idiot. He killed that kid. Period."

"So cool off."

"Cool off? You're telling me to cool off?"

"Just hold your voice down, I meant. Christ."

Manny massaged his eyebrows, lit another cigarillo. "I've come close to going over the edge these last few days, Leo."

"You've been on the spot."

"If the whole crock with George wasn't enough, Phyllis had to pick this weekend to go loony."

"Giving you a hard time?"

"She took pills."

"To kill herself?"

He nodded. "Just for a show, a horror show, but I had to call an ambulance, doctor, the whole bit. They pumped her stomach. She's home the next day bawling me out right and left. Like she's a martyr. She took pills, so she's a martyr, right? And me? I'm the goddamn Spanish Inquisition. I'm the tyrant. I made her take the pills, her book."

"Rough."

"I had to tell her to say we went to the dinner Friday together, just in case somebody asks. She looked at me funny. Jesus, if she suspects, she'll crucify me for the rest of my life."

"She was pretty well corked that night."

"She's always corked. She can still put two and two together."

Leo poured an ice cube into his mouth and crushed it.

Manny winced. "Now, what about Chi Chi?" he said.

"Good boy. I like him. I'd say, normally, send him somewhere—Cuba—for a couple of months, he'd be okay. But this—"

"This we take no chances. None. No room for chances. We're up against it."

"I agree. Plus, Chi Chi's kind of a mama's boy. Up to a point, you can trust him. But this thing, my opinion, is going to keep eating him. Not George, the little girl. Sooner or later it's going to eat him up."

"It's eating him already, you say."

"I'm sorry to see what I see there. He's a good boy."

"What do we do?"

"We gotta take care of him, Manny. I hate to. I like him. But I don't like him that much."

"I don't like him at all. You can do it?"

"Me and Gap. We'll take him out in Gap's boat. Tell Chi Chi we're going to fish, talk things over. Go way, way out."

"Do it quick. Tomorrow." Manny jabbed his half-smoked cigarillo into the ashtray.

"Check. And Manny, don't let this get to you. Know what I mean?"

Their eyes met. Manny gripped his hands together to stop the tremor. A distracted look flickered across his face.

"This—it's going to come out all right, isn't it, Leo? It'll be forgotten, won't it?"

Leo shrugged. "I already forgot all about it."

June 25

As the green Imperial swung out of the lane leading to the cemetery, a spattering of summer rain began to wet the windshield. Carlo flicked on the wipers. He wore a black band on his arm. Bea unpinned her veil. In back, Madeleine sobbed into a handkerchief.

"I'd been in school with nuns," Bea was saying. "Can you imagine the thrill I felt to be engaged to this man, so strong, so alive? And a good man, too—generous. You know he was."

"Sure," Carlo said. "George cared."

"He took me to a dance hall. The band was playing music that went all through you. The air was full of laughter. George had a beautiful pewter and leather flask. He put something into my drink that tasted wicked and made me giggle." She paused, smiling inwardly.

"A man came up to me. What did I know? He was friendly. I suppose he'd drunk too much. He asked me to dance. I said I didn't care to. He touched me. Not harshly, just on the arm. He said I was a looker. Really. George came over and they began to argue. Then they started to go outside. I was supposed to stay at the table. I was dying of curiosity, though. What did men do when they went outside? By the time I reached the alley, George was already beating the man who'd touched me. I just stood there with my mouth open. Blood, so much blood. And George wouldn't stop. His friends, three or four of them, had to pull him away. After, I told George I thought it disgusting. But secretly, it thrilled me to think this fire burned for my sake. It made life sparkle. I'll never leave this man, I said to myself. His hands were still swollen at our wedding."

Madeleine blew her nose loudly. Bea checked her face with her compact mirror.

"I always knew, Carlo. I knew what he was. I knew he killed men."

"Now, Bea."

"Oh, I never let on. When he had to be away, I never questioned. When he was in prison that time, I went down every week and took him his strawberry jam and cupcakes, as if nothing could be more normal."

"George was a prince," Madeleine said, sniffling. "And so good with kids."

Bea held her elbow in one hand and covered her mouth with the other. She looked out at the trees that lined the road, lush and slick with rain.

"We'll all miss him," Carlo said.

"It wasn't right, was it, Carlo?"

"No."

"Not the way they did it."

He shook his head.

"Not Diane."

"No, no, it wasn't right."

They dropped Bea at her house. Madeleine offered to stay with her. Bea said her sister would be there. Anyway, she wanted quiet, wanted to rest.

Madeleine moved to the front seat and lit a cigarette.

"She'll have to go to Diane's tomorrow," she said. "That'd kill me, seeing that little casket. They're usually white, I think. Except, she was twelve. That might be the age when they're considered—you know."

Carlo said it was a shame, the whole thing was a shame.

"What did she mean, George killed men? Why would she say that? George never hurt a fly."

"That's right. She said it because she's upset."

"I'm going to miss that big lummox. I liked George."

Carlo said nothing. He kept noticing out the window the raw look that death gave to everything. The most common sight—the jutting legs of a guy fixing his car, the limp flag in front of the American Legion, a trash pile smoldering in a field—was tinged with mortality.

"Do I look good in black?" Madeleine asked.

"I already told you."

"Do I?"

"You look good in black." You'll make a swell-looking widow, he almost said. He drove on in silence.

"Why did they kill George, hon?" Madeleine asked.

"He was sick. You know that. Sick in the head. Remember Christmas?"

"You said that was nerves."

"I was wrong. The man was sick."

"So he's sick, so they kill him? Who are they, God or something?"

"Anybody with a gun can be God."

"But what kind of a man would do that? And murder a child, an innocent little kid?"

"That's enough, Mad."

"I'm worried, is all."

"Enough."

She drew on her cigarette and said no more. Enough was their code, the door shutting.

Carlo didn't understand grief. On the street he'd learned that when things got wild you watched your back, you figured your opportunities, and you acted. You channeled your energy into alertness, not weeping; into retribution, not regret. For him, George's death was not the end. Not by a long shot.

June 27

Manny poked the soft folds of gray satin, ran his fingers along the glossy mahogany, touched the brass fittings. The small placard said THE WEDGEWOOD.

"This is for me, Vinnie. This is the one I want. Manny Petrone, they'll say, real class."

"You'd better get some money down on it now, Manny. Your old lady might not want to part with eighteen bills after you're gone. She might would rather spend it on a trip to Cape Cod." The roly-poly man was lounging in a red velvet armchair. He twiddled his thumbs over the waist of his trousers, which rose almost to his collar. He had rheumy eyes, a thick roll of fat under his chin, and hair combed forward from the back of his skull to cover his baldness.

"Eighteen hundred bucks for a damn coffin?"

"Hey, where can you buy a Caddy for the price of a Dodge? That one's got an adjustable box-spring mattress. We've got miser models. Nice plywood veneer. No brass. But hell, how many are you going to buy? That's what I tell them. Splurge a little. Live it up."

"Ha. And you're going to be spending some time in it. You want something snug."

"Sure you do. Get a nice Simonize job on it, too."

"And a case of champagne, a TV, you're set."

"Christ, Manny, you'll have all your friends down visiting."

"Better put a phone in to call out for catering."

They both snorted. Manny moved on to examine other caskets: THE AMBASSADOR, THE MAJESTIC, THE EMPIRE, THE FUTURA.

"Were you down at the big meeting there last fall, Vinnie? I don't remember seeing you."

"No, how could I? We had two stiffs here. I couldn't go off hiking in the woods."

"You heard what happened to me, right? Goddamn Leo got all turned around. We traveled in circles a good three hours. Cold? Pouring rain. We—in the end we were lucky the bulls did find us. We could of frozen our balls off out there if it'd gotten dark. I mean it. Mr. Ruggiero, he was about the only smart one of the bunch."

"Sure. Went inside Joe's house, hid in the can. Cops came up, looked around, but they never went all through the place. Hell, those other bums, they caused their own problems, running like niggers from a melon patch."

"Cost me a seventy-dollar pair of shoes, brand new."

"Well, What were you running from? Guilty conscience?"

"I don't know. It made sense at the time."

Vinnie lit a cigarette and picked a fleck of tobacco

from his lip. "So what's this about George Lombardosi, Manny? Bad business, hey?"

"Well, the man was sick. He was sick." Manny tapped his temple with his finger.

"I knew him," Vinnie said. "Knew him for years. Used to be Charles Atlas in the old days. Worked out like a fighter. I remember one time he shakes hands with this punk. *Crack*. The guy's face turns white. *Crack, crack*. Five minutes later, his hand looks like a catcher's mitt. George could make people afraid, I'll tell you."

"Yeah, he was sick, all right. In the end, it got bad."

"Nice fellow, though, if you knew him."

"Don't I know it? I loved the man. I really did. You shoulda seen the wreath I sent."

"He did a job," Vinnie said.

"Sure he did. You had to respect him. He could be a hammer, but he had dignity too. Damn, I'm going to miss him. Some'll say he was dumb. I say you could count on him. It's a loss. But a man gets sick, what can you do?"

"That what the old man wants you for?"

"Hey, Vinnie, they call, I come. I don't know what the hell he wants till he tells me what he wants. Maybe he wants to congratulate me. You hear? I got an award from the City Club. Citizen of Achievement."

"Hey, all right. I didn't know I had the privilege of talking to one of those. What's it mean, anyway?"

"Prestige. Nobody has the connections in the city that I do, the standing. Nobody has the rabbis that I have. I'm a power in the city. I'm in. Politicos come to me, I don't go to them. I'm big, I mean it. I'm a mover, a goddamn mover."

Manny walked around a coffin and stared out the window. The sharp morning sunlight stung his eyes. Several couples were strolling past on the sidewalk in front. June brides, Manny thought. Off to see the

Falls. The idea filled him with remorse. He turned back to the hushed room.

"You hear any talk, Vinnie?"

"Talk?"

"About George, the whole incident, that kid and all?"

"Me? Nah, I hear nothing. Like you say, he probably wants to pat you on the fanny for being a citizen of whatchamacallit."

"How about Ted? I don't like the way he's got the boss's ear."

"Ted don't say much to me."

"The guy gets on my nerves. He despises me because I have my own thing, where he's just Ruggiero's stooge." Manny plugged his nose to imitate Ted's nasal twang. "Yes, Mr. Ruggiero. No, Mr. Ruggiero. Look at these numbers, Mr. Ruggiero. Let me wipe your hind end, Mr. Ruggiero."

Vinnie laughed. "Good old Ted."

"He never liked me."

"Ted had his friendly bone taken out years ago."

"I'm just afraid he's talking dirt about me to the old man."

"Don't worry about the old man. Never worry about him. He knows Ted."

"I can explain this thing. I really can."

"Sure you can. Hey, you ever hear that rumor that Ted's got fourteen?"

"Bull."

"What they say. Has to do it with an Amazon or he can't go all the way."

"Oh, come on, tell me another one. That little—" A door opened behind him.

"Manny," Ted said. "Want to come in?"

Manny winked at Vinnie. "Sure, Ted. How you been, buddy?"

He received no reply. They passed into a room whose heavy drapes, thick Persian carpet, and wall of leatherbound books gave it a religious quiet. A patch of sunlight fell through the leaded glass window.

"Sit down."

Manny took a chair facing the big oak desk, unwrapped one of his cigarillos, and lit it.

Ted's harelip wasn't noticeable except in the lopsidedness of his infrequent smiles and the sinus ring of his voice. Two vertical lines were etched above his nose by his perpetual frown. He sat in the high-backed chair behind the desk. Manny thought him presumptuous. This was Mr. Ruggiero's office.

"Beautiful day," Manny offered.

"Is it?" Ted brushed imaginary dust from the corner of the desk. "So, Manny, how's your wife? How's your lovely wife?" He tasted the word *lovely* as he said it.

"She's fine."

"Feeling a little blue?"

"Whataya mean?"

"Phyllis, isn't it?"

"So?"

"We hear she's not so happy."

"What are you talking about? You're outa your tree."

"Don't play games, Manny. We know." Ted's stiff smile looked like a sneer. "We know about the pills."

Manny dragged on his cigarillo. He crossed his arms. He thought of something smart to say, but it was already too late.

"Now, let's hear it. What happened and why?"

"With George, you mean?"

"You're very swift on the uptake, Manny."

"Well, I'll explain the whole thing to Mr. Ruggiero."

"Mr. Ruggiero won't be here. He doesn't want to see you right now. He wants me to handle it."

"What do you mean? I come all the way up here and he doesn't even want to see me?"

"You talk to him through me. He's interested. Believe me, he's interested."

"I'd rather give it to him personally."

"Maybe you'd rather it rained whiskey, too. Start talking."

"Okay. I have nothing to hide. I did it right. I talked to Mr. Ruggiero about it before. I had no alternative, not after the church business. Not the way Lombardosi was running his mouth. That was agreed. He okayed it. Told me to take care of it personally. I had no problem with that. That's the way I wanted it too. Even if the guy was cuckoo. I wasn't afraid of him. The kid, that was completely his fault."

"Start from the beginning. I want to hear all the juicy details."

"The beginning? Well, I planned it for the night I was going to receive this award. Perfect cover. We got this guy Chi Chi, a very reliable boy, to drive."

"Reliable?"

"We thought. Leo was close to him. Anyway, he steals a car, picks me up near my house. He's got this thirty-ought-six carbine. We drive down near a bridge and wait for George. Cars are just starting to turn their lights on, but it's not dark yet. I knew George's car, a Lincoln, and ten minutes later, here it comes."

"You didn't see the child?"

"No, you kidding? Of course I didn't see her. She—I don't know—she was a little thing, or slumped down maybe. I saw Lombardosi plain as day, no mistake."

"Careless."

"Come on, I'm giving you what happened. He looked like he was alone, I'm telling you. So he turns down along this park and we're right on his ass. We have a place picked out—no houses for a good two hundred yards on one side, a park on the other, and a flashing red. He'd have to stop."

"You didn't see two heads?"

"It's getting dark. You can't see that well."

"And?"

"And we come to the spot. George stops. Chi Chi pulls up alongside. Perfect. The boy's a good driver.

I'm ready with the carbine, holding it like this. I swing it. George looks. Turns his head right toward me. Just at that instant, *bam!* The slug caught him right in the eye, right here. So there he sits, staring at me with one eye. Weird. I couldn't believe it. Big red tear dripping down." Manny pointed to his cheek. "Then his face sort of turns into a clown face—I don't know how to describe it—as if his brain was shorting out. Really bizarre."

"You must have laughed. What about the kid?"

"What kid? I still didn't see any kid. But I cocked the gun and I'm getting ready to give him the insurance when he peels out. It must have been a nervous reaction. Because, I swear, he was a dead man. And here he is, tearing down the road. Chi Chi goes after him. George's weaving a little, but he's hauling a pretty good clip. Chi Chi didn't want to pull next to him because he could have wrecked us. Pretty soon, George is swerving bad. He goes off the road and into the park. Now, by the road they have a culvert and a guard rail where this ravine cuts through. But where George is headed there's nothing. Bushes. He goes over and flips. The drop is about thirty feet. The car lands on its roof. We pull up and look. No point in getting out. I know he's dead. So we take off."

"To pick up your award."

"Chi Chi has his car stashed about a half mile away. We switch to that, he drops me at the hall. He takes the carbine down to the bay, bends the barrel, gets rid of it. Meanwhile, I'm giving a nice little speech to the City Club, telling a few jokes, mixing it up. Leo's waiting outside in my car, he hears it on the radio. Two dead. A child. Comes running in to tell me. Maybe he shoulda waited, but—"

"Was that the way Mr. Ruggiero told you to do it, Manny? Is that the way one of our friends deserves to go?"

"Hey, you can talk. George was a madman. Spooked. He carried a cannon in his jacket. Always. And he was touchy as hell. You couldn't get anywhere near him. I couldn't. Try it and it would have been worse. This was the only way."

"Dignity, Manny. The man served us. He had a family. He deserved more dignity. Mr. Ruggiero thinks so."

"Let me explain it to him, then, if he thinks that. Lombardosi was beyond dignity. I had to face reality."

"So you killed a child."

"Get off that. That was George's fault, not mine."

"Mr. Ruggiero doesn't look at it that way. The death of the child has moved him very deeply. He's doing a novena to St. Francis."

"Well, I was sorry about it too. Terrible. But I'm not going to beat my breast. He never should have had a kid in his car."

"You're a crude man, Petrone."

"I don't see any crocodile tears in your eyes."

The slender man did here's-the-church over and over with his fingers, staring at Manny.

"Anyway, what's done is done," Manny said.

"Done? Mr. Ruggiero is concerned about the consequences of the tragedy. The consequences for our thing, for you."

"Bound to be some flack. It's temporary. Minor inconvenience, that's all."

"Inconvenience? That's how you look at it? What about your driver?"

"He came down with a case of the shakes. The kid getting killed bothered him. I thought it would be best if he took a trip, considering how touchy things were getting in the city. No problem. Nice long trip."

"That raises the question of Leo."

"What do you mean?"

"Leo helped you plan it."

"Leo? Are you joking? Leo's stand-up. All the way. Give him life, the chair—give him the chair tomorrow, he wouldn't tell you his middle name. Christ almighty.

I've known Leo years. I'll vouch for Leo. I'll go on the line for him."

"Maybe your vouching for him won't carry much weight."

"What's that supposed to mean?"

"I can't read Mr. Ruggiero's mind. I know he's unhappy."

"Hey, I want to see him. Tell him it's urgent. I can explain. You go tell him. Right now."

"Settle down, Manny. He doesn't want to see you."

"Who the hell do you think you're talking to? Huh? I'm Manny Petrone. I run that city. Look at the produce markets. Ruggiero knows. Look what I've done with those markets. Look at the revenues coming out of that. Don't forget that."

"Who was it handled that for you?"

"I handled. It was my idea. I built it. Carlo helped, sure. But it was my baby. Still is. Ruggiero knows."

"There you're right. Mr. Ruggiero knows. He knows you. And he's very concerned."

"What the hell have you been telling him about me?"

"Me? I told him a long time ago to kick your ass. Now I'm telling him you're a liability, a minus."

"Listen, Ted, you're making a big mistake. Nobody's got my connections in the city. Nobody can take my place. I don't roll over. You'd better remember that. Mr. Ruggiero knows it. He knows me. He doesn't need a worm like you to sit around here and poison him on me." Manny was on his feet, jabbing with his finger, shouting. "I'm warning you. I'm Manny Petrone. I'm big, my friend. I'm a mover."

"See you later, Manny."

The brilliant sun outside brought tears to Manny's eyes. As he walked to his car he kicked the air. He wore his cliffedge grin.

June 30

Link hitched his body around again, trying to get comfortable on the angular Danish-modern couch. Across from him, Dave Ryan, stiff as a praying mantis, was explaining the delay.

"Gail, Sherry's sister—I don't know if you knew she was expecting. She didn't feel well after lunch, so Sherry went over to stay until her husband gets home. She should be along any minute now. I don't know what's keeping her." He looked at his watch again. "I think it's good—not that Gail's ill, but good for Sherry. She needs something to take her mind off of Diane. You can imagine—the shock."

"Sure."

"This morning, when she told me you were coming by, that she was going to ask you this favor, I didn't think it was right. We hardly know you, really, though I guess you were friends with Sherry in school."

"Yeah, we hung around a little together." He kept watching Dave for a sign.

"But this has become her crutch since the tragedy. Better to let her get it out of her system."

"What is it?"

He shook his head. "She should explain it to you. I—"

The silence made the warm, closed room oppressive. Outside, the summer sun was relaxing in the west. Link stopped fighting the urge and lit a cigarette. Dave leaped up to find an ashtray.

"How's work?" Link asked. "You back at work?"

"I took last week off, of course. I'm going back on the late shift tonight. I really prefer that, you know. It's cooler, much cooler. Not as hectic. And it gives me a chance to work around the house during the day."

"You're building one of those—what do you call it, bomb—"

"Fallout shelter."

"How's it coming?"

"Fine, fine. I'm finishing the concrete. I've started to do a little work inside. You always run into problems, of course. Maybe—I don't know if you're interested, but maybe you'd like to have a look."

"Sure, great. I've heard about them."

Link welcomed the opportunity to move. He followed Dave out the kitchen door and into the backyard. Mounds of sod and clay were piled around the excavation. A concrete cube, its sides tarred black, nearly filled the hole. Lumber, gravel, reinforcing rods, and empty cement sacks lay scattered on the lawn. A robin perched on the cement mixer, serenading the declining day.

"A plank door will cover the stairs here," Dave said as they descended the cinder-block steps. "Then I'll have a steel door that will seal off the actual shelter, here." They passed down a narrow corridor, turned into a black, musty room. Dave flicked on a light bulb dangling from a cord.

"The walls and ceiling are twenty inches of reinforced concrete. I'll be piling on another foot and a half of soil when it's finished. One problem I've had—you can see it there on the wall—is with the damp. The ground holds water so bad. But I think I've solved that. I really do."

"Yeah, all this clay. This is quite a project. Very, um—"

"Of course, I have a lot of work left to do in here. Bunks. I'm getting a diesel generator—ten kilowatt. Ventilation, you can see where the pipes come in there. The pump will bring air in through charcoal filters. Sanitation. Supplies: food, water, first aid, radio. Another thing, and this is my own idea, seeds. You don't know what'll be available after. Could very well want to grow things."

"Hey, I bet most people don't think of that. Garden, sure."

"Do you know about the bomb, Link?" He moved so close he made Link feel uncomfortable.

"Atom bomb?"

"Well, actually, the hydrogen or thermonuclear bomb has replaced the original atomic device. They have them—they tested one in the Marshall Islands recently—fifteen megatons. That's fifteen million tons of TNT—*million.*"

"Jesus."

"But what you're likely to get hit with, the standard size, is something like two megatons."

"Bet that'll still break a few windows."

"Eight miles away from ground zero it would rupture your eardrums, the pressure. At twelve miles, the heat would raise blisters on your skin. Even fifty miles away, exposure to the fallout would kill everybody within two weeks. What I'm talking about is unprotected, of course."

"That's why the shelter, I guess."

"Right. Inside here we're completely protected from the initial blast and heat—except in the case of a direct hit. But what's more important, the fallout doesn't reach us. Say we have fallout that's giving off five thousand roentgens an hour. I know this is a little technical, but figure a chest X-ray gives you forty roentgens, and seven hundred an hour will kill you. So there's five thousand up there soon after the blast. Okay? Deadly. Seven hours later, that'll drop down to five hundred. Okay? Two days and it's just fifty. Two weeks, five. Nothing, if you're careful. You go up, hose things down, start rebuilding. The crucial thing is the shelter. An inch and a half of lead equals six inches of concrete, equals nine inches of soil, equals twenty-six inches of wood. Okay?"

"You've studied up on this stuff."

"All government reports that anyone can get from Civil Defense. Oh, and I forgot, games. Some people don't think of this, but they've done research on submarine crews. Keep busy, that's vital. I'll have Monopoly, checkers, cards, crossword puzzles, brain teasers." He smiled.

"So you think it's coming, this World War Three?"

"I know it is. It's going to happen. We'll only have a few minutes' warning once the ICBMs are in the air. At night, when I hear the siren blow for a fire, I always get up and turn on the radio to make sure it isn't an alert. Just a matter of time. It's foolhardy not to have a shelter, once you know. I mean, there are peaceful uses of the atom. But do you know what the half-life of strontium ninety is? Any idea?"

"What about your neighbors? Say they don't have a shelter. You know how they're talking about the people with shelters will be shooting those that want in?"

"I would accommodate whoever I could. But there are limits—food, water, space. You have to draw the line. You can't endanger everyone by overcrowding."

"You mean you'd shoot?" Link laughed.

"You have to draw the line."

The glare of the light hid Dave's eyes under his brow. Link stopped smiling, scratched his neck.

Both men turned toward the click of footsteps that broke the silence.

"All clear. All clear." Sherry entered, smirking. "Time to go up, hose things down, and start rebuilding. Right, Dave?"

He forced a smile and shrugged.

"Hiya, Link."

"Sherry."

"How's Gail?" Dave asked.

"Just swell—for swelled, I should say. She has a touch of indigestion, she's in labor. Little does she know. So what do you think of our new rumpus room?" Her strained face didn't participate in the banter. Bluish circles highlighted her eyes.

"Nice."

"I wanted a TV, but Dave said there won't be anything to watch, didn't you, hon? The bomb just wrecks your reception."

Dave looked away. He began straightening a stack of boards in the corner.

"Let's get out of here," Sherry said. "This place gives me the willies."

Link watched her hips move as they mounted the stairs. Outside, a dirty orange sun was hovering on the horizon like the fireball of a nuclear explosion.

"Could I get you something, Link?" she asked when they reached the kitchen. "Beer?" Link nodded. "Dave?"

"Coffee."

"Want a cookie with it?"

"Please."

She put the kettle on the stove. They sat around the kitchen table.

"Hey, I never did thank you for giving me a ride home that night," she began. "I told Dave how Frieda let me down."

Link glanced at Dave. "Sure, nothing."

"It still seems like a dream."

"I can imagine."

He took a swallow of beer. The kettle whined and Sherry busied herself pouring a cup and stirring in instant coffee. She placed it in front of Dave, along with a plate of macaroons.

Dave said, "The neighbors sent so much food in, we're still eating it."

"People were so nice." Sherry lit a cigarette. "Link, you know us, don't you?"

"I guess, sure."

"I mean, we went to school together, we live in the same town, we see each other occasionally."

"Yeah."

"Because we want you to do us a favor."

"What's that?"

"Find out who killed Diane."

He stared. "You kidding?"

She shook her head.

"How could I find out? I'm no cop."

"What Sherry was thinking," Dave said, "is that maybe you'd know somebody you could ask. According to the paper, and what the police have told us, it has something to do with gangs in the city. Apparently, Sherry's uncle was mixed up in that kind of thing and somebody had a grudge against him, and— well, you read the paper."

"You're saying I'm involved in that?"

"No, no, no," Dave protested. "But she has an idea you might know who to ask, that's all."

"Are you crazy? I don't hang out with hoods in the city. Even if I did, what's the point? What do I do? Say, 'Hey, bud, know who killed George Lombardosi? Why am I asking? Oh, just curious, just want to keep up on the latest.'"

"When you put it that way," Dave said, "it does sound silly. Maybe, Sherry, we—"

"No. I'm pleading with you, Link. Do this. Try, if nothing else. For my sake. For old times' sake. Anything."

"What about the police?"

"I guess," Dave said, "she thinks the police aren't doing a good job."

"They aren't. They're never going to find out. They practically admit it."

"What do they say?"

"We spoke with a sergeant in the city police," Dave said. "He told us they're doing all they can, but it's difficult. They think professional criminals are involved. Anybody who might know is afraid to talk."

"But they're going to tell me?"

"She'd like you to try. We'd pay you, of course. Whatever you think is fair."

"Pay me?"

"Anything, Link," Sherry said. "Dave has money saved."

Link groaned. "You're picking at a scab."

"It's not a scab. It's a wound, Link, an open wound.

It's going to kill me if I can't do anything. Understand? Kill me. Diane meant everything to me. Somebody murdered her. And now that somebody's out there enjoying life, just like it never happened. I can't stand that. I won't stand it."

"Sherry, even if I got a line on who was responsible—and I say that's virtually impossible, but what if I did?—then what? You have to have evidence just to arrest him. Maybe he is arrested. These guys have lawyers. They know how to play the technicalities. The system's rigged in their favor."

"I know."

"Leave it alone."

"No. I want him dead."

"Sherry," Dave said. "For God's sake."

"I know we didn't discuss this part, Dave."

"You're talking foolishness now," Dave said. "It's wrong. I don't want to hear anything more about it."

"Then you'd better leave the room, because I'm serious."

"Link, I'm sorry. She's upset. She doesn't know—"

"I'm upset! Of course I'm upset! Somebody murdered my little girl. I want you to kill a man, Link. Find him and kill him. Kill him like he killed Diane."

"That's not right, Sherry," Dave said. "We can't even talk about that. Nothing will bring Diane back, and thinking about killing isn't the way to remember her. I know it's hard, but—"

"Will you?" She turned to Link, pleading. "For me?"

He frowned. "You've been watching too much television. You can't go around—"

"No, I can't. Dave can't. But you can. You, Link, you."

Dusk had settled in. Dave got up and turned on the overhead fluorescent light.

"I think we'd better forget the whole thing," he said to Link. "I didn't realize she was going to talk this way."

"All I want is an answer," Sherry begged. "So I'll know."

"It's no use, Sherry," Link said. "Can't you see that? It's just a fantasy."

"Link, this is all I want now. I know you think it's a mother's grief. I know you think it's not likely you'll be able to, anyway. But I just want to know if you'll try. For me. Please? Please?"

"No."

"Well, God damn you to hell, then."

"Sherry," Dave said. "I think you'd better go lie down."

"I will not lie down. I want revenge for my little girl or I want to die." She covered her eyes with both palms.

Dave stood over her, hesitating to touch her. "Mommy," he said. "Mommy, please don't cry."

"Oh, Jesus," Link muttered. He got up. "I've gotta go. Sorry. I—sorry."

He hurried out the kitchen door. The sky still held a hint of turquoise, though dark was pouring from the east. He rounded the corner of the house, walked toward his car, stopped to light a cigarette. He heard her call his name. She'd followed him out. He hesitated, turned. She stood looking at him for a moment, her eyes swimming, lost. He nodded imperceptibly. Carefully she wrapped her arms around him. He smoothed her hair. They kissed. She shuddered once, clung to him with desperate strength. He glanced toward the house.

"Oh, my God, Link."

"I know it's been bad, but how could you ask me to come when you knew he was going to be here?"

"I don't know. I thought he'd be at work. I got the shifts mixed up. Then I just didn't—it didn't seem to make any difference. I thought maybe he could help."

"Are you going to leave him?"

Yes—I mean, eventually, I guess. I'm too confused right now. Dave's helped me not to go out of my mind. I can't just leave him alone all of a sudden. I—it wouldn't look right. And he needs me too. He doesn't show it, but this has hit him hard."

"What did you tell him I was, anyway? A killer? A criminal?"

"I didn't tell him anything. Just—that I thought you could help us. I thought you might know someone."

"Listen to me. Drop this revenge idea. What's happened to Diane is done. You're just making it worse for yourself with these crazy notions."

"No, I can't drop it. If I did, I think I'd have to kill myself."

"Don't talk like that."

"Why not? It's true. I've come close. All that stops me is the thought of getting back at whoever did it. And you have to help me. You're my only hope. Can't you see that?"

"Please, Sherry. Please." He rubbed her back. She became still. She pulled away and looked into his face.

"Link, Diane was your daughter."

He stared at her.

"Not his. She was our daughter, yours and mine."

"What? What are you saying?"

"I didn't want you to know. Dave suspected, but he treated her like his own, always. But I know. She was ours, Link."

"But why? Why didn't you tell me?"

"I had to decide. I had to choose. At the time, you know how it was. You were so young when it happened. I was too. I just wanted the best for Diane. I was going to tell you. That night at the lake? Remember I said I had a secret? I was going to tell you."

"Holy—"

"I could see you in her. You know how when you took her in your car—you told me she kept staring at you with my eyes. Well, she looked at me with your eyes. She smiled your smile. I hoped, over the years, as we kept coming together, I hoped—I don't know."

"You should have told me."

"I wanted to. I did. But I never felt the time was right. And I really didn't see what good it would do, the way things were."

"You should have anyway. Now—"

"Now you have to help me fight. For us. For our child. Won't you?"

His eyes burned into hers. He nodded.

"I love you, Link. I always have."

She gave him a wet kiss on the mouth and turned back to the house. Link saw a curtain move.

Night overtook the last of the twilight, the crickets shifted gears, and the sky suddenly blazed with stars.

July 1

Link climbed Petey's back steps and hammered on the screen door. He waited. A cicada let loose its urgent rasp.

From inside the house came a giggle, the sound of someone moving furniture, footsteps. Link shaded his eyes against the sun and looked in.

Petey appeared. He was shirtless. His arms were brown to the biceps, but his hairy chest and four-quart beer belly were white.

"Link. Hey, buddy, where you been? I've been trying to get in touch. Come on in. Hot one, hey?"

The house was cool after the loud sun outside. Petey removed two bottles of beer from the refrigerator, opened them, and gave one to Link. He noticed a brassiere crumpled on the kitchen table. He picked it up, grinned, tossed it into the hallway. They sat.

"Been keeping to yourself."

"Yeah."

"Hey, I heard about Sherry's kid. That was a damn shame. Jesus, that's a shame. How's she taking it?"

"Bad."

"I can imagine. That was a cute kid, too. God. I was sick when I heard. I suppose it's shaken you up, too."

"It has."

"Bev and I sent a mass card. We didn't go to the funeral. Bev gets too teary at those things. Hey, here's the better half herself."

"Hiya, Link." Bev came bounding down from upstairs and burst into the kitchen.

"What are you supposed to be, Lady Godiva?" Petey asked. She had on a mauve bikini printed with orchids.

"She didn't wear anything at all, idiot. And she rode a horse."

"Can't get much closer to nothing than that handkerchief."

"What am I supposed to do, dress like Mother Hubbard? How do you expect me to get a tan?"

"Whataya, wanna look like a nigger?"

"I just want to be bronze, is all. You like a girl with a tan, don't you, Link?"

"Sure I do."

"Just keep out in back, like I told you," Petey said.

"He's a real namby-pamby, isn't he, Link?"

"Report you to the Legion of Decency, I'm telling you."

"Nyah, report yourself too."

"Come on, we have things to talk about."

"I'm going. See you later, Link." Her hand rode her hip as she descended the porch stairs.

She put on a pair of sunglasses and crossed the scrawny lawn to her chaise longue. She loved the summer scent of suntan oil. She rubbed it on until her skin glistened. She lay back and leafed through a *Good Housekeeping*. The sun was a hot hand pressing on her body.

She was already hot inside. The recipes, the margarine advertisements, the wordy stories failed to nour-

ish her imagination. It occurred to her that the way
Link smiled at her, he must have been thinking—what?

She never aroused herself with raunchy thoughts.
Expectation, anticipation did the trick for her. She
focused on the preliminaries—a wink, a word, a gesture, a touch, a secret rendezvous, what he would
wear, what she would wear, their intimate conversation.

She knew Link was giving her a sign, right before
Petey's eyes—the way he rested his ankle on his knee,
his hand on his leg, meant Meet me; the way he
looked at her, looked through her, said, I ache for
you—and she'd tossed her head to tell him she could
hardly wait—wait for his face in the window of the
car, the lean lines of his smile, the rebellious strands
of his hair arching over his forehead, his collar rolled
up, his shaven chin, his gray, blistering eyes that said,
Get in—the feel of the seat, the scenery speeding by,
their talk—their deepest, most heartfelt thoughts, the
knowledge they'd always had of each other—his response to her inner tenderness, her fears, her passion—
her instinctive understanding of his thirst, his gentleness,
his complicated need, the things that can never be
said, his smile, the sweet air pouring through the window—

They come to a glen, a precious valley that smells of
wind and earth and roses—he takes her hand, gently,
gently—they step on a carpet of wildflowers—the air
shimmers like glass—a storm sweeps over them, a
sudden shower—they race for the shelter of a tree—
the sky sprays them with tears—her dress clings sop-
ping to her breasts—he strips off his shirt—rainwater
beads on his shoulders—he touches her damp hair—
she holds her breath—

Beverly felt fidgety. She sat up. She picked a dande-
lion with her toes. She strolled over to the corner of
the house for a drink. The water gushed out hot from
the hose. She waited for the cool. She sprayed her
feet. She wandered around to check the progress of
the pansies she'd planted by the kitchen window. The

cool shade soothed her. In the stillness, she could hear the voices from inside. She stopped to listen.

" . . . has to know, Petey," Link was saying. "Has to."

"Why? Why should he?"

"You saying Lombardosi didn't work for him?"

"Okay, there was some kind of connection there, I grant you. But that doesn't mean Manny knows."

"He has to have an idea."

"I don't know about that. Lombardosi—listen, the man was off his rocker. I know that. Probably had plenty of enemies."

"Maybe, but even if Petrone isn't positive, he can at least point me in the right direction. He's supposed to be Mister Big, isn't he?"

Petey said something that Beverly didn't catch.

"Well, make out it's a family thing," Link said. "You're—his wife's your cousin, isn't she?"

"But I just don't think that pestering Manny about it—I don't know."

"Look, Petey, you know Sherry. We all went to school together. Something like this happens—think of that little girl. Look—" He lowered his voice. Beverly moved closer to the screen.

"I know him," Petey was saying. "Of course I know him. I do business with him—sometimes. But, see, we're not really pals. I can't say, 'Hey, Manny, do your old buddy a favor.'"

Link said something.

"Phyllis is the one," Petey continued. "We knew each other as kids. Phyllis likes me. Fact, she's supposed to come over this weekend to go to the fair with me and Bev. Manny, he's distant. His nose is out of joint."

"So get her to ask him."

"How could I—"

"Just put it to her. Tell her we want to talk to her old man and why."

"I'm not sure, Link. Manny's my in. I have to keep on his right side. If he . . ."

Beverly walked back to the chaise. She lay on her stomach and unbuttoned her top. She knew they were talking about the killing. Such a terrible, terrible tragedy, especially when it was someone you knew, or nearly knew. Tears came to her eyes. A chill of anxiety for her own children, yet unborn, shot through her. She tried to read again, dozed, woke up feeling sticky and thirsty.

Link was standing by the door when she entered the house.

"Hey, beautiful," he said.

"Going so soon?"

"I have to run."

"We never see you anymore, Link. Why don't you come over more?"

"I might catch you on Saturday," he said. "At the fair."

"Oh, yeah? I adore carnivals, don't you?"

"Sure."

"We'll see," Petey said. "You want to look at those tires, Link?" He swung the screen door open and stepped outside.

"Link," Beverly said. He turned. She hunched her bare shoulders and grinned. "Um—I'll be looking forward to it. Know what I mean?"

He winked and continued on out.

July 2

Leo was driving. The other man, tall and heavy-boned, rode with his elbow hanging out the window. He was bald and wore thick horn-rimmed glasses.

"So what's this nut Shargoff like, anyway?" he asked.

"Hustler. Has a storefront on Norton. Blue movies

for the newspaper-on-the-lap crowd. A few two-buck whores. And he peddles greefa, horse. He's nobody, really. Lombardosi was supposed to look after him, but the guy didn't pay his dues. I can't say I blame him. I wouldn't have either. Old George wasn't hitting on all six.''

"I hate perverts. Buncha nuts. Dope fiends, they're nuts too.''

"Shargoff's no nut. He has brains. Very reasonable guy.''

"This mean Manny's trying to tighten up?''

"Trying. He's worried, Gap. He really is. I don't know what they told him up to the Falls there, but if they pinned a medal on him, they didn't put it on his chest.''

"They're not happy.''

"They think Manny sucks the big wamboozle.''

"Does he?''

"Hey, I've been with him a long time. I like him. He gives you the benefit of the doubt, he don't pick nits, and he has a sense of humor. I like working for him. But he made it through politics, not this.'' He held up his fist. "He knew people, cooked up deals. He's slippery. But he doesn't have it where it counts, y'want my opinion. He thinks too much.''

"That's bad.''

"I'm the one saves his ass. I mean, I could have taken out Lombardosi with one hand. But they wanted Manny to do it personally. Mistake.''

"Think Manny's headed for a tumble?''

"I don't know. Doubt it. The girl getting killed sucked, but those things happen. Chi Chi—well, what can you do? I'm sticking with Manny up to a point, but I'm not going down with any ship.''

"You aren't the captain, you don't have to.''

"Way I look at it.''

They parked on a quiet, dirty street and walked up the sidewalk for half a block, their shadows tap-dancing beneath them each time they passed a streetlight.

"They've got boons in this neighborhood now," Gap said.

"No shit. They're all over the ward."

"I hate boons. Ever meet this Jew?"

"Sure I met him. He's okay. He's a fun guy. Laugh a minute."

Next to a propane dealer stood a long box of a building, windowless on the side, with its storefront glass whited out. The whole structure was sagging. No sign hung over the entryway, which was illuminated by a red bulb. Leo rang the bell.

An expressionless gray-haired man opened the door.

"Shargoff here?"

"Might be."

"Better be. We have a date. Leo."

The man jerked his head and stepped back. In the white light they could see that the gray extended beyond his hair. His skin had a dull pearl cast, his lips were blanched, his eyes had the tint of zinc. He wore a dust-colored suit and seemed to be supporting an invisible weight on his shoulders.

"He's upstairs."

"Great," Leo said.

"This way."

"We want to look around first."

"He'll show you around."

"Don't worry about it, old man." They strolled into a room crowded with racks of books and magazines. The gray man followed them impassively. They wandered up and down the aisles, fingering the publications.

"This stuff is dirty as shit," Gap observed.

"Hey, get a load of this," Leo said. "She could fit a lawn mower up it."

"Here they got three guys humping one girl. What's the point?"

"Lookit the prices. Four bucks for a goddamn magazine? The place is a gold mine."

The half dozen men browsing in the room watched Gap and Leo suspiciously. One clicked his tongue, as he might have at someone talking too loudly in a public library.

They ambled out and down a short corridor. As Leo started to open another door, a pimple-faced youth rose from his folding chair and said, "Hey!"

Leo stopped and looked at him. The older man shook his head at the boy.

The room behind the door was dark. Old church pews were lined up facing a home movie screen. About twenty patrons were staring intently at the flickering image of a trouserless man in shirt and tie. He was lecturing a naked girl, who looked cold. Leo stood and watched, chuckling. Gap moved over and began to make shadow figures on the screen—lecherous ducks and crocodiles, who nipped at the actress's full bottom. Complaints arose from the audience. Leo guffawed.

"You're all nuts," Gap shouted. "Nuts! Perverts!"

They finally climbed the stairs to the second floor. Their guide knocked at an unmarked door, spoke Leo's name. A voice answered. The man opened the door and motioned them in.

Shargoff greeted them cordially without getting up from his desk. He was a man of about fifty with very close-set eyes. He wore a toupee the color of coffee grounds.

"Sit down, fellas."

They sat. Shargoff opened a small tin box, extracted a pinch of snuff, jabbed it up his nostril, snorted, closed his eyes briefly, then repeated the procedure on the other side.

"Too bad about Lombardosi, ain't it, Stinky," Leo began.

"I was devastated," Shargoff answered. "Man was a prince.

"Shows what can happen."

"Yeah. Here today, gone tomorrow. That's what they say. George, he deserved better. We were pals, you know."

"I didn't know that."

"Oh, sure. Brothers, practically. I cried when I heard. I don't mind admitting it—broke down and cried. And that little girl, that made it even worse."

"Real shame."

"He'll be missed."

"Listen, Stinky, we were talking with a friend of yours the other day."

"Who's that?"

"Oh, you know, friend who's done you a lot of favors. A real pal of yours. Only, he says, you don't seem to appreciate what he does for you."

"You talking about Manny?"

"I'm talking about your friends. Friends you shafted. I mean, George Lombardosi was a sick man. You knew that, didn't you."

"Sick? No, what did he have?"

"He was nuts," Gap said.

"That's too bad."

"Wasn't too bad for you, was it, Stinky? Poor George under the weather, you took advantage."

"Hey, hold on there."

"You took advantage of a sick man, don't say you didn't."

"I'll say I didn't. Know Byrne?"

"Byrne the pervert?"

"He's a sergeant on the vice detail."

"That's him," Leo said. "Wanna hear a story? A guy I know went a little off his rocker last winter. Drank too many bottles of crème de menthe and went out and exposed himself on the Ellis Avenue Bridge. Eighteen degrees and he's out there waving his weenie. Cops came, it's Byrne. They put my friend in the back of a squad car, Byrne gets in with him. Next thing he knows, Byrne's got his fingers on the guy's meat. My friend couldn't believe it, a cop. He's pissed, but he figures if he goes along they'll drop the charges. And know what? They didn't. He gets a twenty-dollar fine for indecent exposure, and when he tells them about Byrne, they laugh. That's Byrne for you."

"Think that's news? Byrne, when he really wants a kick, he shoves a cardboard tube up his tuchus and pushes a little mouse up there. Then he pulls the tube out and the little mouse goes wild. Byrne loves that."

"God, what a nut," Gap said. "The guy's nuts."

"Let me tell you," Shargoff continued. "Last fall Byrne came by to visit. Brought some friends with him. Wagon, too. Warrants. I have a catwalk out this window over to the garage roof. I jumped down into the next yard with a suitcase full of files and contraband. That saved my ass, but it was a close call. This place died for a month."

"Tough."

"Tough, you say. But you'll agree, Leo, that it should never have happened."

"What?"

"If George had been on his toes, that never would have happened. Look, come in here and pay to see an art film, what the hell do you get, huh? You get an art film. You don't get a cartoon. You don't get a sermon on the mount. You get what you pay for. Okay? That's all I want. Why should I pay George when he's not handling his side of it? Sick or not." Shargoff started his snuff ritual again.

"Byrne hit you in November, right? When did you last settle with George?"

"I think, let's see—"

"September."

"He was already screwing up then. Two of my runners had taken falls."

"What kind of runners?" Gap asked.

"Tea."

"What do you mess with that shit for? Know what you're gonna do? Turn white people into niggers. Peddle that dope, turn them into lazy, bone-headed, sex-brained boons."

"Ninety percent of my customers are as colored as they're going to get. Besides, I've never heard of it curling anybody's hair."

"Some nut sold that crap to my kid," Gap said, "I'd kill him, so help me God."

"The point is, these two runners were aced. I talked to George. Sure, he's going to do something. He's got friends here, friends there. Nothing."

"How many times do I have to tell you, Stinky? Lombardosi was sick. Cracked. Now, you aren't kicking about the dues, you're kicking about the service that goes with the dues."

"You're a scholar, Leo. Except, I do have a problem with the dues. Three a week, George wanted. I pay three a week, this place, I'm in the red. I don't generate the cash. What am I, sending some cop's kid through college? Three is way out of line, the little operation I have."

"I'm glad you're seeing it our way, Stink."

"I'm a businessman. I want value for my money, is all. I had some kids, they came around and gave the customers a hard time. I asked George to talk to them. Just talk. His specialty, no? He wouldn't do it."

"Why should he? That's your business."

"Because I'm paying, that's why." He blew his nose into a stained handkerchief.

"You're paying to run your operation. Period. How, that's up to you."

"I just thought—"

"Run. Just to be. No pay, no be."

"Well, be reasonable. I want Byrne off my back at a bare minimum."

"We have that puppet in our pocket," Leo said. "But if you want him off, you pay, you pay in full, and you pay on time."

"I also think a bill a week is plenty, for what I'm getting."

"Think again. Five, two weeks up front."

"I can't handle that. I'll have to shut down. I don't take in five some weeks, what with expenses."

"Shut down. Who cares?"

"I'll agree to two-fifty."

"Five."

"Three-fifty. Okay, four. That's it." He crossed his arms to mark the finality of the offer.

"Five. Two weeks now."

"That's a grand."

"As a kind of remembrance of George."

"Listen, Manny's a businessman. Let me talk it over with him. Reason it out—you put me on the street, Manny gets zilch."

"Gap, hear what I hear?"

"He's nuts."

"You're making unreasonable demands, fellas. Never heard of the goose who laid the golden egg? You're going to ruin me."

Leo let his head loll forward, pretending to doze. Gap sat staring at Shargoff.

"I'll give you seven-fifty. That's all the cash I have on me, swear to God."

Leo let out a long snore. Gap pulled his fingers one at a time until they popped.

"Okay, but I'm telling you, I'll have to close up at this rate. I really will."

"Hand it."

Shargoff reached carefully inside his tweed jacket. He dropped his hands below the desk to count, then placed a stack of bills in front of Leo.

"Tell Manny, though. Tell him he's not being reasonable. This will never work. Tell him."

Leo wet his thumb and slowly totaled the money.

"A week and somebody'll be around to collect. Don't get into bad habits, Stinky, because we'll be watching you. You don't want trouble. Not the kind we'll give you."

"We have to work together, fellas. Do what's reasonable for everybody."

"You got it. Pay your dues, you're reasonable."

"Tell Manny, though. Huh?"

Leo and Gap both rose. Gap was halfway out the door when Leo said, "Gap, wait a minute."

"What?"

"We forgot to give the guy a receipt."

He stopped, looked at Leo, bulged his upper lip with his tongue. "Oh, nuts, you're right. A receipt."

He closed the door.

"We took your money, Stink, and we didn't leave you no receipt."

"Hey, now, hold on. What?" Shargoff stood up. The two men came around opposite sides of the desk. Gap yanked his belt off and wrapped it around his hand.

"Just a receipt so you can say you've paid. That's reasonable, isn't it?"

"Reasonable as nuts," Gap said. His short punch caught Shargoff in the temple. The smaller man's toupee fluttered to the floor like a bird with a broken wing. Leo pinned his arms.

The next punch split Shargoff's lip. Pleading through clenched teeth, he sprayed a mist of blood. Gap hit him on the side of the neck. Leo thrust a knee into his tailbone.

Shargoff folded over. Leo pulled him upright as Gap slammed both fists into his kidneys. His final blow sank deep into his gut. Leo let Shargoff drop to the floor. They left him lying there, crackling sounds seeping from his throat.

July 4

Beverly yanked the steering wheel to the right, and her little car slid through a gap in the traffic. She watched Link, two cars in front of her, oblivious of her presence. Another car clipped his bumper as he started into the curve. He skidded on the steel floor, began to go out of control. But a deft maneuver brought him to rest near the guard rail.

Beverly pressed the throttle so hard her foot ached.

She strained for acceleration. She hunched over the wheel. She took aim at Link's rear. She bore down. She crashed full speed into him. His head snapped back, his hands flew up, he spun wildly, he came around to face her, his mouth let out a laugh, but the sound was lost in the din. Beverly squealed, twisted her car back into the traffic.

She looked behind. Link was after her. She'd gotten him good, now he was stalking her. She wanted him to hit her, wanted him to plow into her. The springs that carried the juice from the ceiling to the electric motors sparked furiously. The pavilion boiled with collisions, caroms, and curses.

Link had his eye on her. He was maneuvering for the most crushing angle. She sat helpless in a corner. She inched her car over to receive the blow head on. He was coming fast. Her eyes rounded. She touched her cheeks with her fingertips. Her mouth opened. He was going to ram her—

The power died. The ride was over.

"Damn!" Link shouted in the sudden quiet. Beverly giggled to cover her disappointment.

He put a hand on her back as they stepped gingerly across the slippery floor, both laughing. She walked as close to him as she dared. They moved down the wooden ramp and into the flowing crowds of the fair. Beverly felt excited, as if the electricity that drove the bumper cars were pulsing through her body.

"Run out of gas, Link?" Phyllis asked. She and Petey had been watching from the side. "You looked good out there, Bev."

"She can drive," Link said.

"Yeah, that's just how she drives our Olds," Petey added. "Like a damn bumper car."

"You never let me drive."

"And that's why, dummy."

"I creamed Link. Didn't I?"

"Oh, you shook me. Next time I'll pay you back, with interest."

Bev beamed. "Let's go back on right now."

"I thought we were going to play miniature golf," Petey said. "Come on."

Bev was determined. "Later. You come too, Phyllis."

"Want to see me puke my guts out? I'm not going on that."

"Let's go," Petey insisted. "It'll be cooler there in the shade. We'll play for a round of drinks."

Beverly liked Phyllis. Before, she'd always thought of her as an older woman, very conceited, very distant, very adult. But today she seemed girlish. Her yellow Bermuda shorts showed off her dark legs. Her terry pullover draped the kind of tight, generous figure that Beverly wished she had. Plus, Phyllis had a way with people, a swagger, while Beverly often felt self-conscious, awkward. Phyllis established instant intimacy with all of them, kidding Petey like a little brother, embracing Beverly with a sympathetic hug, whispering something in Link's ear that made him laugh.

Oh, Phyllis had Link exactly where she wanted him. Beverly had seen his reaction when she'd thrown a spray of red nails from her white convertible. Phyllis had insisted that he drive them to the fair in her car. She'd urged him to tell of his feats on the racetrack and had mooned over his daring. She'd dazzled him with smiles, disarmed him with looks, and roped him in with the seemingly casual gestures that Beverly recognized as sexual snares—similar to ones she herself practiced before a mirror. Link had remained cool, but in his very coolness Beverly saw his fascination. His bantering, offhand attitude she knew was a disguise for boyish arousal. As they watched the firemen's tournament, Link and Phyllis began to hold hands. Phyllis made him lick her Fudgicle. She laughed at his jokes, flattered him brazenly, planted a lipstick smear on his neck. Beverly hated her.

"Sink this and you're only twenty-three over par, Petey," Phyllis was saying. "Does he take this many strokes in bed, Bev?"

The two women shrieked. Petey hunched over his putter. His eyes moved back and forth from his ball to the hole in the green felt. He held his breath and nudged the dimpled sphere. It rolled slowly two thirds of the distance to the hole and died.

"Can't seem to get it in the hole." Phyllis smirked. Bev tittered.

"What the hell are you laughing at?" Petey snapped at his wife.

"Oh, touch-y," Phyllis said. "We're laughing about those drinks you he-men are going to be buying us when we finish wiping your backsides."

"Yeah," Bev said.

"Stupid game, anyway. Half luck."

He knocked his ball in and they moved to the last hole.

"You're pretty good at this game, Phyllis," Link commented. "You're killing us all."

"I have to confess, my husband's a member at the country club. I've put in some time on the putting greens. Who says marriage is a total waste? And what's your secret? You stroke a pretty good ball yourself."

Link shrugged.

"I think it's nerve," Phyllis said. "I love nerve in a man. It's what makes a man, if you ask me. Nerve, pure and simple."

"Oh, boy," Petey said. "It takes nerves of steel to play goddamn miniature golf. Takes a regular Marciano. That what you're saying, Phyl?"

"There's winners and there's losers, Petey."

"Dumb game."

Afterward, the women staked out a picnic table near the ladies' auxiliary tent while Link and Petey went for drinks. Link bought a pint of Seagrams under the counter at the Wheel of Fortune. Phyllis poured generous shots into each cup and added Seven-Up. She proposed a toast to Link. He smiled. She emptied her cup in one gulp. She declared that she was glad Manny hadn't come, glad he had business. The old fart, she said. They didn't need him. They were young. And the night, the night was young. She laughed.

"So tell me more about racing, Link. It's so romantic."

"Romantic?" Petey said. "It stinks. You ever go? Stinks, those fumes. And the noise'll drive you out of your gourd. Call that romantic?

"I like the idea of danger, of courage. Are you ever afraid, Link?"

"Never. Not because I'm so brave. It's just, if you're afraid, that's when it gets dangerous. If you're going to think about it, you don't belong out on that track."

"Fascinating." Phyllis fixed another round of drinks. "I'd love to see you drive sometime."

"I'm out there about every week."

"And you win, too, don't you, Link?" Beverly said.

"Try to."

"I'll bet you do," Phyllis said. They traded smiles. "So, Bev, when is this guinea going to get you in the family way? Don't you want some little Peteys around the house?"

"Oh, I don't know. I'm not in any hurry."

"I already had Rick when I was your age. Hell, get it over with."

"You have kids?" Link asked.

"Two. Does it make a difference?"

He shrugged. "I just wouldn't have thought, is all."

"Not the motherly type, hanh? Good. Actually, I wish I was in your position, Bev. I'd have my tubes tied no matter what anybody said."

"Not if you were my wife," Petey declared.

"Anybody."

"Why?" Beverly asked.

"Hey, I love my kids. Don't get me wrong. It's just, they cement things. As long as you don't have kids, you can change, you're still free. After, it's too late. But you've already got a baby, Bev. Gweat big bootifoh baby, aw." She took hold of Petey's cheek and shook a smile onto his face.

The women decided to go to the ladies'. Petey suggested that he and Link drink a beer to wash down the liquor, and they all meet at the clambake.

The beer tent had open sides. They took a place beside some sloshing, sunburned farmers and ordered two bottles.

"So what do you think of her?" Petey asked.

"She's got balls, I'll say that."

"I told you. Beautiful body, am I right?"

"She's okay."

"You know, hers was the first one I ever saw."

"You're kidding."

"Nope. I was, I guess, ten. She must have been thirteen. We were playing Ping-Pong in her cellar. We got bored and started talking about this and that, boys and girls. Next thing, she's showing it to me."

"Take advantage of it?"

"I was scared stiff." They laughed. "But, oh, did I dream about it. You ask her yet?"

"No, I want to get to know her a little."

"Feel her out, huh? Or up? But even if you hit it off, is she going to want to get Manny to talk to you?"

"I'll explain the whole thing to her, Diane and all."

"She's a wildcat."

"She's not a happy broad, I can see that."

"Married wrong, that's her problem."

"What's he like?"

"Manny? His head's too big for his hat. She needs somebody who's devoted to her. He's devoted only to him. But it's both of them, really. They're one of these couples that thrives on grief."

"She beats his time?"

Petey smiled on one side of his mouth. "She's an industry."

The bare bulbs along the edge of the tent lit up, marking the onset of evening. They ordered two more beers.

"You want to watch out, though, Link. Phyllis chews them up and spits them out. Always has. She has all the moves down pat. She'll leave you skinned alive before you can say pretty please."

"I've had some experience in that line, Petey."

"Sure you have. Just check your jockstrap on your way out. Another thing, Manny's no lightweight. Not the kind of guy you want to throw anything in his face. He plays the game every day. It's his bread and butter."

"All I want—all—is to get to him, have a talk."

"Uh huh."

By the time they left, the sky had given up its struggle with the electric light and the fair had changed into a hot yellow world of its own. At the clambake, Petey said, "Hey, here's a couple of beautiful broads."

They slid onto the benches beside the women.

"You boys get lost?" Phyllis asked.

"Sure. You having a good time?"

"We're lonely. Couple of yokels came over and wanted to take us on the chair swings. We almost went."

"He said I was cute," Beverly announced.

"Yeah? What did you say?"

"I said I thought he was pretty darn cute too." She giggled.

Petey frowned. "What?"

"Well, he woulda been, except he wore glasses and had big Elmer Fudd ears and a tooth missing right here." She lifted her lip. Phyllis screamed with laughter.

"You're pie-eyed," Petey said to Bev.

"Am not."

"Keep your pants on, Petey," Phyllis scolded. "We're having fun."

"Yeah, keep your pants on."

"Oh, yeah?" he muttered. They all laughed at his solemnity.

After a meal of steamed clams, barbecued chicken, sweet corn, potato salad, cole slaw, and stale rolls, washed down with pitchers of beer, Beverly decided the feast wouldn't be complete without a caramel apple. She and Petey went off in search of one.

Link and Phyllis shared the remainder of the liquor and she urged him to buy another bottle. When they'd gotten one, they traded raw swigs. The whiskey vapors cut them loose. They wandered around the sawdust as if on a stage, immersed in scenery, intense color, light, bells and sirens, music, and air that had the bright tang of popcorn, manure, stale beer, and cotton candy.

They took a place at the Over-and-Under booth. Phyllis lifted her hands toward the darkness, praying for lucky seven. When it failed to come up she erupted in curses. She twisted her body in a slow jitterbug to influence the dice, pulled at her hair each time she lost another dollar, and kissed Link full on the mouth when she finally won.

"Wanna sit for a while," she said.

"How about the Ferris Wheel?"

"Great. Haven't been on one, years. My papa used to take me. Loved it."

They handed the Negro operator their tickets and climbed into the seat. He swung the bar across. They ascended haltingly while the ride loaded. They took fortifying swallows of whiskey. At the top they could see the entire fair burning before them and, beyond, the immense dark. Link put his arm around her. She laid her head on his shoulder. They began to revolve.

"Fantastic. Just the way I remember. 'Cept, when I got scared, used to hide my head on Papa's chest. Thought we were gonna fall."

"Like this?" Link leaned forward to rock the seat. Phyllis gasped and clutched at him. He laughed.

"Link," she said. "Oh, Link, you know, we—we're the wild ones. We're the ones know what it's like once you pass the edge. Hanh? Black and empty and lonely. God, it's lonely. Isn't it? Isn't it?"

"I don't mind being alone."

"You don't—oh, you're crazy. You're a wild, crazy man. And I haven't had so much fun in a long time."

"Good."

"There's Petey and Bev. See?"

"Where?"

"I think. Over there by the Twister. Here, give me a drink." They shared the bottle again. "Yeah, we—we're both out for fun. Hanh? Both out for a good time and we don't give a damn what the world thinks. Do we? Do we? Hanh?"

"Nope."

The ride slowed, came to halt, leaving them swinging at the peak.

"Oh, I love this part," Phyllis said. "I could stay up here forever."

The fair moved below them like the works of a fantastic glittering clock.

"I'm bad, Link. Know? Just a dirty, fun-loving broad, that's what you'd think. But I'm bad. Very bad."

The wheel began to revolve downward notch by notch. The fantasy below solidified into real faces, real people waiting to take their places on the machine.

The tide of the fair was moving now toward the mowed hay field beyond the beer tent, and Link and Phyllis let themselves be carried with it. The field sloped up a hillside. People were picking out spots for viewing the fireworks. Phyllis led Link all the way up, close to a row of birches at the top. He spread his jacket for her. They stretched out on the prickly ground. Link put his hands behind his head and stared up at the stars that sliced through the yellow glow of the fairgrounds. Phyllis propped herself on her elbow, leaned across, and kissed him, slinging her leg over his.

"Baby," she said, "did you ever think about going to the moon? Ever get choked up because there isn't enough time to grab all you want in this life? Ever wish you could rip your heart open and let out whatever monster that's in there? Have you?"

He looked at her, shook his head, laughed. She joined him.

"I don't want it to be cheap with us, Link. For once. Let's not let it be cheap. Let's aim for the stars."

"Sure."

"I mean it. I need something, one thing, that's solid in my life. A plastic smile and a poke in the dark, what the hell does that mean I don't want that. I want—"

Her desire was drowned out by the cannonade that opened the fireworks. She rested her head on his chest. They watched the green and red and white rockets burst in the air. Phyllis ohed and ahed the unexpected blossoming of fiery roses, the sudden expansion of great spheres of blue, the sneaky delayed booms. The barrage of the finale was accompanied by swishing pinwheels and an American flag in red, white, and blue flame. A recording of the national anthem blared over loudspeakers. "The home of the brave" brought whoops of appreciation from the crowd. The flag sputtered and died.

"Phyllis, there's something I want to talk to you about," Link said.

July 5

"Not true," Petey said. "I don't care what you say, it's just not true."

"She told me."

"She's full of it."

They were traveling along a country road in Link's car. A hot sun had left embers in the western sky.

"To begin with, why would he do it to one of his own? It doesn't make sense."

"Lombardosi went crazy, you told me that yourself. Petrone couldn't control him, thought he'd blab to the cops."

"But even so, Manny— Okay, I know, you know, Manny has a lot of say in the city. He gets his say because he's willing to bust people up. But that also means he'd know what he was doing. He wouldn't let—what happened."

"You don't know that."

"She was drunk."

"And she's used to being drunk. What she told me was the truth, Petey. About setting up the alibi, everything. No mistake."

"Even so. Even if it was true. What you're talking about is out of the question."

"Why? What are we here for? To these people, we're insects. They do something like that without even thinking. Am I supposed to lie down and take it? Me?"

"Do you have any idea what you're saying?"

"There's a time for kidding around, Petey. And there's a time for standing up and doing what you have to do. Sherry's family to me, as good as, and—"

"And what?"

"And that's enough. There's Ronny."

Ronny was sitting on the steps in front of the coffee shop with two high school boys. He strolled over when he saw Link and Petey pull up.

"Hey," Petey said. "You haven't told anybody about this, have you?"

"He's all right."

"No, no, no. Don't—"

"Hey, Ron boy, pile in."

Petey leaned forward to let Ronny crawl into the back seat.

"Link. Whataya say, Mush-face?"

"Not much, Bent-tinkle," Petey answered. Link cruised slowly through town, then turned onto the highway toward the city.

"Ronny's in love," Link said.

"Aw, leave it alone, will you, Link?"

"In love? Is it true love, Pimple-prick?"

"I wouldn't talk, Turd-for-brains. I saw your wife's fanny last week."

"Go to hell."

"I'm not joking, man. I was driving by and she was

doing the vacuuming right in the window, stark naked bare-assed nude."

"You're a goddamn dog-licking liar. And you'd better leave my wife out of this, or I'll do some dental work on you, no novocaine."

"Hey, I'm petrified, BB-balls."

"Better be. So where's your little Miss America? How come you're spending Saturday night with the boys?"

"She's working. She's a nurse," Ronny lied. "Nurses really know how, better believe they do."

"Cause they have so much practice. Easiest lays in town. Maybe she thinks you're a medical curiosity."

"You couldn't get close to a nurse if you had double pneumonia," Ronny said.

"Har har. I used to carry a baseball bat to keep the nurses away from me."

"At least," Link said, "he's a hell of a lot easier to live with, now that he's getting some regular."

"I ain't knocking it," Petey said. "That's the key to life. What's she like?"

"Combination of Jayne Mansfield and Natalie Wood," Ronny replied.

"Uh huh. Spare me, please."

"Thirty-seven chest."

"Just don't let the air out."

"Fuck you, Charlie."

They drove a few more miles along the straight strip of concrete. Link pulled up in front of a small grocery store.

"Hey, Ronny, run in and grab a couple of six-packs, will you?"

"And a bag of pretzels," Petey added.

"Say please, Dipshit."

"Please, Dipshit."

"Link, look," Petey began as soon as Ronny went inside. "*Maybe*. Okay? Maybe Petrone did do it. I don't know. I can't believe he would, but maybe. But listen to me. Don't keep thinking the way you are."

"Why not?"

"Because you're smart, you're tough, you know your way around. But you're just not in the same league as these guys. You're a good class-A hurler. They're the majors. You never hurt anybody. They do. I know. I had a deal with this farmer—that meat business, remember? They wanted to make sure he wouldn't talk, so they fed him a mouthful of caustic soda, held his jaw shut. Know what that does?"

"So they're animals—great. It makes them that much more predictable."

"Link, the freaking cops are afraid of them."

"Maybe they are. Just happens I'm not. What am I supposed to do, take a correspondence course in chicken shit? They hurt people, all right. And this time they hurt the wrong people."

"Then listen to me. I mean, listen. You remember that stuff last fall? Apalachin? Remember? Link, this isn't just Manny. It isn't just in the city. It's everywhere."

"What do you mean?"

"There's an organization, a secret organization, all over the country."

"Come on."

"I swear to God. I'm not part of it, but I know a little. It's big. It's bigger than the goddamn government."

"You're just barking."

"No, it's true. And you touch one of them, they all turn on you. Don't mess with them, Link. Believe me, don't—"

"Let's roll," Ronny said, approaching the car with a paper bag under his arm. He handed it to Petey and climbed in. Petey punched holes in the tops of three cans with a church key. Back on the highway they drank, ate pretzels, traded insults. Twenty minutes later Link turned onto a rutted dirt road.

"What's here?" Petey asked.

"You'll see."

They crawled past a ruined barn, then along two grassy tracks that had once been a lane. Cresting a knoll, they came upon a gravel patch where five other cars were parked. The sky opened into a broad expanse. The main road ran along the bottom of the hill. Beside it, the huge screen of a drive-in faced directly toward the knoll. Its brilliant colors blared into the night.

"Cripes, this is something," Petey said. "Free show."

They climbed onto the hood of Link's car. The others were mostly teenagers. They huddled in back seats, sat on car roofs, stretched out on the grassy hillside. Ronny recognized someone and went over to talk.

"You know, you're exactly the same as you were in high school, Link," Petey said. "You've never changed."

"So?"

"Nothing. Just so long as you're not worried that the world'll pass you by—or run you over."

"I've seen the way the world goes, Petey—heavy on the throttle but shaky in the turns. I have the knack. I know I do."

"Well it's one thing to be able to hustle a living or chat up a broad. It's another to—you know, go on the trapeze without a net."

"That's right, it is."

"Don't say I didn't warn you. . . . Hey, I've been wanting to see this. These guys get captured by the Japs and they make them build a bridge out in the jungle. What's he saying? Look at that Jap bastard. Oh, he has to go into the box there. Look how he's sweating."

The sky was a slow explosion of stars. The dreamy halflight, the quiet, the giant ghostly images on the screen gave the night an unearthly quality. Petey went off into the bushes by himself. When he returned, Link was sitting on the hood, talking to a redheaded girl in black slacks and a pink sweater.

After a while, the girl wandered off and Petey climbed up beside Link.

"Christ! You know, I envy you, Link, when it comes to women. I thought I'd lose the urge when I tied the knot. Remember how I told you I was in heaven? Used to be, every time I'd think of Bev, *twang*. But now that I've been eating my dreams breakfast lunch and dinner, I find myself dreaming about others, about what it'd be like with this one or that one. Even when I'm doing it with her, I think that."

"It's the itch."

"Maybe. Funny thing is, I'd kill Bev if I knew she was thinking the same—about guys, I mean. I'd kill her."

"You're insecure."

"I don't know what it is."

From, the last car, a girl's voice yelled out, "There's a shooting star!" They all looked, too late.

"Is that how it goes, Link?" Petey said. "Does anybody ever really get what he wants? Have you ever gotten what you wanted?" He drained his beer can and tossed it into the weeds.

"I never knew what I wanted. I just took what I could get."

"It's just—sometimes I feel like I'm going in the wrong direction. Ever get that feeling? I'm leaving it all behind me, somehow. I don't know."

"Let's get out of here," Link said, sliding off the hood.

"What? Hey, wait a minute. This is the best part of the movie."

"Ronny!" Link already had the engine going. Ronny and Petey climbed in. They bounced along the lane back to the road.

"Okay, let's look for kicks," Ronny said. "Let's get into some trouble. Let's go to the hop. Yeah, let's go to the hop."

"Count me out," Petey replied. "I'm getting off probation in two months. I don't even want to get stopped for speeding. Damn open container or something could screw me. Let's just hit a bar, have some drinks, maybe pick up some quiff."

"Oh, man, you are all corners," Ronny said.

Link said, "I have to see about my friend's car."

"What do you mean?" Petey asked.

"A friend of mine wants me to steal his car so he can cash in on the insurance."

"Oh, yeah?"

"Sure. I sell it, we split the take."

"Sounds like a good racket."

"Pumps up your insurance rates, but he needs the cash."

"You're going to do that now?"

"Sure, why?"

"I'm not riding around in a stolen car."

"Chickie?" Ronny said.

"Don't worry, Petey. He won't call the cops until later. It's all set up. If I'm stopped, I say he lent it to me and he backs me up. I've got copies of the keys."

They turned down a driveway that led to a party house along the lakeshore. The building, a rambling, dilapidated hotel, perched on a bluff. The gravel parking lot down the short slope was crowded. The diluted strains of a dance band wafted in the air.

"There's the one you're looking for, Link," Ronny said. "Over there."

Link made a turn, cruised down the row, pulled in at the end.

"You guys know what you're doing?"

"Hey, Petey, don't curdle your milk," Ronny said.

"I can't afford any trouble. What if—I don't know—somebody sees us?"

"I told you," Link said. "My friend will back me up. Once I have the car in the barn, that's when he reports it to the cops."

Link got out, walked along the row to a red convertible, and climbed inside. Petey watched him. Ronny moved up to the driver's seat of Link's car. He had the engine running and twisted the rearview mirror so that he could watch the entrance. The other car puffed exhaust and rolled over beside them.

"Come on, Petey. Let's go for a ride."

Petey went around and got into the convertible. Both cars left, turning in opposite directions. Link stopped at a tavern down the road and Petey ran in for another six-pack. By the time he came out, Link had lowered the convertible top. They continued along back roads into the country.

"What's this, a Pontiac?"

"Yeah, a Bonneville, after the salt flats. They came out with it last year. Has a three-seventy with fuel injection. Zero to sixty in eight flat. One-thirty top right off the assembly line."

"Sporty."

Link fed the car some gas. The acceleration pressed their shoulders back.

"Okay," Petey said. "I believe you."

"This thing with Manny—what I told you, you have it down?"

"Jesus, Link, I don't know. What if he won't?"

"Convince him. I'm a guy you've done business with, that's all. I got you the Chrysler. Don't be too eager—just, the deal sounds hot and you thought he'd be interested. Any car, any color, tell him."

The blackness swirled around them as they drove into the country night.

They'd just finished the last of the beer when Link pulled up in front of Petey's house.

"Well?"

"I'll have to let you know. Okay?"

"Make it soon. If you don't want to, I'll try something else."

"All right. Say, how much does your friend make off this insurance deal, anyway?"

"What friend?"

Petey shook his head and said, "Shit."

"This one's for me, Petey. I might need it."

He gunned the engine. The Pontiac disappeared.

July 9

The butt-heavy revolver jutted precariously from the pocket of Link's jeans. He stood with his legs bowed, his elbows wide. The wind jerked an ash tree in the hedgerow. He slapped his hand onto the checked grip and yanked. The sight snagged in his pants. He swore, freed the gun, snapped it at the tree.

The hot turbulent air and petulant clouds promised a storm. Link opened a box of bullets, picked six of them from their neat rows, inserted them one by one into the chambers of the revolver. He walked up the slope and through a field until he came to an eroded gully that served as a graveyard for old appliances, perforated stovepipes, corroded buckets, broken sleds, and the anonymous skeletons of prewar cars. An enameled washing machine hunkered halfway down the slope.

Link took aim at its white abdomen. He cocked the gun, hesitated, pulled the trigger. The revolver barked, shuddered, twisted upward in his hand. The washer regarded him defiantly, unscathed. He pulled the trigger again. The sharp report cut the wind. His hand leaped. The machine grinned at him with its wringers.

He fired four more quick shots. He heard glass break somewhere in the undergrowth. The washer remained unmarked. He emptied the spent casings, selected more cartridges, and reloaded. Now he aimed with care, tensing his arm against the expected kick. He squeezed, squeezed, squeezed. The explosion was accompanied by a thud as the bullet sliced into the side of the tub. The washer didn't crumple, didn't pirouette in cowboy death, didn't moan a dying curse. It just began to bleed. Link squinted. No, not blood but the rusty accumulation of many rains, oozing through the wound.

Link felt a drop on the back of his neck. Thunder rumbled out of the forest beyond. The wind took on a sudden chill. He clicked the safety on, jammed the gun under his belt, picked up the box of shells, and headed back down toward the house. Bullets of rain began to pelt him—a blow on the shoulder, a flesh wound on the thigh, a direct hit in the spine, the heart, the head. He jogged the last few yards and strode up the steps to the shelter of the porch. He stood watching the downpour, breathing the wet dust. The screen door banged behind him.

"What was that noise, Link?" his mother asked. A slender woman, she had long bony hands and an elastic face. Her hair was set in elaborate curls. Her rouged lips made stains on the cigarette she was smoking.

"Nothing."

"Wasn't nothing. What's that you've got there?"

"Pistol."

"You a fool? For what? What do you need a gun for?"

"Just to have."

"Just to have? You in trouble? I don't concern myself with your business, boy. But you start with guns, you're going to end up in jail, or hurt, or killed. Then what?"

Link shrugged.

"Yeah, you didn't think of that. Then where am I? All alone. And you told me you'd stick. I'm counting on that."

"I told you I would, I will."

"Well, all I can say is you haven't been you lately. What's gotten into you? What are you worrying about?"

He thought for a long moment. "Diane, Sherry's child—she was mine."

"What? That poor little girl? Don't talk rubbish."

"Diane was mine, my blood. Sherry told me last week. She was your grandchild, Agnes. Maybe the only one you'll ever have."

"I don't believe that for a minute."

"Don't matter, it's true."

"Well, why'd she tell you now?"

"Someone murdered our child. We have a score to settle—I do."

"Are you dumb or what? If she was yours, how come you didn't know? Ten years, more, you're sneaking around courting another man's wife and you never figure that out? But now you believe her? Now?"

He laid the pistol on a wicker table. "Why would she lie?"

"Why? You haven't thought about this enough, son."

"Yes, I have. Even if Sherry'd asked me for her own sake, I'd help her. You know I've always lived my life just from day to day. But I have two spots in my heart, one for you, one for Sherry. The fact you can be a pain in the rear or that she's married doesn't matter. I have the feelings and I have to go with them."

"You're like your father, Link. You can't get a grip on things, neither could he."

"I'm not like him. I know how to get along."

"Where you getting to? Where you headed? You're like him, all right. Except, after that blizzard, when I got a taste of what alone was, having you here saved me. And you made me laugh. Like the time you painted flames down the side of Mrs. Bulmer's Packard."

"Hell, you whipped me for that."

"Course I did. She was a once-a-week customer. And remember when I came home early from visiting Doris and you had that skinny girl here—what was her name?"

"Barb."

"And she ran out here on the porch in her undies. You came downstairs and started looking around with an expression on your face I'll never forget. Lord, she turned blue." Agnes laughed her dry laugh.

"We've had some times," Link said.

"Just remember, son, without you I've got nobody." He nodded.

"But hold on there," she said. "Just wait right there." She hurried inside. When she returned she was fixing a bulb in the flash dish on the side of her camera. Link lit a cigarette while she lined up the shot. She handed him the gun.

"Hold it right out in front of you. Higher. That's it. Pretend you're shooting somebody. That's pretty. Now smile."

July 10

Ronny's Hollywood mufflers rumbled as he slowed to turn. His '52 Hudson was decked out with wheel skirts, louvers, a spotlight, dual chrome exhausts, a whip antenna, mud flaps, a bare-breasted hood ornament, a continental kit, and curb feelers all around. A raccoon tail decorated the stick, the tassel from his graduation mortarboard still dangled from the mirror, and the amber eyes of a swollen-bellied hula dancer on the back deck winked when he signaled a turn. He palmed the suicide knob and pulled to a halt in Link's driveway.

"Yo, Rhett!" he called, getting out. "Come here, boy. That's a boy."

A lazy black mongrel ambled over, his tail wagging, to be petted. Link started down from the house.

Ronny found a stick, held it for Rhett to sniff. "Come on, Rhett, babe. You ready? Huh? Here it goes!"

His tongue hanging out, Rhett grinned at Ronny.

"Go get it, boy. Fetch! Come on. Go, go!"

The dog yawned, strolled to the shade of Ronny's car, lay down, and scratched behind his ear.

"Christ awmighty, Link, I thought I was going to sit there forever waiting for you to go by last night. You had problems?"

"You could say that."

"What the hell happened?"

They walked up the driveway toward the paintless barn.

"Dog," Link said.

"Oh, shit. How'd you get the 'Vette?"

"Before I got there I thought it'd be easy. You saw how far the garage was from the house. But as soon as I came in the driveway, this police dog tore over and started yapping his head off. Then the porch light went on and I was up a creek. I kept coming right along the drive. I rang the bell. A maid—I guess she was a maid—answered. I said I needed to use their phone, my car had broken down. She told me to wait. I stood there and stood there. Finally she came back and said okay."

"So you went right in the house?"

"Yeah. I guess the husband was out. The lady was very nice. Maybe forty-five and wishing she wasn't. I gave her a lot of maple syrup, apologized all over the place. Dialed a number, started talking, saying it's me, car's broken down, yeah, it's the frazziwazzle again, borrow Thelma's car and come pick me up, dear. Yes dear, no dear, like that."

Link unfastened a padlock on the barn door and they went inside, with Rhett following.

"Meanwhile, this woman is spread out all over the couch and flashing leg. She said I could wait for my wife there. She'd have the maid fix me a drink, even. I said thanks, but no thanks, I wouldn't dream of imposing. I would like to ask a favor, though. The dog. I'd been bitten as a child, on the face, and I was deathly afraid of them. Right, Rhett?" The dog hummed a high note at the sound of his name. "Would she mind tying him up while I left? She said she didn't like dogs herself. Her hubby insisted they keep one. She told the maid to put the shepherd on a rope in back of the house."

"That's slick."

"So I strolled down the drive, waited till the light went off, doubled back. The garage wasn't even locked. Eased the door open, wired it, took off."

A shaft of sunlight pointed through the dusty air and nicked the rear bumper of the white sports car.

"It had to be a Corvette?"

"That's what he wants. And white. Our gimmick is custom service, model and color you want."

"I love Corvettes. They're cool as hell."

"Good thing I'd seen this one parked in that driveway."

"It's like a little girl, a little virgin." Ronny ran his hand along the fender. "Boy, I'd never have the balls to pull off something like that."

"Bullshit. You have the balls to pull off anything. Be sincere, that's the trick. Be sincere when you lie."

Ronny opened the door of the Corvette and slid behind the wheel. "This is what I call sincere."

"See the four-speed stick? It's got hydraulic valve lifters and the suspension package with the sway bar." Link picked up an empty oil can and arced it into a barrel. The barn had been converted into a full-scale workshop. Four other cars, including the Fugitive, were parked around the room, yawning or propped on car stands. An engine was suspended from a hoist. A drill press stood at attention in the corner.

"It's a work of art," Ronny said, admiring the car's commanding instruments.

"Something to hold his attention. I expect him to be suspicious. We use this to dangle in front of him, then we sucker-punch him."

"Any chance we can keep it?"

"Depends. Might be messy."

"Oh. Oh, yeah. Well, I can't wait."

"Listen, if you want out, just say so. It's nothing on you if you do. We're not talking about grand larceny auto anymore."

"Out? Hell, I'm up for it. I'm in all the way. Don't worry about me."

"Just so you're going in with your eyes open."

"Wide open. Hey, look at this. Guy hasn't changed

the oil in eight months. That's a crime, car like this. Why doesn't he take care of it?"

"Because he's stupid, stupid and rich."

"I'm going to change it." He started the car and rolled it over a hole in the floor that served as a grease pit. Climbing down underneath, he said, "I wanted to tell you, Link, the way things are going with me and Marsha, after this is over I might—"

"Don't say it. Didn't you ever see those war movies? Guy says something like what you're about to say, you know they're going to be sending his dog tags to his girl back home. Kiss of death, man."

Ronny's too-loud laugh echoed through the barn.

She arrived twenty minutes late. Her big Cadillac glowed in the dark. Top down, fins erect, it turned the heads of the people outside the cocktail lounge. Phyllis swung in a slow arc past the entrance. Link got out of his car and waved to her.

"Hiya, handsome." The sparkle of her smile matched the car's chrome. "Glorious night."

"Warm enough," Link said. "That car does things for you."

"Think so? I love white, just love it." Her white middy blouse and short white skirt brought out her tan.

"What's up?" Link asked.

"I have to talk to you, Link. I was going to let you buy me a drink, but I have a better idea. Both my brats are off at Boy Scout camp. The maid's on vacation. And my illustrious husband just left for his stinking club. So follow me over to my house. We'll have a party, little private party, and talk. Just, don't park in the driveway."

"I don't know if that's—"

"If that's what?"

"Wise."

"See you there." She gunned her engine. Link had to drive quickly in order to keep up. She ran one stop sign without even slowing. She led him through quick turns as they entered the posh residential neighborhood where she lived. She swept into her driveway and jerked to a halt. Link drove a hundred yards farther and parked by the curb.

"Think I could drive a race car?" Phyllis greeted him.

"You'd tear 'em apart."

"Lead foot. Can't help it. The tickets I've gotten, I should have lost my license ten times. Manny pulled strings, natch."

She led him up the brick path to the house. The cocoa shells beneath the shrubs gave off a sweet chocolate odor.

"Quite a mansion you have here."

"Like? I did the decorating myself." The house had a Spanish flavor—beaten brass coffee tables, terra-cotta lamps, woven throw rugs, and wrought iron wall hangings.

She fixed them highballs in unwieldy glasses. They settled onto the couch, she facing him, one leg drawn under her.

"Do you believe in love?" she asked.

"What do you mean?"

"You know, love. Like in the songs. Heaven and hell. Something more than I-want-you-want. Not being alone."

"I guess."

"You guess."

"I'm not too sentimental."

"Oh. No, you're right. Absolutely. I'm being vague. I'm afraid to say—to say I've fallen for you. Ha. Yep. Me. I'm out of control, Link. I want you. Want to make a run for it. With you."

He looked at his glass, swirled the cubes.

"Not trying to make you say you love me. Maybe you don't even like me. Just, I have to go through with this. Like I said, out of control."

"I like you, Phyllis."

"But I'm boring you with all this serious claptrap. Here, drink up. Let me freshen that for you. I'm afraid I've had a little teensy head start."

As she refilled the glasses, Phyllis wondered how she could say what she wanted to say. But what did she want to say?

"Look, Link," she said, joining him again. "Let's forget all that. Let's make it this—I want to get to know you better. You don't love me, but we won't let just a word stand in our way. We'll get to know each other. Whataya say?"

"When you told me it was urgent, I thought you had something particular in mind."

"Love is urgent with me. What could be more urgent?" She took a large swallow from her glass.

"I think I'd better go."

"Okay, truce. No more crap about love. Okay? I want you. Period. I'm crazy about you. I had to see you tonight. So let's get in the mood, hanh?"

"I don't know, Phyllis. I don't feel right, being here."

"Why? I told you, Manny won't be home for hours. Sometimes it's four, five in the morning."

"Still."

"What, you afraid? You?"

Link stood, paced across the living room, looked at his reflection in the black window.

"I shouldn't have said that," she said. "Come on, let's go outside. It'll be nice by the pool. You go ahead—through there. I'll fix us some more drinks and join you. Go on."

She had to be alone to sort it out. In the kitchen she dropped a half-full bottle of Canadian Club. She stepped over the broken glass and sat at the table, breathing heavily.

The day had been hot. That afternoon she'd needed a highball to soothe her prickly skin. And she'd needed another to take care of the empty feeling that always came after the first. Anyway, she didn't want to be rock-bottom sober when Manny came home. He'd been rubbing her the wrong way lately. Talking too much. Ever since the business with the kid. Talking like Rick and Stevie talked when they'd been into mischief and wanted to put off the moment of reckoning. Talking, blustering, ranting.

Under it all, she knew he was scared. Heap scared. Wake-up-sweating scared. She almost felt for him. She almost admitted they were members of the same species. But no, she'd earned her pain. He'd only come by his out of stupidity.

And the thing with Manny was, it was all Manny. One time. If one time he'd think of her, her needs, her anxieties. If he'd—just once—really see her.

But no. Manny in a rush. Manny no time to say hello. Manny look, no see. Never see. Manny have important business. The son of a bitch.

She'd given him hell. Given him hell the way she did when she was looped. But she hadn't been looped. Had she? She wasn't looped now. Or was she?

Anyway, he'd stormed out—so predictable. Manny and Phyllis, exit Manny. She'd chased him with curses. And, oh, she could curse. She'd cursed him, his whore, his mother, his ancestors, and especially her own goddamn self.

Then she'd skipped dinner. Not hungry. She'd had more drinks by the pool, watching the sun, red as a maraschino cherry, sink into the neighbor's maple tree.

Link had been on the edge of her mind since the weekend. A rube, for sure. A stud, or thought he was. Thought he was because he had his way with a bunch of loose-hipped adolescents. But his eyes, the way his eyes looked directly at her. Nobody else did that. Everybody else looked into a mirror when they looked at her. But this one, those eyes connected.

And something more. What she'd said, said that night, about Manny. She shouldn't have told, she knew that. Why had she? Why had she said that, about the kid, what she suspected—knew. She was sorry she'd said that and she wanted to see him and erase it somehow, take it back. Because he'd said the little girl had been—what? He'd wanted to know—why?

She'd gotten in touch with him through Petey. Urged him to meet her. Insisted. She'd built up an elaborate, anxious fantasy of how he would lay her bare—at last—and cleanse her. He'd show her how to step out of herself. And she'd fix things about what she'd said, what she should never have said. She'd fed the fantasy with more highballs.

But now that he was here, he was like someone who'd arrived late for a party—out of the spirit, way behind, awkward, ill at ease. He seemed so distant. Beyond her. He seemed, for a moment, like her father. Unreachable. She blinked away a tear.

The fumes of the spilled liquor smelled like ether. They drove her out of the kitchen. She went up to the bedroom to change her clothes. She came down and knelt by the liquor cabinet. She puffed her cheeks and blew out a big breath of air. She opened another bottle, poured a big straight shot, and dropped it down her throat.

Outside, the only light came from the underwater lamps in the pool, a soft bluish glow. Frogs charged the warm air. Phyllis carried two glasses and the fresh bottle on a tray. She wore a white velveteen bathrobe. Link smiled.

"Sorry to be so long. Thought we might like a swim."

"I forgot my trunks."

"Well, guess you'll just have to bare-ass it then, won't you, mister? Hanh? Hanh?"

"I guess."

"You know, my husband, if he ever caught you here, caught me, you with me, like this, he ever, why he'd—" She laughed.

"Maybe we should move the party somewhere else."

"Scared?"

"I hate to be interrupted."

"Fraidy cat. Nyah nyah."

"Something wrong? Was there something you wanted to tell me?"

"Hanh? Yeah. No. Oh, no. Just wondering who in hell you think you are. Hanh? Who?"

"You called me, remember?"

"I'll tell you who you are. You're nobody. Got that? I never told you nothing. Got that? You're nobody. Nobody."

"Okay."

"Nobody. And I? I am Missus Manny Petrone. I am." She said it with a careening smile. "And you're a punk. You're a punk with a carrot in his pocket. You don't know nothing about nothing. Understand? Nothing."

"You're drunk."

"Ha. Ha ha. It's hot. It's so damn hot. And I'm so damn lonely. And you're so damn smug. You think it's easy."

"No, I don't think it's easy."

"Shaddup! Just, shaddup! I tell you what you think. You think it's so goddamn easy. You're just like my husband. And I'm gonna tell him. Tell him you tried to rape me. Hanh?"

The night sounds mounted to a shrill stillness. Phyllis turned away. Link gripped his bicep and watched her. She leaned unsteadily on the arched handles of the pool ladder and wagged her bare toe through the water.

"Like bath," she said. "Wanna go in?"

"No."

"Come on, party pooper. Come on. Didn't mean all that. The whole world stinks. We all stink. Come on."

She drained her glass as she walked around the end of the pool. She tossed it into the water. It glugged once and sank. The light wavered through the ripples.

"Come on." She stepped onto the diving board,

walked its length as if it were a tightrope. "Come on, Link. Show your stuff, hanh? Come on, lover boy."

"One thing I hate, Phyllis, it's a tease."

She yanked at the knot of her belt and violently pulled the robe down from her naked shoulders.

"This look like a tease, baby? Hanh? Does it? Ha ha. You're nothing. You're nobody. Ha ha ha."

Laughing, she twisted out of the robe and whipped it away. She clutched her hair and turned slowly around. The pulsing glow from the water cast a sheen on her bare skin.

"You're nothing and nobody. You hear? Look at me. You're nothing. Nothing. Ya ha ha." Inebriation turned her laugh into a sob, then twisted it back to a laugh. She struggled to keep her balance.

She took two steps backward, caught her breath, squinted at Link. He wasn't looking at her. He'd turned his head. He was frowning. Listening. She heard a car door chug closed.

"Manny."

He was gone before she could say another word, sprinting across the dark lawn toward the row of shrubs that grew down the side of the property. From there he could make his way to the street undetected.

The night turned suddenly breathless. She heard the front door slam. She felt a horror of nakedness. She grasped her shoulders, bent at the waist. She murmured, "Wait, I didn't mean—"

July 11

"Be a beautiful night to be out fishing," Leo said. "Smallmouths just eating it up. Drag 'em in as quick as you can cast. Moon sliding over you. That's the life, Manny. You ought to take it up. Do you good."

They were seated in a window of the Santa Lucia, a

restaurant overlooking the small bay. The sun had just set, the dinner crowd was beginning to thin. Leo was finishing a bottle of Utica Club while Manny fingered a glass of port and smoked one of his sour cigarillos. Across the water a motorboat was disappearing through the reeds on the far shore.

"I don't like to touch them. They're slimy. Go out and get chilled to the bone, bored as hell, not exactly my idea of a good time. Give me a nice broiled fillet, couple of pats of butter, that's fishing."

"Relax you, is what I mean. Eases your mind, that's the thing about fishing."

"How the hell am I supposed to relax?" Manny's fist crashed down on the table. Leo looked at the floor. "Goddamn it. Fucking Ted's after me day and night. You know, Mr. Ruggiero hasn't spoken to me since it happened. Ted's either on the phone or he's down here looking over my shoulder. Every time I take a shit, he's counting the turds."

"So he sees the job you're doing. Sees you're on top of things."

"Truman saw the job MacArthur was doing too. So he fired him. Coulda brought Red China to its knees."

"Ted's a brown-nose. Ruggiero loves you. It's just his way of slapping your wrist."

"Thing is, thing that pisses me, I've busted my hump for them. I've got revenues coming in they never dreamed of. I've got connections you can't buy. Shit, we own that produce market now. Signed, sealed, and delivered. We own those nigger lotteries. We have friends over at Local Four-seventeen. What do they want?"

"You're the power here, Manny. The mover."

"And I don't sit on my hind end and rake it in, either. Like this thing tonight. Could turn out to be a big operation, big money. I'm working. They don't appreciate."

Leo drained his glass and nodded to the waiter. "The old man appreciates, you know that. Wait'll he hears. Your cousin coming?"

"Phyllis's cousin, you mean."

"Take your order, gentlemen?" the waiter asked.

"No, we're waiting for a guy," Leo said. "Another round."

Manny watched the waiter's back. "Musso ain't coming. I don't want a middleman involved. Always deal direct, much simpler. Also, nobody's going to be screaming it's his idea or something. I want to talk to the guy who'll be handling it, and that's all."

"And he'll get you any car you name?"

"Claims. Says in a week, ten days he can deliver whatever you ask for—Caddy, Lincoln, anything—plus the color you want, at like half the price in the blue book. What he needs is a way to move them. Course, you can't advertise them in the paper."

"Sounds good."

"Okay, I said, have him bring me a Corvette. A white one. Says fine. And he'll give it to me for nothing to ace the deal. How's that?"

"Beautiful. Those are beautiful cars."

"I'd never want one."

The waiter came back and set new drinks in front of them.

"I'd never want one," Manny repeated. "Too cramped. Reason I asked for it was Phyllis. I'll give it to her—complete surprise. She'll wet her pants."

"That's a nice gesture."

"And I can sell that damn Cadillac, damn coon car."

"Right."

Manny looked out at the darkening water. He twisted a swizzle stick in his fingers. "I don't know what to do about her, Leo. She always drank, you know. But she's getting to be a total lush. Pathetic. She can't leave it alone. And the kids see it, that's the worst. See her stinko. Their own mother. Can you imagine?"

"Sad, all right."

"Last night—good example. Came home, the house reeks of booze. There she is, out by the pool, vulcanized, naked as a ham bone, bawling her eyes out.

Thank God, I said, the kids are at camp. What if they'd seen you, the whole show on view, lit to the gills? I hit her. Not with the fists, but I hit her. Had to."

Leo scratched the back of his neck. "You've got enough troubles without that."

"My feeling. Plus, she's constantly giving me hell. Suspicious? I can't turn around."

"Jeez."

"I'm not saying it's not partly my fault. We've—Phyllis and I have been drifting for years. Lately, I haven't had the time to pay attention to her. I'd sooner spend it at the club. Donna, she worships me. But I figure I'll show Phyllis some consideration, give her the car, show I care."

"And it's for nothing."

"Sure."

"This must be him."

Across the room, tropical fish glided lazily through a large aquarium. Beside the tank they could see a young man in a burgundy blazer talking with the waiter. The waiter pointed. The man began to cross the room toward them.

An hour later, Manny and Leo and Link sat around a table full of dirty plates. Leo was saying, "Manny can arrange that easily enough can't you Manny?"

"What? What did you say?"

"I was telling Jeff here that you could arrange bail if need be. That's no problem, is it?"

"Problem? I—why, I have half a dozen bail bondsmen in my pocket right now. Want one?"

Leo and Link laughed.

"That reminds me of the story," Leo said, "about the guy who was in jail for, like, five years. All that time, of course, he'd never seen a single dame. But he was even afraid—"

"I'll be right back," Manny announced, rising.

As he crossed the room, Manny dug a tin of Phillips tablets from his pocket and chewed four more. Christ, he couldn't eat anything. Simple steak and potato, his belly was griping.

He entered the empty men's room, chose the farthest stall, took a seat. Pain in the kazoo—literally. And it distracted him. He just couldn't think, couldn't keep his mind on anything. This might be an opportunity, yet all through dinner his attention had wandered. Leo had handled most of it. He'd gathered the details and had beaten the guy—what was his name? Jeff?—beaten him down on the cut. Sounded all right, Manny guessed. Real dough if it developed the way the guy said it could.

Sitting in the cool tiled room, Manny breathed through his mouth, trying to relax. His stomach still churned with gas.

If only Phyllis was on my side, he thought. If only I didn't have her attacking from behind, I could face it. Jesus, nothing worse than to see a naked woman crying. She still had a dynamite body, even now. But that way, hardly able to stand up, that made her seem phony, cheap, like costume jewelry.

Donna, she didn't have the chest, or the hips, or the face, even. But what a gem.

How the hell do you get it back? When you have your confidence, it's easy. The bigger your bluffs, the less likely anybody is to call them. Talk big, look big, act big, and you are big. But once it's gone, how do you call it back? Everywhere—risks, threats. You become so cautious you're afraid to turn around.

Of course, Ted smelled blood. He'd always hated Manny. And that damn idiot Ruggiero let him—no, not Mr. Ruggiero's fault. Manny would have to face Ted himself. But how? What was that crack Ted had made about Phyllis? About the pills?

Phyllis. Damn Phyllis. What the hell did she want, after all? What if the kids had seen her last night?

And why did Ruggiero listen to Ted? Manny was the one with the contacts, the rabbis, the influence. You couldn't buy the contacts he had. What contacts? A smile, a glad hand, a bottle of booze at Christmas?

Hang on and see this through. When they heard about this car deal at the Falls, they'd realize. Sorry, Manny, we underrated you—as always. Now we see. You're a mover.

This Jeff seemed to know his business. Talked a good line. Almost too easy.

Manny bore down, forced the darkness from his brain. No, no need to panic. It all made sense. He had it under control.

He flushed the toilet. His stomach had settled down to a dull rumble. He washed his hands, lit a cigarillo.

He stopped at the aquarium. The filmy, iridescent fish looked wise, unemotional. He glanced across to the table. Leo and the young man were laughing. By the time he reached them, they'd stopped. He sat back down.

"Jeff agrees with you about Cadillacs, Manny. Says they suffer from overweight and drive like plates of Jell-O."

"Yeah? Nigger cars, didn't I always say? I told my wife that but she insisted on the Eldorado. Anything to keep the little woman happy."

"You getting this?" Leo asked.

"Getting what? What the hell are you talking about?"

"The damages, boss," he said, pushing Manny the check.

"Oh, sure." Manny peeled some bills from his roll and dropped them on the table.

They rose. Link headed for the door. Leo hung back. He said, "You all right, Manny?"

"All right?"

"You here?"

"Of course I'm here. I'm fine. Damn gut, is all."

"Okay, okay."

Leo strode ahead and caught up with Link. As they went out he asked him if he fished, if he'd ever been night fishing for smelt out on the lake. Manny grabbed a handful of mints from the bowl by the cash register.

It had rained earlier in the day. Breaths of chill rising from the bay laced the musty, humid air. A canopy covered the walk to the parking lot. The macadam angled away down a slope. The Corvette was parked in the far corner, practically out of sight of the restaurant's entrance. Twenty yards of grass separated it from the shore.

Manny walked along behind the other two men. He chewed his mints and stared out at the water. Lights from the opposite side wormed their way across the undulating surface and disappeared. Far in the distance, the blue flasher of a buoy blinked.

How would he find Phyllis tonight? Manny wondered. She couldn't leave the bottle alone. Maybe he'd come home in the new car and . . . give the damn thing to Donna. Sweet kid, she deserved it. She'd go wild. No, that would be too much. That was the kind of thing he might have done back when. Shit, he had to find a way around Ted. The Lombardosi business was not . . . Ruggiero had to . . . Phyllis had to. . . .

Maybe this car business would do it. When they heard—he'd tell the old man, Any car you want, I'll have it for you. Fucking Rolls. Guaranteed. All my idea. Yeah, the old Manny Petrone. Mover. Manny the mover.

He focused on the sports car now. Creamy white, top down, gleaming.

Leo and Link stood by the car, waiting. As he approached, he heard Leo say, " . . . caught three carp and one smelt. So I said, 'Which one?' " They both laughed.

"Manny, look at this baby, will you," Leo said. "Ain't she a beaut? Jeff tells me she'll crack a hundred without even thinking."

"You guarantee it's good, right, Jeff?" Manny asked.

"Yessir, Mr. Petrone. The reg is from one that got wrecked in Batavia. Here's the papers, signed over to you. Go down, put it in your name, on your insurance, throw the old plates away."

"Looks nice."

"Lot of car there, Mr. Petrone. And it's all yours."

"No strings?"

"I could ask maybe twelve hundred for that car. I'm giving it to you to show how I do business."

"I like the way you operate."

"Yeah, can't beat it." Leo laughed.

"Why don't you try it out?"

"I think I will. I've never—Jesus, these things are low to the ground. You have to stretch your legs right out." Manny climbed in. He took hold of the wheel and patted the gearshift. "Nice. Nice feel to it."

"Why don't you try it, Leo?" Link said.

"Me? I don't fit in them sporty cars."

Manny looked at the sparkling instruments, the tach-ometer, the gauges and knobs and dials. He tried to pry open the ashtray in order to stub out his cigar. It wouldn't come. He got his nail into the crack and pried. Damn thing. How in hell—?

He heard a shout behind him. He turned. Leo and the car thief were dancing together. Horseplay. No. Oh, shit, he has a gun.

As if to confirm his fear, at that instant a shot crashed through the night. It rebounded a second later from across the bay. Manny hunched his shoulders. He tried to find the handle to open the door. The car clung to him. His sleeve caught on a knob. His legs were wedged in. He looked back again. They were wrestling now. On the grass. Sprawling. Punching. Twisting.

Manny's mouth was dry. He managed to pull his heavy body up. He tried to hoist himself out of the car over the door. He fell. His palm burned along the blacktop. He scrambled to his feet.

The other two had rolled closer to the water. Manny stood petrified for a moment. He took a step forward. Something came rushing at him from behind. He leaped. He was in the air before he even saw it. He sprawled

across the hood of the Corvette. A red car roared past.
It heaved over the curb at the end of the pavement, tore
across the soft grass.

The brawlers broke apart. Leo was reaching inside
his jacket. Manny yelled. Leo spun, jumped. The car
sideswiped him. It fishtailed in a long arc, spraying
mud. The passenger door flew open. The car thief
sprinted, leaped inside on the run.

The convertible hesitated now. Its wheels slipped.
Leo clambered to his knees. The car wavered, crawled
forward, whined. A lick of flame shot from Leo's hand.
Again the crack, the echo.

The car gripped the blacktop. It let out a scream of
rubber as its tires caught. It rushed forward. Leo's
hand jumped again. The car careened around the
driveway.

Manny, frozen, trembling, watched the taillights disappear.

July 12

The blue-dyed carnations that Link carried were already wilting with the heat. He entered the carbolic air
of the hospital, found the room number, and proceeded
to the third floor.

"Hey, hey, hey," Petey honked as Link entered his
room. "Here's the boy."

"What's this, private room? Class. Hiya, Bev."

"Hi, Link."

"I can't sleep if there's anybody in the room with me.
Except her."

"How you feeling?"

Petey's right arm was in a cast and sling. His left leg
was plastered and suspended from a pulley. Bruises
made a Lone Ranger mask around his eyes.

"Oh, fine. I have a couple of baked tomatoes up my

nose. I can't get at the itch on my shin. It hurts to swallow. They won't bring me a beer. And somebody's playing the bass fiddle off-key in my crotch. Plus, I thought they had air conditioning in this place."

"You should feel it outside. It's murder."

"Thanks for the posies, man." His voice was sand-paper.

"I'll get some water," Beverly said. She took a plastic vase to the sink. "We're so glad you could come, Link."

"When did it happen?"

"This morning," Petey said. "About ten thirty. They caught me out back. I was taking some trim off a Studebaker. These two heavyweights. I said, I'll take both of you to school, long as it's a fair fight, not two on one. But they didn't care about any fair fight. Bev got home from the store right in the middle of it and scared them off."

"I wish I'd gotten their license number," she said.

"I'm really sorry about—"

"Don't say it, Link. Just don't say it. I'm all right. What don't kill me makes me tougher—who said that?"

"Shakespeare, I guess."

"Tell you one thing, when I'm back on my feet, my shoe leather is going to be making contact with some behind, you better believe it."

"Oh, Petey, now," Beverly said.

"Guys are going to be plenty sorry."

"Sure they are," Link said.

"But I'm okey-dokey. Bev didn't even want to leave me alone here once she got a look at the destroyer who's my night nurse. Why do you think I'm really shelling out for a private room? Have some fun while I'm in here."

"Best therapy there is."

"Hey, Bev, whyn't you take a break. Go down, get a cup of coffee, relax. Link can keep me company awhile."

She looked at him. He jerked his head toward the door.

"Okay. Could I u

something, Link?"

"No, thanks."

Petey waited a moment after ‥
the hell happened with you last n‥

"About what I told you on the ph‥

"They jumped you, or what?"

"The whole thing goes very smooth," ‥ ‥,
perching on the edge of the bed. "The car is ‥ice
touch. Petrone climbs right in, but his buddy, that guy
Leo, he wouldn't. Still, I manage to get the gun out.
Leo doesn't even notice. I'm going to give him one
right in the kidney, then go for Petrone. I pull the
trigger. Keep squeezing and squeezing. Goddamn, I
thought my hand had gone to sleep. I thought God had
me by the balls. Nearly broke my finger trying to get it
to go off. Finally, he sees it and grabs me. We get into
this wrestling match."

"What was it?"

"Safety. I forgot about the safety. I didn't want it to
go off in my pants, you know. But then, it was so easy,
I forgot about the damn safety."

"What a kick in the ass. I'm glad you scraped out of
it."

"I have to hand it to the kid. Ronny's waiting up the
hill in that Bonneville to pick me up. He sees, comes
tearing down. Almost clipped Petrone. Gets between
me and the gorilla. The guy's shooting at us, Petey.
Bang, bang—I mean really shooting."

"You know what they thought?" Petey said. "Thought
you were trying to rob them. This guy Fantino—the
Gap, they call him—and a pal of his come by this
morning. At first, I thought they just wanted to bawl me
out. They're saying how Manny's boiling over, and I
put you onto him, and you pulled a rod, tried to stick
him up. I'm saying, That's totally unbelievable. You'd
always played straight with me, I said. I'm shocked and
all. I'm mortified. They want to know where to find
you. I said, I don't know for sure, down in the South-

......ere, around Olean. They liked that not
.....anny's really p.o.ed, could have been killed,
....nks it's my fault. Now they start roughing me up a
little. I keep on with the same line, say I'll go down
there and look for you myself, I'm just as ticked as
Manny. We go on waltzing like that for a while. Then
they get tired of it, just start giving me my medicine."

"Rough."

"Guy has this thing, like two steel bars with a hinge,
that he uses on my leg. Hurt?"

"I wish there was something—"

"No. I'm not blaming you. But remember what I
told you about the organization, the syndicate? No joke.
Now you see what I mean."

"I should have done it on my own."

"Hey, I wanted in. I decided. No beef now. Only,
give it up, Link. Manny'll always have that goon with
him. Leo's his bodyguard. Just let it be. You took your
shot—let it be."

"No. Petrone's a dead man. Petey, he's scared. I
could see that. I know I can take him."

"You're kidding yourself. I told you from the beginning—"

The door swung open and a nurse entered carrying a
tray. She had a narrow face, like a collie's, and droopy
auburn hair.

"Hello, beautiful," Petey said.

"Time for your pills, Mr. Musso."

"What about the beer? I want my cold beer. How am
I supposed to get better if I have to lie here day and
night dying for a cold beer? That hankering can get to
you. Can't it, Link? I knew a guy dropped dead just
because he couldn't get a cold beer."

The nurse chuckled, shook her head at Link. "Need
the bedpan?" she asked Petey.

She stood over him while he swallowed the three pills
she handed him in a paper cup.

"You'll find that these will make you drowsy," she
said. "Try to sleep."

"Yeah."

She sipped her beer and wiped both eyes with her hand.

"Well, he won't be truthful with me, so I'm not staying at my mother's, so there. I think I'll go upstairs and powder my nose. Would you be a sweetheart and turn on the lights down here? All of them? I'd feel better."

She went up the stairs. Link heard water running. He switched on a fluorescent light over the sink and an electric chandelier hanging from the ceiling of the dining room. He looked at the wedding picture on one of the lamp tables in the living room. Back in the kitchen, insects were divebombing the fixture in the ceiling. He mopped sweat from the back of his neck. Suddenly he gasped and spun around.

Beverly giggled. She'd padded up behind him and jabbed her fingers into his ribs.

"Ticklish? Petey, I could just tickle him to death. They say men who are ticklish aren't any good in bed, but Petey—" She giggled again.

"Too hot for tricks, Bev."

"Sorry."

They sat back down at the table. She'd changed into shorts and a cotton chemise that showed off her tan shoulders. She pulled one knee up and rested her chin on it. She said, "Poor Petey. The doctor says he's really going to be sore tomorrow. I wish there was something I could do."

"You're all he needs, Bev."

"He has the nicest skin, his skin is very smooth for a man. I hate it whenever he gets scrapes and cuts working." She rubbed the red nail of her bare big toe.

"He'll be all right."

"Of course, if he walked in here right now, found us like this—ho ho. Jealous? That's his one big fault."

"Because he loves you."

"That's what I tell myself. But you know the temper

he has. Sometimes he scares me. And it's so silly. I mean, we're married. Why should he be jealous?"

"Jealousy's a scavenger. Feeds on anything."

"But he's all over me if I so much as look at a guy. Course, I like living dangerously." She picked at one of the ribbons that hung down the front of her shirt, twisted it.

"You do?"

"Sure. I like to look nice. I like to think I'm making them hot." She hooked a finger inside her shirt, pulled it out, and blew down her chest. "Whew, I'll never be able to sleep tonight. Just lie there and roast."

"I have to be running."

"Shoot, do you have to?" She propped her cheek with her palm. "Link, do you think about girls?"

"What?"

"Girls. Do you think about them?"

"Yeah, I spend quite a bit of time thinking about them."

"You do? So do I. I mean, about boys. I like to imagine the most fantastic things."

"Like what?"

"You know, like being lost in the desert with them, or going to fancy parties, all kinds of things. Sometimes I'm a princess, with the most gorgeous dresses that I only wear once and throw away, and boys have to do whatever I say or else they get thrown into the dungeon."

"Sounds like fun." Link stood up to leave.

"Link did you—have Phyllis?"

"Phyllis?"

"You know what I mean. Even though she's married? Did you?"

"No."

"She wanted you to. I could see that when we were at the fair. She didn't even try to keep it a secret. If I was a married woman, I'd at least try to hide it a little."

"You are a married woman."

She closed her eyes and laughed. "I forgot. I mean, though, if I was like Phyllis. Don't you think? And she has children, too."

"You're younger than Phyllis. You see things differently."

"I guess. What do you think about?"

"How do you mean?"

"You said you think about girls a lot. What do you think about?" She bit lightly at the fingernail of her pinkie.

"I think about ripping their clothes off and throwing them into bed."

"Oh, Link, for God's sake."

"I have to get going. It's really too hot for me here. See? I'm sweating. Thanks for the beer." He started for the door.

"Link, wait."

"I can't, Bev. I can't play games. Not with you. Not now."

"But wait."

He stopped, holding the screen door open, on the top step. Her eyes were level with his. Perspiration beaded on her nose.

"Who?" she whispered. "Who do you think about?"

He winked. "You, angel."

She ran to the side window to watch him climb into his car. He never looked back.

July 18

The tan Lincoln showed a three-day beard of rust on its front fenders. Once an elegant town car, it now crouched in the middle of the infield and scowled with hurt arrogance, like a broken businessman forced to squabble over a bottle on a skid-row street corner. Suddenly it leaped backward to avoid the rush of a purple Mercury station wagon. The Merc's ferocious grille snapped at the Lincoln's front bumper, sending a piece of chrome, like a detached tooth, flying across the dirt.

Ronny was reclining on a stack of used tires in the pits. He enjoyed the orgy of destruction, like a Roman emperor bemused by the battle of metallic gladiators. He'd never suspected the wealth of simple riches the world could lay at your feet.

Of the twelve cars that had begun the contest, eight had already given up the ghost. They lay scattered about the field, steaming and smoking, tires gashed, doors caved in, fenders amputated.

Now a green coupe of anonymous make and year was careening toward a crippled '51 Olds. The Olds whimpered, tried to hobble out of the way. The green car whipped around backward and crashed into the front bumper of its rival. The cars locked like mating dragonflies. The coupe spun its wheels, wailed in consternation, but couldn't free itself. The Olds quivered, coughed sick yellow smoke, and lurched forward, pushing the smaller car before it.

The public address announcer was having hysterics. The crowd howled a cruel laugh. But farce turned to tragedy as the Olds's engine first sang a high lament, then seized violently and died.

Link returned with two bottles of Nehi. He handed one to Ronny.

"Down to two now," Link said. "My money's on the Merc."

The Mercury was drifting around the third turn, panting. The Lincoln roared and surged. The crowd stomped the bleachers for action.

"Link, I have something to tell you, or ask you. I mean, I'm going to—I'll be getting a job. Or, I have a job. I'm starting next week at Banion's Buick."

"Full time?"

Under the floodlights, amid the dust and carnage, the two cars gathered energy for the final conflict.

"It's a great place," Ronny said. "They have all this electronic shit, scopes and that, to do the timing, get inside the engine. You'll see me wearing my white coveralls, 'Ronny' sewed right here on the pocket. You get hospital insurance, vacation, discount on parts—I can probably get you stuff you need cheap."

"What I need's a new partner, is that what you're saying?"

"I can help you out race nights. But I won't have time to work with you regular. Unless maybe I can get Banion to back the Fugitive, work on it there in the shop."

The Lincoln suddenly gunned its engine and charged. The spectators rose to their feet. The car wheezed up the short slope. Its clutch began to give. It tapped the Merc impotently in the rear and allowed it to escape.

"No more action?" Link said.

"No, I don't . . . this last thing, it kind of shook me up. I feel like I'm over my head, Link. I can't take it."

"Take it? You're a barbarian. How many times do I have to tell you? You had your chance to prove what you could do when your ass was on the line. And you did it. Saved my life. You want out, fine. Get the hell out. But don't say you can't take it. Don't say that."

"I guess I was pretty on the ball there that night."

The Lincoln stumbled, confused. The Mercury roared across the infield, skidded onto the back straightaway, accelerated down the track. The Lincoln hesitated.

"I just wish I'd, you know, mashed the fuck," Ronny said.

"We tried. We did what we could."

"But I've done a lot of thinking since then. About everything. I don't want you to get the idea that I'm letting you down, or that I don't appreciate."

"You want me to give you a medal? Bend over."

The Merc crashed broadside into its victim. The tan sedan turned a clumsy somersault and thudded back onto its wheels. It continued to roll, eased onto its back, and rocked to a halt.

"What I wanted to say," Ronny said. "What I was going to say, what I was going to ask you: I wanted to know if you would, like, be my best man. If you wanted to."

Link coughed a laugh. He slowly shook his head, looking Ronny in the eye. Ronny glanced away, then back, held the look, and finally grinned.

"Marsha?"

Ronny nodded, his face splitting. He said, "I figured, what the hell. She's a great girl—well, you know that. I mean, and stacked too, heh heh, that can't be bad. And, it's just time. You know what I mean? All of a sudden I feel time is going by. I'm wasting time."

"She's the right girl for you, kid. The perfect girl."

Ronny beamed. "I know."

The Mercury had blown a tire, but it managed a galumphing circuit of the track to acknowledge the ovation. Its grille grinned now, the weary satisfied grin of survival.

"For you it's different," Ronny was saying. "You're on top of things. You're in charge. Me, I figured, well, if I'm ever going to do it, I'd better ask her. I didn't think she'd want to, to be honest. I thought, I'll just pop the question. And, whataya know, she said she would. And so we are. I never thought it could be so easy."

"And she had the apron strings ready for you—in a noose."

"Hey, that's not fair."

"No, you're right, it's not. I'm just a little sore, I guess. She's a fantastic girl and you deserve her."

Link looked away. Ronny suddenly became aware of the gulf that was already opening between them.

Link said, "I'll tell you a secret she told me a long time ago. The only reason she ever went out with me was so she could get to meet you."

"Get out of here," Ronny said, pleased.

"God's truth, so help me. Yeah, I'll be your best

man. I'll throw you a real bachelor party. We'll get so drunk we don't know who we are."

They laughed. Link put on his helmet, climbed into the Fugitive, and headed onto the track for the feature.

July 20

Agnes looked out again at the car that had been parked in the driveway for the past ten minutes. A summer wind was clawing the trees, sending sea waves across the field of unmown grass beyond.

The car's door opened. Sherry started toward the house, leaning into the wind, the gusts plastering her dress to her thighs, whipping her blond hair.

"Sherry, honey, you all right?" Agnes greeted her at the kitchen door. "You're crying."

"No, I'm fine. Just the wind, some dust."

"Come on in. Get you some coffee? Gosh, it's wild out there. Like to blow up rain, I'd say."

The gale made the house tremble. Sherry sat, wiped her eyes. Agnes placed a mug in front of her. She clutched it with both hands.

"I've been thinking of you, dear," Agnes said. "I know about loss."

Sherry nodded, sipped the coffee. A clock was ticking above the stove.

"Is Link here?"

"Was. Him and Rhett went out wandering somewhere. Should be back soon."

Agnes watched the face across from her. She saw the finely etched lines of sorrow that would never leave, that would just turn into age.

"You forget, you see," she said, half to herself. "At first that's the most awful thing. You blame yourself, scold yourself. Oh, God, I've forgotten, you say. For a second, for a minute, an hour, you've forgotten all about them. You think if you can hold onto the memory always, every instant, they won't be gone for good. Then, time comes, a whole morning goes by, you don't think about them. You panic. But you know they're gone for good anyway. They're at rest. Forgetting is the only balm. So you let yourself. You let yourself forget."

Sherry's face hardened, resisting the sympathy of the older woman's words.

"You all right?" Agnes asked. "You're white as chalk."

"I'm fine. It's just that . . ."

Sherry jumped up and ran out into the gulping wind. She sprinted up the slope to where Link was emerging from the woods. Mare's tails were reaching across the sky, forming a nimbus around the sun.

Breathless, she fell into his embrace. The wind snatched a single bark from the dog's mouth. She couldn't press herself closely enough to him. She whispered, "Dave's dead."

Link kissed her forehead and held her. Fingers entwined, they walked down the slope. She told him the details. The note: *Don't come down in the shelter. Sorry. Love always.* Her terrible indecision. The silence, the utter silence. Her descent. The peace in his eyes. The gun. The wound. The blood. More blood than could possibly be inside a person.

Her own peace. Her frightful calm. The gentleness of it all. The slow drama of police and ambulance, of friends and relatives, of sympathy, shock, and tears.

It had happened yesterday. Dave must have come home early from the night shift. She'd heard nothing. But when she awoke, the note was there. *Don't come down in the shelter. Sorry.*

All day she'd tried to feel sad, to break her oppressive, numb peace. She had loved him. She'd failed him, they'd failed each other. She wanted to grieve for him, but she couldn't. She told herself he was a tortured soul, a fearful soul, that it was better this way, that it was a blessing.

But she knew that what filled her was the guilty joy, the agonizing exhilaration of her freedom. Tragedy had left her naked, ready to abandon herself to Link's love.

She gripped his arm. She stared into the pupils of his gray eyes. No remorse. She asked him to say it. Always. He said it. That he had always loved her. That he would always love her. Always and always.

July 23

The town languished at midafternoon. In the coffee shop a big fan turned its head from side to side, stirring the hot air.

Link entered and stood by the candy counter while his eyes adjusted from the glare outside. Paul, the vinegary proprietor, was leaning over the sink washing dishes, a cigarette in his mouth, one eye squinting to keep the smoke out. A fat meter reader sat on one of the stools. Two adolescent girls occupied a table along the opposite wall. The only other person in the shop was a man in a light blue seersucker suit who sat alone in a back booth.

Link strolled back. "You're Carlo?"

The man nodded. Link slid in across from him, introduced himself, reached to the middle of the table. They clasped hands briefly.

"Hot day," Carlo noted. A cup of black coffee steamed before him.

"It's a griddle out there. Petey said . . ."

"Yeah, I've run into Petey from time to time. He knows me. When I heard, I went to him and laid my cards on the table. I told him to put me in touch with you."

"So he said."

"How's he doing?"

"Okay. Doctor says he'll have a little limp."

"Something to think about," Carlo said.

"Why?"

"What's yours, Link?" Paul called to him.

"Bottle of Orange Crush." To Carlo he said, "Why is it something to think about?"

"Everything's a lesson, ain't it?"

"Depends on how you look at it."

"I look at it real close. Especially broken legs and missing teeth and blood in the piss. Real close."

"Thanks," Link said as Paul placed the bottle and a straw in front of him. He tapped the straw on the table, pulled the paper off, sucked some orange. "What's it teach you?"

"To be careful. Not to screw up. He told you, in general, how come I wanted to see you, right?"

"Yeah. You know Petrone?"

"Manny? I know him."

"Friend of his?"

"I have no friends. Me and Manny do some business together, some trucking."

Link waited for him to continue.

"Listen, I used to stop in to a joint, have a drink once in a while. Got to know the guy who owned the place, a hard-eyed dago who could lift a truck. I was like you, I didn't need nobody—I thought. This guy showed me different. Everybody can use a hand, especially when you're coming up and are too smart by half. He put me on to the right people. Even lent me jack, back when jack was hard to come by. I'm not a palsey guy, but we got to be pals—brothers, kind of. We watched out for each other."

Link looked at him as he talked. Carlo's small eyes bored into him.

"Now it happened my buddy did some work for Manny Petrone. We both did. My buddy had some tough luck. He got sick. Here." He pointed to his forehead. "Manny didn't give a shit. Manny didn't give a shit that my pal had helped make Manny what he was. Manny didn't give a shit that my pal had no control over what was happening to him. He didn't give a shit about my pal's wife. He didn't give a shit that my pal was a man, a man—you know? And Manny didn't give a shit that the guy was my pal, my friend. He just didn't give a shit. And he did to my pal like you'd do to a dog—just like you'd do to a dog."

"Lombardosi."

"George Lombardosi. That's my why. George is my why."

"Why what?"

"Why I'm going to help you."

Link slipped a cigarette from his pack and took his time lighting it. "Help me?"

"Because Manny did a little child, George's niece's kid. That's your why."

"She was my daughter."

Carlo hesitated. "That I didn't know."

"I didn't tell Petey."

"Listen, I'm no assassin. I'm just a businessman. Anyway, I'm tied in too close to Manny. The cops would be all over me. And if they weren't, Petrone's friends would."

"What friends? Apalachin friends?"

"I don't know about Apalachin. I just—like I say, I keep my eyes open. I see what happened to Petey. But I owe George, and I plan to do right by him somehow."

"What can you do for me, Carlo?"

"I can dish him out and hand you the fork."

Link swallowed the last of his Crush. "When?"

"Tomorrow."

"Simple as that?"

"Why shouldn't it be simple? He's so scared he's fooling himself. Tells himself it was just a holdup. I knew different as soon as I heard. That's why I went to Petey. There's only one complication."

"What's that?"

"You had him cold and you couldn't do it. Think you'll be able to pull the trigger next time?"

"The gun jammed."

"Yeah? I hear guys'll say the gun jammed, it's really them that jammed."

"I don't care what you hear."

"Because if I'm going to help a guy, I want to know that he's going through with it, straight through."

Link crossed his arms and the two men looked at each other. The fat man at the counter ordered another Mexican sundae.

"Don't tell Petey more than you need to," Carlo said. "Everybody else—your girl, everybody—you tell nothing. Now or later. Far as you know, Petrone just had enemies."

"What's your plan?"

"My plan is we meet tomorrow night and I tell you what my plan is. All you'll need's a sport coat."

"What if I don't like it?"

"You'll like it." He told Link where to meet him. "Deal?"

Link nodded. Carlo slipped a dime under his saucer, fit a narrow-brimmed straw hat on his head, and went out.

Link paid for his drink and bought a package of gum. One of the girls called him by name. He waved bang-bang-you're-dead with his thumb and finger. The girls exploded with laughter.

July 24

"You bum!" Manny shouted. "You dirty, rotten, filthy bum! Whyn't you open your eyes? Outside! Outside!"

"Manny, for the love of God," Phyllis said.

"Mile outside. Come on, babe. Make him pitch. Milk him."

"Do you have to?"

"That's it! Go! Run it out!" The ball skidded through the grass between second and third. The shortstop scooped it up and pegged to first, ending the inning.

"They needed a run there, too. Damn umpire."

"How much longer, anyway? My derrière doesn't like these bleachers."

"This is the last inning coming up. They need to hold them here, then pick up a couple of runs."

The Petrone Produce Giants jogged onto the field, while the Jim's Esso Cubs filled the bench on the sideline, waiting for a chance at bat.

"Where's Stevie?" Phyllis asked.

"I don't know. I saw him over by the ditch there with some other kids."

"Rick doesn't even notice we're here."

"Sure he does. Can't show it, but he knows. He's proud as hell."

"He'd better be."

"Hey, there's that Tommy Doyle. They say he's thinking of running for city council. I'm going over, say hello. Be right back."

Phyllis shifted her weight. Watching Manny descend in his plaid summer suit, she wished she'd brought a thermos of Manhattans. She slapped at a mosquito.

The fried-egg sun was sliding down the hills now, stretching spidery shadows across the grass. Her eyes drifted to the coach of the opposing team, a young gym teacher at the elementary school. Why did he wear those silly knickers that fit so tightly around his crotch?

No, no gym teacher, no race car driver, nobody. Nobody was on her side. She was doing her penance. Not no booze, but less booze. Not no men, but seeing them for what they were. Say this for Manny, he was no worse than the rest, and he had a bank account. And he was the father of her children. All she had to fight against was hope.

"What's going on?" Manny asked, taking his place beside her. "Oh, Jesus, they have a man on first. Come on, guys!"

"Do you really have to scream your head off, Manny?"

"Yeah, I have to scream my head off. That's my boy out there. Hey, let's hear some chatter! Come on, talk it up! Rile 'em!"

The infielders looked at each other, then began to chant: "Batta-hey-batta-hey-batta—*whing!*"

On the third pitch, the batter did swing, bouncing the ball sharply to the first-base side of the mound.

"Double play, Rick!" Manny screamed, jumping to his feet.

The ball took two quick hops, leaped up, and smacked Rick in the mouth. By the time he retrieved it, the runner had passed him on the way to second. He spun and fired to first. The ball sailed four feet over the first baseman's outstretched glove, bounded past the bleachers, and rolled into the wide drainage ditch beyond. The runners stopped at second and third—one base on an overthrow.

"Okay, those are the breaks, Rick. Bad bounce, boy. Settle down." As he sat, he said, "That was pathetic."

"Manny, he's bleeding. Is he all right?"

"Just cut his lip. What's bad is that error."

"I think he's crying."

"He's all right. Let's hold 'em, guys!"

Rick kept wiping his mouth and nose on his wrist. Phyllis looked away.

No hope. A comforting twilight thought. Accept what you have. Don't chase rainbows. Don't pile one disappointment on another. Be decent, for a change, even if the world treats you dirty. Grin and bear. Manny, the kids. Don't keep looking and grabbing. That was her new philosophy.

Swallows were slicing the air in the field beyond, swooping precariously low, darting at impossible angles. Phyllis felt a warmth settle on her as she watched, almost a peace, a sadness that, because it couldn't be uttered, verged on beauty. She felt as if she'd become a saint, as if the scarf she'd tied around her hair were a veil. She smiled inwardly. A martyr. A saint.

"Beautiful! Way to go! Let's bang in some runs, you guys!"

"Is it over?"

"Jesus, aren't you watching? Our boys held them to one run. This is their last ups. Need at least two." Manny's face was all enthusiasm. "And Rick's batting clean-up. Let's go, Rick, baby!"

The Cubs were tossing the ball around the infield. Manny said, "That Doyle guy is a real dope. Even the Republicans won't give him a tumble. Talks like he just crawled out of the cradle. They'll eat him alive."

"What is he, honest or something?"

"You're funny. He's the old-fashioned reformer type that went out with Prohibition. Thinks he doesn't need friends. He'll see."

"Maybe he knows something you don't."

"What the hell is that supposed to mean?"

"I don't know, Manny. I don't know why I said it. I'm sorry."

"They'll eat him alive, I'm telling you."

The gym teacher flashed a grin. Phyllis made her eyes icy. She hadn't been looking at him. Not on purpose. What right did he have to leer? No. Definitely not. No more hotshots.

"Run, goddamn it! You could have run that out, you little son of a—" Manny sat back down. The boy who'd grounded out returned to the bench.

The hell with them. The hell with them all. She didn't need them. She didn't need anybody.

The crowd moaned. One of the players came dragging his bat back, his lips pressed into a pout.

"Is it Rick's turn yet?"

"He's on deck. Two outs. I hope to hell he gets up."

She watched Rick on the edge of the field, swinging two bats, stretching his legs, bending down to touch his cleats.

"All right!" Manny whooped. The batter had cracked a ball into right field. It bounced over the fielder's head and rolled on. The boy dug around second and slid safely into third. He stood, brushed himself off, and preened over his feat by pretending nothing had happened.

"Come on, Rick! You can do it! Hum, babe, hum, babe!"

Rick hitched up his pants, crumbled a handful of dirt, took a last practice swing, and stepped up to the plate.

"Let's go, Rick!" Phyllis shouted. Manny looked at her. She shrugged.

The first pitch came right down the pike, a rib-eye steak. Rick unloaded, whiffed, fell down in the dirt. The opposition howled. Rick grimaced, rose, glanced briefly back to his own bench.

The players in the field raised their chatter to a crescendo with every pitch: "Easy-out-easy-out-easy-out-easy—*whing!*"

Rick looked at a ball high and outside. Manny began to stomp his feet on the bleachers. Soon, the whole crowd was sending up a rumble in unison. Rick golfed at a low ball, fouling it down the baseline—strike two.

"Make him pitch to you, Rick babe!"

Two more balls went past high and outside. Full count. The pitcher pawed the mound, shook off the catcher's signal, nodded, wound up, hesitated, stretched, and hurled. The ball veered inside and struck the spinning Rick square on the seat of his pants. Boos exploded from the bleachers.

"Come on!" Manny bellowed.

"Is he hurt?"

"Rick's all right. You're tough, Rick! You can take it! Way to stick in there, boy!"

"That's terrible," Phyllis said. "Where's he going?"

"Gets to go to first."

The catcher went out to the mound for a conference. Next up was a gangly youth who'd outgrown his uniform. The crowd was restless and eager. Cadenced clapping splattered through the bleachers. The big kid studied the first pitch carefully and heard it called a strike. He spit in his hands, rubbed them together.

"Take the bat off your shoulder!" Manny yelled.

The second pitch headed for the fat part of the plate. He swung. The bat connected. The sphere sailed into the twilight, traced a long arc, hovered. Then it dropped squarely into the waiting glove of the center-fielder. The game was over.

They gathered the equipment. Each team huddled to yell, "Yea! Boo! Giants!" and "Yea! Boo! Cubs!" The players and parents began to disperse.

"Dirty trick, son," Manny said, draping an arm on Rick's shoulder. "He knew you could pound him. That's why he did it. He knew you had his number. You would have taken him downtown, won the game. He was scared."

"Let me see your lip," Phyllis said.

"It's all right, Mommy."

"Sure it is. Fat lip, is all. And you didn't rub where he hit you. I like to see that. It smarts, but don't rub. That shows class, Rick."

"Didn't hurt that much."

"You're tough, that's what it is."

"Where's Stevie?" Phyllis asked. "Stevie!"

"No whining. That's what it's all about. You got on base anyway. You did your job."

"Stevie, come here. Where have you been? Look at you."

The younger boy came running over, one pant leg rolled up, the other dragging, his sneakers covered with mud.

"Where were you, Stevie?" Manny scolded. "Didn't you want to see your brother play ball? Year or two, you'll be out there. Won't you want us to come see you? Aren't you interested?"

"Naw. We were down by the creek catching frogs. There's millions of them down there. I caught this gigantic one, a greenie."

"Tuck your shirt in, Steven. You look like a little bum."

"And—and Dad, we caught all these frogs, and Bernie had some firecrackers, and we were—we'd take the frogs and—and open their mouths and—"

"I think we deserve a little celebration even though we didn't win, what do you say, Rick?"

"I don't know."

"Did Rick get hit in the can, Dad? They said he got hit right in the can."

"You played a damn good game, son. Nothing to be ashamed of."

"Rick got hit in the can! Rick got hit in the can!"

"Stevie, hush," Phyllis ordered.

"Learn from your mistakes, Rick. That's the important thing. We'll stop at Ferguson's Dairy on the way home, and we'll all have banana splits."

"Oh, boy!" Stevie said. "I want a Pig's Dinner."

"You're not having any Pig's Dinner," Phyllis told him. "Manny, you'll spoil their appetites."

"We'll eat there. I'm hungry myself. We can all have a burger platter, then a split."

"Wait a minute. I thought we were going out to dinner."

"No, I'm going to the club. Out? Thursday night, isn't it? I always go to the club Thursdays. It's my night."

"What? What are you saying?"

"Hey, come on, boys. Let's race to the car. First one there gets an extra scoop." They tore across the field to where Leo was waiting in the car.

"Manny."

"I'll be home early, hon."

"Manny, don't do this. After I—"

"Now, don't have hysterics. I go to the club Thursday nights. Why shouldn't I tonight?"

Phyllis's throat burned. "Manny, I've tried. Haven't I tried? Haven't I made an effort? I figured you would too. Just come partway to meet me. Can't you do that? Can't you even try?"

"Effort? Listen, I'm not the one who has the problem. You are. I'm not the one who can't keep it under control. You are. I'm not the one who runs around the neighborhood naked and shot-in-the-neck drunk. You are. You, Phyllis. You."

"Manny, you're sick. You're a monster."

"Oh, don't push that sob scene on me, baby. I don't want to hear it. I really don't."

"Monster. You're—"

Manny gave her the back of his head. He started for the car. Phyllis followed, walking toward the liquid red sun. She'd guessed it would be like this. She'd guessed he'd hurt her. Part of her penance. It made her feel good, the hurt. It made her feel warm and good.

———

"She'll raise and lower the shade twice. That's when you get out of your car. No hurry. Just give the name and get upstairs without any ruckus. The window with the cross."

"Why is she doing this?" Link asked. They were sitting in the Bonneville, parked in a turnoff on the side of a hill. Above them, on a billboard, a gigantic orange bottle was pouring a perpetual stream of neon liquor into a blue cocktail glass. The trees cast a lacy pattern of color on the ground around them.

"The girl used to do a strip act in a bar on South Avenue," Carlo said. "But that was all she did just a kid who could dance a little and didn't mind taking her clothes off. I saw her. She was a turn-on. Manny talked her into working at his club. He calls it a club, it's really a jazzed-up cathouse. He'd keep her in style, he said, and she'd satisfy his sweet tooth and put on a tease for his pals. First night he had fourteen guys in. After the show they gang-shagged her. Everybody took a turn except Uncle Carlo. I'm her friend now. I hold her hand, she tells me about Manny. Tells me everything about him. Told me he'd be there tonight."

"The guy's an animal."

"He's not so much worse than anybody else. He has his blind spots. We all do, especially when it comes to pussy. But she's pissed because first he turns her into a whore, then he comes around and whines on her shoulder about how his wife don't love him."

"So the girl's cashing in her meal ticket."

"Know why? Not just the grand I'm laying on her. That's not it. It's the little girl. When I told her about that, about what Manny did, that cinched it."

"She knows to get out of the way?"

"Oh, yeah." He took a handkerchief from his lapel pocket, patted it across his brow, and replaced it, adjusting the corners precisely. "Now, tell me once more, Link. We're putting our heads on the block here, both of us. You're ready, aren't you?"

"Don't ask me that."

"I'm thinking about the last time. Freeze up here, you won't walk out."

"I told you what happened."

"I know what you told me. But I'm not shitting you. This isn't playtime."

"This isn't playtime?"

Carlo smiled, but his eyes didn't smile. "Anyway, with that thing you won't have to worry about any safety. You don't even have to aim."

Link lit a smoke, flicked the match out the window. "You cook this plan up yourself?"

"Me? No. This is the way guys have been doing it for, I guess, ten thousand years. Guy's sleeping, he can wake up. He's eating, he can have a pistol in his lap. But when he's humping, he's wide open. He ain't looking over his shoulder, he don't hear you coming, and his mind is occupied. So if you can get a guy with his pants down, why do it any other way?"

"I thought you said you were just a businessman."

"I am. But the business I'm in, you push or you get pushed. People I deal with understand a knee in the groin better than they do a profit-and-loss sheet."

"Tough guy."

"When I need to be. That's one of the reasons I'm doing this. George, okay—I loved him, I owe him. But I'm doing it for Carlo too. See, Manny pushed me when he hit George. He don't look at it that way, maybe, but I do. And if you don't push back, and push back harder than you're pushed, you've gotta learn to like the taste of brown."

Link turned away, tapped the steering wheel with his palms, looked out his window into the overgrowth of brambles, dragged on his cigarette.

"When you go in," Carlo said, "don't hurry. Walk. You've got all the time in the world. You'll feel a hand at the small of your back hustling you along. Lean against it. Keep your eyes open. Notice things. Stay loose. Once you've done it, give them the pretty-boy smile. Shit'll be flying, but you can slice right through it if you stay calm. Go nervous, you'll catch a face full. It's a funny feeling. Giddy."

"I've been there."

"Maybe, but this isn't hooking cars. This is keeps. This is business."

"Business, huh?"

"Okay, I'm talking too much." He held his right hand up, looked at it, offered it to Link. They shook. "I'm not saying good luck. You've got it."

Link flashed a smile.

"Know Skinny's?" Carlo said.

"Downtown?"

"Yeah, behind the Y. I'll be there making sure a lot of people see me. When you finish, stop by and have a beer. When you walk out, I'll be right behind you. I want to know what happened."

"Okay."

"Anything goes wrong, you're on your own. That's understood."

"Think I'd squeal?"

"I don't know. You don't know yourself. I'm just reminding you. It'd be a lot better for you if you didn't."

"Don't worry."

"And Link—when this cools off, I might be able to steer some work your way. I like you."

"I'm independent. I don't need any work."

"Sure, I understand. Independent. But who can't use a friend sometime?"

Link nodded. "Totally independent."

Carlo opened his door and started to get out. "Remember—the window with the cross."

"They could have been in first place if they'd given it half an effort," Manny said. "My day, hell, we played ball for keeps. We didn't need the fancy uniforms and all. We played dirty, cutthroat, sandlot baseball. These kids don't have any spunk."

Stretched out on the bed, Manny had his jacket off, his hands folded behind his head. Circles of perspiration stained his short-sleeved blue shirt. He wore a black leather harness across his shoulders. A holster containing a small automatic hung down his left ribs. He'd removed his shoes, and his feet, in dark-gray socks with green clocks, were crossed. Donna sat beside him, picking her nose delicately with her pinkie. Her yellow robe, loosely tied, revealed glimpses of complicated underwear.

"But Rick's okay. He's going to make me proud, I know it. No crybaby. No mama's boy. He takes it, stands up for himself. Smart as paint, too. Had a ninety-two average last year in school. And popular. It amazes me, considering. You'd think with Phyllis carrying on the way she does, it'd turn the boys rotten.

Thank God it hasn't. Not yet. But it puts a double burden on me—mother and father, sort of."

"Yeah." She looked at him with her large umber eyes.

"I mean it. Last thing I need. Hey."

He held up two fingers and wiggled them. Donna reached to the bedside table, unwrapped one of Manny's cigarillos, lit it, and placed it between his lips.

"Like tonight. She knew I was coming here. Don't I come here every Thursday? No big deal. But she goes and makes like it's news to her. Shocked, she is. Thinks because she agrees to go see Rick play ball she deserves a medal of honor, night on the town. As if it was some kind of penance to spend time with your own kids. I said, Phyllis, it's you. You're the one who's sick. And she—hey, I'm giving you a funk. Let's forget the bitch."

"No, Pumpkin. You know how I feel for you. It's not that. I'm just moody, I guess."

"Probably your period coming on."

"Maybe. Whyn't you go ahead and divorce her, Manny?"

"I told you a million times. We're Catholic. Besides, she'd skin me. My business is too delicate to drag out in court. I'd have to settle. She'd pull my fingernails out with tongs. She'd probably even go for custody of the boys out of spite. No, Phyllis is my cross to bear."

"Poor Pumpkin. It's hot as a tamale tonight, isn't it. Let's take this icky thing off, get comfy." She reached for the strap of the holster.

Manny slapped her hand away. "Never touch. Haven't I told you? Accidents happen when somebody who knows from nothing about firearms starts messing with them. I'll take it off when I feel like."

"I just wanted to help you relax."

"I don't feel like relaxing."

She tucked in the corners of her mouth and bowed her head.

"Know what I've been thinking?" Manny said apologetically. "Someday, when I can work it out, I'd like to set you up in a place of your own. Be our little hideaway—just you and me. Even have a maid to bring you tea and toast in bed."

She forced a smile. "And silk sheets."

"Silk sheets, silk towels, silk drapes, silk everything. And we'll go on trips. Europe, Vegas, Hawaii. We'll go around the world. Let 'em talk."

"Oh, Manny."

"People'll envy me. Manny Petrone—there goes one son of a bitch who didn't let life get the best of him. And he had his crosses to bear, too. But he faced it like a man, a real man. They'll be in awe, like they were talking about the president."

"Like the Pope."

"Like the fucking Pope of Rome. He makes things go. Sets 'em up and knocks 'em down. The guy's a mover, they'll say."

"I'll be a lady and nobody can say different."

"Lady? Whataya mean? You're a lady now."

"Yeah, but here, this—"

"This what?"

"You know. I thought—" She sniffed wetly. "You—I didn't know about the others. I didn't know—"

"Oh, don't start. Not Rebecca of Sunnybrook Farm. You were flashing your skinny little ass for the world to see, baby. Don't start on how I dragged you out of the convent. Don't start that yapping."

"I just meant—

"I don't care what you meant. Shut up."

She rubbed her slightly bucked teeth with her knuckles.

"Let's have a drink," she said, smiling. She started across the room in her high-heeled slippers.

"No," Manny barked. "I don't like the smell of booze on you."

"Okay." She returned to the head of the bed and began to rub his temples with her fingertips. "Manny?

Pumpkin? I've been waiting for you, lover man. I've been dreaming about how you make me sing. Know how I sing? I blush when I see Althea or one of the girls after we're together, because they always know. They razz me, but I think they're jealous."

Manny closed his eyes. She leaned to his ear and whispered. He smiled, chuckled. Her hand strayed downward. He lifted it away.

"I don't know, Donna. I'm so wound up, one thing and another. I don't know if I feel like it."

"Oh, I know, Pumpkin. Just leave it to me. Relax. Don't I always find a way? Hmm?"

"Just let me unwind awhile."

"Oh, Daddy." She brushed his cheek with the back of her hand. "Little girl wants to play. Please, Daddy. Little girl wants to play horsey. Pretty please? Hmm? Oh, Daddy, what is this? What in the world?"

Manny laughed. She half stretched out beside him and kept murmuring. Five minutes later he sat up and removed the holster. He hooked his hand around her neck. Her robe hung open.

"So hot," she said. "Gonna open the window."

He nodded. She walked barefoot across the room. She raised the shade. The window was already open, but Manny didn't notice.

"If only for a minute I didn't have so much shit hanging over me." He sighed. "I can't enjoy anything anymore. I can't even think straight."

She pulled the shade down, let it up, yanked it down quickly again and left it.

"Nobody blames you for an accident, Pumpkin," she said, crossing back to the bed. "Just try and relax and think about good things."

"What accident?"

"Come on, Daddy. Time to tuck little—"

"I said, What accident?"

"Huh?"

"Nobody blames me for what accident?"

"I don't know, any accident. If it's an accident, it's

not your fault. Come on, now. Please. I'm burning for you. Please."

"You mentioned an accident. I want to know what the hell you meant."

"Nothing. I meant nothing."

"Why'd you say it?"

"I don't know. Cripes, it's just a way of talking."

"You meant the kid, didn't you?"

"No, what kid?"

"Somebody told you I was responsible for the kid."

"I don't know what you're talking about."

"The kid that died. Who told you that?"

"Nobody, Manny. Golly."

"Althea?"

"What do you mean? I just—"

"No, she doesn't know anything. She wouldn't, anyway."

"Manny, you're acting crazy. You're talking crazy. it's me, your little girl, your little Donna."

"Crazy? Why are you shaking like that?"

" 'Cause I'm scared, is why. I don't like it when you act like this. It makes me nervous."

"Ted."

"Manny, stop."

"Ted told you, right? Wait a minute."

"Please."

"Ted knew about the pills. About Phyllis and the pills. I always wondered about that, about how he found out. Nobody else knew. Leo, but he wouldn't have told. Nobody knew. Except you. I told you, didn't I? Didn't I?"

"What?"

"Didn't I tell you Phyllis tried to kill herself with pills?"

"I don't—yeah, you told me that."

"Took pills and got sick all over the place and almost croaked?"

"So?"

"And you told Ted. You've been spying on me for

them. Haven't you? You dirty bitch! You dirty little bitch!"

"No, Manny. Don't call me names. I don't know anything about what you're saying. I love you, honey. Please." She tried to caress him. He aimed a slap at her face but barely grazed her chin as she snapped her head back.

"Everything I told you, you passed on to them. Everything!"

"No. I'm Daddy's little girl. Remember? Daddy mean to little girl." Slouching into herself, she became a child.

"You—"

"I never did, Pumpkin. Don't say I did, 'cause I didn't. Watch. Watch this. You love this." She flung off her robe.

Manny sat on the edge of the bed, his bottom teeth slicing along his upper lip.

Donna dropped to her knees in front of him. She writhed to the frantic bump and grind in her head. Wrapping her arms around herself, she bent backward. She doubled over at the waist, stretched herself until her head touched her heels. Her hands crawled over her body like two crabs.

Manny pounded his fist into his palm. "You filthy sneak. What'd they pay you? Huh? Huh? How much?"

Swaying upward, she began to do an anxious hula. She forced a grin onto her face. She threw him a lurid wink. But her eyes were filling with tears.

———

He was approaching the house. For almost three hours Link had been watching it from his car, parked fifty yards down the road on the other side. The broad veranda, the gingerbread, the roof peaks, the dim upstairs windows, the silhouette of the cross against the yellow light—all had etched themselves onto his eyes. Now the building was looming.

It had to have been a funeral parlor once, or the

home of a bishop. The porch stretched around to a portico at the side where cars could discharge their passengers in dignity. The house bristled with gables and cupolas, weather vanes and spires and lightning rods. It regarded his approach with authority.

The sport jacket made him sweat. It tugged at him, constrained him. The hard weight where the butt protruded from the lining slapped his hip. The pavement pressed against his feet.

The house yawned, scooped him up its steps. The night waited with bated breath behind him. He pushed the lighted flesh-tone button. Chimes sounded in the distance. Crickets filled the air with question marks.

They'd mown the grass that day. The aroma still lingered in the air. A car passed on the street. He watched its taillights disappear. He looked back to his own car the way a skin diver glances to his boat above.

The solid front door contained a brass peephole. Link felt himself being examined. He cranked up his smile. A latch snapped. The door swung open.

"My goodness." A mouth returned his grin.

He mentioned the name Carlo had given him, one of Manny's business associates.

"Oh, you're a friend of his? How is he? Haven't seen him in a month, at least."

"Crazy as ever."

"Crazy, that's good. He is crazy. I'm Althea."

He said he was Wayne.

Her laughing salmon tongue flicked against small teeth. He followed her inside. She closed the door behind him, slid two bolts quietly into place.

"Been here before, haven't you?" The small black eyes glittered up and down him.

"No. No, I haven't."

"No? I thought you had. Well, any friend of—" She had a mole on her left temple that was not completely hidden by her makeup. Her hair was frozen into hard little spools. The diamonds in her earrings and choker were of a size that screamed glass.

Someone tickled the back of Link's neck. He looked quickly behind. Only a trickle of perspiration. The stairs, which rose from the spacious entryway, beckoned him. Don't hurry.

"Like a drink? What can I get you? I mix a mean martini. Dry. Veddy, veddy dry."

"No, no thanks. I'd rather—he said I could—"

"Oh, yes, of course." An audacious leer contorted her lips. "A companion. No problem, boy like you. Fact, I, heh, I myself, heh heh. Know some tricks, believe you me Bob."

He laughed with her.

"But I know what you want." She took his hand in her fat ringed fingers. "Nice duckling, huh? Nice young chick. Come with me, handsome."

He could imagine corpses laid out for viewing in the hushed parlor to which she led him, could imagine the gaudy, rancid flowers, the powdered impatience of the face anxious to decompose.

"In such a hurry," Althea was saying. "I know, you young men just can't wait."

"That's right," his voice answered. "Been awhile."

"Oh, ho ho. Been awhile. You just hold on. Please, sit." She reached inside her dress to hitch up her bra strap.

He sat on one of the stiff, decorative chairs. Again she pressed him to drink. Water was all he wanted. She sprayed some from a siphon. He wet his mouth. The glass had a smear of lipstick near the edge.

"What line did you say you were in, Wayne?" she asked him.

"Cars. I sell cars."

"Oh. New or used?"

"Both."

"Fascinating. Would you buy a used car from this man? I sure would. I hate driving, though. So—crude. Wish I had a chauffeur. Probably never will. Think?" The big boggy bosom sighed.

Link lit a cigarette.

"Be right back," she said. "You'll like her. Fun, lotsa fun. Funny bunny. You relax, will you? Don't be in such a hurry."

She sidled out of the room. In the quiet, he listened for the tick of the mahogany clock on the buffet. Nothing. Broken. Or not wound. Hands frozen on timeless Roman numerals. He touched the metal inside his coat. He heard someone move through the entryway. From another part of the house drifted laughter and the clink of glasses.

He strode over to the archway through which he'd entered. Crushing out his cigarette, he began to step into the hall. But a voice behind him piped, "Oh, Wayne. Here we are. Where are you headed? Need to go wee-wee?"

He turned. She'd entered the parlor through another door. A face peeked over her shoulder at him.

"Come on, Vicki. Don't be shy. Such a shy thing."

The girl's eyes danced in painted sockets. Her large mouth folded into a rubber smile. Link leered back.

"Just dying to meet you, Wayne," the older woman told him. "She loves cars."

"Oh, I do," Vicki squealed. "Fast ones."

"You two young people have so much in common." She winked at him.

Vicki was eager. Her upswept hairdo, her long, penciled brows, her powdered chest gave her an elegant patina—but her plainness seeped through. Her fingers were too thick, her jaw too ponderous, her nose too wide at the bridge. Her breasts were large but slack, her hips overblown.

She disguised her look of appraisal under one of sexual anticipation. Althea tried to bring them together by wrapping her arm around Link's ribs, but he moved away abruptly. She said something to Vicki with her eyes.

"Well, I'm sure Wayne would like to see the rest of the club, wouldn't you, Wayne? Take him, why don't you, Vick? Little tour. Billiards and TV room and all."

"Yeah, I would," Link said. "Let's go."

"Oh, such a hur-ry. Better watch out for him, Vick. Such a hurry." The two women laughed.

Vicki took him by the finger and murmured something into his ear. He didn't catch the words. She giggled. She led him into the hallway. A crystal chandelier cast hard, fractured shadows. A beveled mirror picked up their reflections. Their eyes met for the first time in the glass.

She said, "I know your type."

"You do?"

"Sure. You're a killer. A killer-diller."

He grinned. The stairs moved toward them. Link could hardly feel the floor. He struggled against the urge to rush. She pressed his right arm.

Just as they reached the first step, a face appeared beyond the stairs, approaching from the back of the house. Link stopped. He watched the gray crew cut come closer. The small, dirty eyes caught sight of him. The thick jaw began working back and forth like a cow's. The face tilted. Its blank expression was hardening into a frown. It stopped. The mouth opened as if it were about to speak, but it said nothing.

The weapon leaped into Link's hands. Vicki fell. She emitted a little "Oh!" of surprise.

The gun exploded. The kick nearly jerked the sawed-off barrels from his hands. He fired again. The grip punched into his palm.

Leo thudded against the wall. He tried to vomit his tongue. His eyes locked onto the oriental carpet at his feet. He studied it. No pain. No surprise. Only curiosity. Breathless curiosity. His fingers clawed at his belly. Gleaming red, they groped deep, deeper into his gut. They disappeared into the hot, liquid mysteries. His mouth, his ears drooled blood. His legs went rubber. His knees slowly buckled. He slid. Inch by inch. He squatted. He peered once more at the carpet already stained with his blood. Hiccoughed. Snored. Rolled his eyes. Toppled. A smear on the wall pointed to him like a greasy red arrow.

Vicki wasn't screaming. She knelt at the foot of the stairs, gazing at Link quizzically, as if he'd just said something to her in a foreign language and she was trying to express her lack of understanding. He looked down the deep soft cleft between her breasts. No one was screaming, yet the air screamed.

Blood pounded in his ears. He broke the gun in half. He extracted the spent casings. Each drooled a wisp of silver smoke. He dropped them into his pocket. He inserted a fresh, brassy one into each barrel. He clicked the gun shut.

Heavy. His feet wore boots of lead. A great weight pressed on his chest. The softness of the stairs kept him from gaining any traction. He looked down—the carpet was much too worn to account for the feeling. He reached a hand to the banister to help propel himself.

At the landing he was already struggling to breathe. Directionless, disembodied sounds reached him—shouts, slamming doors, glass breaking, laughter or crying. Needles pricked into his scalp. His clothes pulled at him as he trudged up the remaining dim stairs.

Winded. If he'd sprinted the whole way he couldn't have been more winded. In the upstairs hall, he tried to regain his bearings. The front of the house? The right side as he'd come in? He moved down a short corridor. He counted the doors. Chose one. Raised the gun. Kicked. It burst open. A woman's razor-sharp scream struck him in the face. She sat on the toilet, dress pulled up, hand between her legs. The scream mixed with the thunder of his own breathing. It chased him to the next door.

This time he tried the knob. It turned. He let the door swing lazily. He crashed inside. Cigar smell. An orange fringed lamp. A bed, still made but wrinkled. Chest of drawers with a liquor bottle and glasses. He crossed warily to the front window. Snapped the shade. It flap-flap-flapped at the top. The crucifix. The writhing Christ.

Gone. A sound spun him. His fingers clamped the gun. Donna lay on the far side of the bed. Crumpled, nearly naked, she propped herself on an elbow and tried to blink her vision clear. The right side of her face, from the corner of her eye down her cheekbone, was split, torn. Her nose bled freely. The blood she couldn't lick dropped off her chin and onto her chest, down along her armpit and the folds of her belly.

"Where is he?"

She shook her head. Then, with her eyes closed, she lifted her chin. Link turned back to the window. He saw a man running up the driveway from the side entrance. He was running the way a man in a suit seldom runs, fullspeed, desperately.

"Son of bitch." He turned and bolted from the room.

———

Bitch, Manny was thinking. Dirty bitch. God, what had she told them? What had he told her? What? What were they laughing about at the Falls? What had he done to her that— His eyes started to go watery. He struggled to control himself. He grinned.

He drove fast, not thinking about where he was going. Leo—oh, Jesus, Leo. He'd just caught a glimpse of him as he rushed down the back stairs and out. Althea standing over the corpse. The man had been alive only—only—only—

The sudden and total unraveling of his life was short-circuiting Manny's brain. Donna kept looming back into his thoughts. The vision of her spilling it all to Ted, of Ted laughing, made his skin crawl.

He'd kill Ted. Had to. Kill him. That was as good as done. Did Ruggiero know? No. Ruggiero loved him. Like a son. His favorite. He'd go to the Falls and plead. Go to the Falls and have it out with Ted. They couldn't do this to him. Go to the Falls. Drive there right now.

But what would they throw in his face? What would Ted throw in his face? What had the little bitch told them? How could he stand up to that? To their laughter? To Ted's nasal laughter?

Maybe it was only Leo they wanted. Ted had mentioned it that time. Have to take care of Leo. Maybe Donna had had nothing to do with it. Just taking care of Leo. Yeah. It made sense. Crystal clear. No need to run. Stupid panic. Everything would straighten out. They hadn't told him about it beforehand because they knew he was close to Leo. But it had to be that way. Had to be.

He chuckled to himself and slowed down. But the idea immediately dissolved in a hot flash. No, the whore had set him up. She'd fingered him. Of course they were after him. The way she'd acted. She knew. She damn well knew they were coming for him. She'd been talking to them all along. The pills. Oh, Christ.

He rolled to a halt at a stop sign. The peacefulness of the evening mocked the clamor in his head. On the opposite corner some teenagers stood in front of a late-night grocery. They seemed to be watching him. He accelerated quickly, throwing stones with his tires.

Should he go home? Were Phyllis and the boys—? No, Ruggiero'd never allow a man's family to be used. But what if Ruggiero didn't know?

Phyllis. She hadn't wanted him to go to the club. If only he'd seen. If only he hadn't wasted it all on Donna.

Cutting down a dark alley and over a one-lane bridge, Manny noticed headlights behind him. With no chance to pass, the other car followed him up a twisting road toward the main highway.

Ruggiero could not know. Manny, he'd said, you are my son. Hadn't he said that? Hadn't he? And when Stevie was born, Manny'd told him: Don Stefano, my son, I'm going to name him—Ruggiero knew what

Manny was worth. Knew Manny had contacts. Knew Manny was loyal. Knew about the rabbis. Knew Manny was a mover. Knew. He'd never let them.

Thing was to get to Stefano and talk to him, plead with him. Ted was running wild. Manny saw himself basking in the old man's affection. Ruggiero would not let him down, not after all these years.

He waited for the green at an intersection. He turned onto the highway. The lights turned the same way. Manny watched them more closely now. He slowed. A three-lane road, but the lights didn't pass. They hovered two car lengths behind. He accelerated. The lights kept pace.

The relief that, in spite of his confusion, had allowed Manny to breathe once he'd escaped from the club now turned to clammy emptiness. He had to find out for sure.

The road was lined with automobile dealers, furniture showrooms, motels, and muffler repair shops. Without signaling, he pulled into the driveway of a lumber company. The lights followed him. He swerved across the parking lot and bounced out onto the highway again. The other car did the same. Manny pulled his gun from his holster and drove with it clutched in his hand.

They were making a mistake. Big mistake. Big, big mistake. Me? Me, Manny. Me, Manny. Me, Manny. Oh, shit. Hold on. His mind was beginning to slip the way a worn clutch slips.

But how could he think clearly? The world had closed down, all at once, completely. Not a single hole for Manny Petrone. Why didn't they try something, those lights? Why just sit back and stare?

He passed a place that sold lawn ornaments. Dark. A Carvel ice cream stand—he'd taken the boys there once. Closed. Used cars for less. Closed. Insurance— all your needs. Closed. Fruits and vegetables, cold beer. Closed. Bridal gowns. Closed. Closed. All closed.

He drove on. The stores were beginning to thin out.

Vacant lots intervened. The night was coming closer. No way out. He longed for an instant to return to Donna, to his little girl, to let her soothe him, reassure him, comfort him—then he remembered.

He drove farther and farther from the city, his city. The lights hung right behind him, relentless, inevitable. His palm was sweating on the butt of the pistol.

The road narrowed to two lanes. Woods and farm fields began to crowd closer. Manny was driving as fast as he dared. The big Chrysler gave a shudder as it clipped a pothole. The car behind crept even closer.

Rounding a curve, he could see a long stretch of straight road ahead of him. An idea lit up in his head. Put some distance between himself and the lights. Then turn off onto a side road and escape. He had the power. Sure. This car? Hell yes.

He pressed the accelerator to the floor and held it. The speedometer crept over ninety, a hundred. Manny felt an electric shimmy coming through the wheel. He gritted his teeth. He was so intent on holding the car on the road, he didn't look back. A small rise flew toward him. He fought the urge to let up. The car leaped over it, sank into its springs, rampaged on. Manny felt free, heroic. But when he glanced into the mirror, his heart sank. The lights were not as close, but they were close enough.

He slowed to eighty. He felt as if he were crawling. The lights rushed up behind him. High beams, now. He had to tilt his head to keep the glare from his eyes. The road became unfamiliar, as if he'd reached another state, another country.

Phyllis. How could he have abandoned her for that slut? Those days, before the kids, when he'd walked into night spots with her and every eye had turned. Oh, they'd seen. They'd all seen the kind of woman that Manny Petrone could have. They'd all seen what a mover he was.

He'd be there again. The contacts he had, the friends he had, the rabbis. He'd be there again. Ted, Ruggiero, they couldn't keep him down. He was somebody. A mover. They'd see. They'd all see.

He slowed. Sixty, fifty. The lights stared, blazing. Suddenly, he jerked the wheel. The rear end of his car spun. He stomped on the brakes. Gravel flew. A squeal. He hit the accelerator. The car fishtailed down a side road.

Over a hill, around a curve. He didn't dare glance behind him. A T-junction loomed. He barely avoided plunging into the yard of a farmhouse. Grating to the right, he peeled rubber.

Before rounding a curve, he looked briefly over his shoulder. Darkness. Blessed darkness. All he had to do was to keep up the speed. He fed the big engine all the gas it could handle. He rocked nearly onto two wheels around a sharp bend. He sped forward. Free. He laughed out loud. Free.

But then, at the end of a long straight stretch, glittering in his mirror like diamond eyes, the lights reappeared. Manny dared more speed. He looked for another road to turn onto.

He rounded a long curve, heaved over two knolls, looked back again. The lights appeared suddenly right on his bumper. The car had gained two hundred yards on him as if in a single leap.

"Ah. Ah. Ah. Ah." He didn't know where the sound was coming from at first. Then he realized it was his own breathing, his own whimpering.

He drove mechanically along the rough, winding road. He crested a hill. A panorama across a small lake valley opened before him. The lights of a few houses sparkled in the distance, as far away as the stars.

Phyllis's face flashed in a bush. His headlights swept past Donna, her hurt eyes staring at him from the roadside grass, impossibly soft. George, the bloody cyclops, laughing right beside him. His tires hissed over a roadway of smiling mouths.

The bright beams sliced into his car, fingered his dash, tickled the back of his neck, wavered, shifted, never blinked. The rearview mirror blazed with light. He couldn't help flicking his eyes to it, over and over. His vision began to swim with colored balls.

The lights were so close they were pushing him forward. He couldn't slow now if he wanted to. The force of the light hurled his car through the countryside.

He calmed. Not a chase. He sighed. A joke. Nothing menaced him but light. All a joke. He chuckled. No one wanted him dead. Not him. No one at all. Not Manny. Not the mover. Just a game. He felt like a child again. He swept over a hill and hurtled down. Soap-box derby. He laughed.

Light. Only light. He glanced into the mirror. Rainbow splinters of light. Throbbing, engulfing brilliance. He stared and stared.

Light swallowed him. Light quietly exploded into his head. Light flashed through him. Light awakened every nerve, every memory, every pain, every joy, every dream. All at once. Forever.

———

Link stopped so that his lights shone on the wreck. The thundering catastrophe was enveloped in an immense, soft silence. The only sound was an intermittent hiss—water dripping onto a hot manifold.

He stepped down the bank to where the blue Chrysler lay hugging an elm. The car's left front fender was mangled, the wheel sprung completely from its socket. The hood, bent nearly in half, recoiled like a sneering lip. The roof sagged in front. The windshield lay half out of its frame, an undulating, frosty blanket.

He bent down to the driver's window. He noticed the lock he'd put in himself. He peered inside, saw the upthrust dash, the obscene angle of the steering column, the glint of open eyes.

Climbing back to his car, he lit a cigarette. He took

one last look. Robin's egg, he remembered someone saying such a sweet color for a car.

July 25

The day had dawned clear but overheated. A haze crept in early. Now the first clouds, gray-white puffs promising showers, were beginning to gather. The thick, sticky air trembled.

The backhoe chewed into the pile of clay, swung around, dropped its load down the cavity, turned back for more. Clods were heaped over part of the hole as over a fresh grave.

Sherry sat on her back steps smoking a cigarette. Link squatted on the grass beside her. Both followed the jerky movements of the mechanical shovel.

"It's going to be all right now," Sherry said. "Isn't it, Link? We did the right thing. The bad's all behind us now."

"You know it is." His smile was a mask. It was like when you were driving and you lost it. You take it down the straightaways, they said, and let Lord Calvert take it through the turns. That was the feeling in his belly now, weightless, riding the edge.

Sherry said, "It took them two days to bust in the roof of that thing. First they used jackhammers. Then they had to go get acetylene torches."

"All that trouble, you should have turned it into a swimming pool. Set up a diving board. Be nice, cool off."

"Jesus, it'd almost make you laugh, wouldn't it—if it weren't so sad? So anxious to save himself if the world went on fire, then he wakes up and finds the war's inside his own head."

"What'll you do if they drop the bomb?"

She shook her head. "The Salvation Army came by

yesterday for Dave's clothes. They were real happy to get them."

"Your yard's going to be a mess."

"Know what I think I'll do? Put in a garden there. I found some seeds Dave had stored down in the shelter. He figured he might need them after he came out, hosed things down, started to rebuild. Funny thing is, they're all flowers. Azaleas, sweet peas, morning glories. I think I'll plant them there, have a nice little garden. Be a comfort to grow pretty things."

"I'll bet you have a regular green thumb, give it a chance."

"Mrs. Meeker's always been a great one for gardening. She spends half her time puttering away out there. Lonely, I guess. She has so many tomatoes by August she has to give them away. Look at her."

In the next yard, a woman in a frayed straw hat was crawling on her hands and knees, weeding a row of string beans.

Sherry turned her eyes to the sky. "Hope it cools off, the way they said. This muggy weather's got me down."

She lifted her hair from the back of her neck and wiped the perspiration. Her face, still pale, was beginning to relax now. Her gaunt cheeks were beginning to fill in. Dark rings circled her eyes, but the eyes themselves were clearer.

"I don't mind the heat," Link said.

"I know you don't." She crushed out her cigarette. They turned back to the hypnotic, growling rhythm of the shovel. Sherry idly twisted the wedding band that she still wore on her finger. "Link, I went to the doctor this morning."

"You sick?"

"I'd been to him before, last week. I've felt kind of off, been throwing up. And I needed more pills to put me to sleep. I just can't sleep anymore. Anyway, he did some tests, told me to come back. Today I got the news. I'm expecting."

"What?"

"Remember that night at the lake? The night Diane— Remember?"

"I remember." He had trouble swallowing.

"I was as surprised as you are."

"I'm surprised, all right. A kid?"

"Ours, Link."

"Goddamn, that's something. A kid."

"Happy?"

"Happy? Sure, I'm happy. Why wouldn't I be? It's terrific."

"You love me?"

"Since you were seven."

"I wasn't sure how you'd take it."

"Well, it seems to me—you know how all these years we've been pulled together? Over and over? Then— *bam!*— everything's turned on its head. Now this. It seems like fate, like our destiny. It has to be."

"I just hope—"

"And don't I have to make an honest woman of you?"

She smiled wanly. "I'm afraid, Link. Scared to death. Because what if what's between us can't survive when we're together? What if it's really only a back-door thing? Because then—"

"Don't say that. We'll make it work."

"Can we? Can you?"

"Hey, we know each other better than two people have ever known each other. Haven't we been best friends, thick and thin, for years? And we've looked life in the eye, both of us. What could come between us now?"

"A kid's a responsibility, Link."

"Whataya mean? Think I can't do anything but hustle and drive race cars? I'll start my own business— real business. You know, all you have to do is get hold of some of these old cars—old Packards, Model A's— and fix them up. You wouldn't believe what people will pay for those. Or hot rods. Kids spend their life savings on hot rods. I could make a fortune with a customizing shop. I don't have to steal cars."

Sherry gave him a long, sad look. Then she smiled. "We'll make it, won't we?"

"Of course. And Agnes'll have a stroke when she hears. A grandchild. She'll die."

"Always. Right, Link?"

"Always."

The backhoe dropped the last scoop of earth onto the shelter. Its engine died, leaving the air ringing with silence. The shadow of a cloud briefly obscured the hot sun.

———

The fat drops of rain pocking the barn's tin roof kept Link from hearing the car pull up outside. A cool gust swept in when the door opened. Two hens that had been pecking grain in the corner clucked nervously and hot-footed away. Link slid out from under the Fugitive and wiped his hands on a rag. Rhett, lazily supervising his work from a stack of feed sacks, growled.

"Whataya say, Link?"

"Carlo."

"Meet a friend. Gap."

Link nodded.

"Hiya, Link." Gap gave him a one-fingered salute. He took off his glasses and wiped them on the tail of the Hawaiian shirt he wore under his sport coat.

"I heard," Carlo said, "what happened. Got some play in the afternoon papers. Nobody saw nothing at the club. And Manny, why, he just had an accident. Driving too fast, lost control. Very neat."

Link laid down a screwdriver and leaned against the fender of the car.

"Too bad about Leo," Carlo continued. "He was just a flunky. Just a Joe. But—"

"Yeah," Gap said. "Shame." He bulged his upper lip with his tongue.

"Course, nobody's blaming you. You had no choice. Did you ditch the gun, the way I told you?"

"Sure."

"Didn't tell anybody, did you?"

"No, nobody."

"Good. You know, I waited for you last night. Got real worried, waiting. Sat around Skinny's for hours. Didn't you remember?"

"I remembered."

"I see. Well, you got the job done, anyway. You proved you could pull the trigger."

Link shrugged.

"You happy, Link?"

"How do you mean?"

"Manny's dead. We both know it was no accident. You got what you wanted. You oughta be happy."

Gap wandered to the back of the barn, inspecting the cars and tools.

Link said, "I was right, wasn't I?"

"What about?"

He lifted a ratchet wrench, tapped it lightly on his palm. "Apalachin. Manny's gone, somebody else has to be Manny. That's the way it works in an organization, isn't it?"

"Sure, you were right, Link. You're a smart boy—I always knew that."

"There's no end to it with you guys, is there?" He leaned over and began tightening the bolts on the intake manifold.

"No, no end."

"So what do you want?"

"Just talk." Carlo's eyes shifted for a second to Gap. "Talk about your future. About business."

Link's elbow moved back and forth. The ratchet crackled in the stillness.

"I told you," he said, looking up. "I'm independent. Strictly independent."

"I know. Independent. I know. You told me."

Two quick shots reverberated from the cathedral

ceiling. A hen squawked. A pigeon fluttered momen-
tarily in the cupola. Rhett barked angrily. After the
third shot, the only sound was the hush of falling rain.

July 26

Outside in the sun, six men carried the casket of a
stranger. A gaggle of mourners shuffled behind. A
bored child turned a somersault on the grass and was
scolded by his mother.

Inside, Carlo forced his attention back to what Ted
was saying.

". . . to be here himself, naturally. But he told me to
tell you he's relieved. This—he's been worried, Carlo.
The way you've fixed things, it's really taken a weight
off his mind. You know, he's had his eye on you for a
long time, before any of this crap with Manny, even.
He knows what you've done for us. He appreciates
judgment. He appreciates a cool head. That's what
Petrone didn't have. He shorted out under pressure.
You, you're different. Mr. Ruggiero knows that."

Carlo filled the pause with silence. Ted swiveled back
and forth in the big leather chair.

"Manny had plenty of pals in the city," he continued.
"That's why it's perfect, the way you've—eliminated the
problem. You won't have his friends pissing and moan-
ing about what happened. We can all shed a tear for the
guy, get on with business."

"Yeah, that was the idea. No loose ends. Just business." He said it with a sneer.

Ted tapped his tented fingers. "Of course."

Outside, the Cadillac hearse pulled away from the
curb, its chrome glittering.

"Mr. Ruggiero knows you, Carlo. He knows you
won't disappoint him the way Manny did. He trusts
you."

"I know what I'm doing."

"Sure you do." Ted attempted a smile. "One more thing. He wanted me to check with you about the arrangements."

"Arrangements?"

"For Manny's funeral. He wants everything first class—couple of cars of flowers, bishop to say the mass—you know."

"I've already taken care of it."

"Good. And the widow?"

"Phyllis?"

"Yes, Phyllis. Make sure she has everything she needs."

He nodded.

"Oh, and a stone. Mr. Ruggiero would like Manny to have a nice stone. A big one. He said to tell you that we'll take care of that. We can get a deal on one."

About the Author

Jack Kelly spent the 1950s in upstate New York and currently lives in New York City. He is the author of four works of nonfiction. This is his first novel.

SPELLBINDING THRILLERS